"You're going to do great, Cole," Kelli said.

"I loved your ideas for the future of the ranch," she continued, "and there's no one in the family better for the job."

"Thanks. I appreciate that. I really do." There was another pause. "Hey," Cole said, suddenly sounding self-conscious, "it's getting late. I should let you go."

"Well, you probably still have stuff to do," she said at the same time.

They both chuckled, breaking the heavy tension.

"Okay," she said. "I'll call you tomorrow morning and let you know how Baxter is doing."

"Have a good night, Kelli."

"You too, Cole."

After they hung up, the house seemed twice as quiet. For a while she tried to go back to her paperwork, but her focus was shot and her thoughts kept migrating back to Cole. To the sound of his voice and the timbre of his laugh. To the fact that he'd apparently wanted to come over and talk to her at the Longhorn, and so maybe he hadn't been there with Miss Tight Jeans. And, most especially, to what he might do now that he knew she and Allen had broken up.

Dear Reader,

My favorite hero has always been the stoic, tormented man who has endured much. One who has gained kindness and compassion through his hardships rather than lost those qualities due to his trials. One who has trouble sharing his pain with others because the right person hasn't come along to help him dismantle his walls. My favorite heroines are strong and independent. They've suffered their own setbacks, but they keep finding their way forward.

Welcome to Tillacos Creek Ranch and a soulmates story with just this kind of hero and heroine in Cole Tyler and Kelli Hinton. I hope you'll enjoy reading their journey of discovery as much as I enjoyed writing it! If you do, I hope you'll continue to enjoy the Tillacos Ranch Romances across all four books in the series.

Happy reading!

Eliza D. Collins

HER COLORADO COWBOY

ELIZA D. COLLINS

HEARTWARMING

If you purchased this book without a cover you should be aware that this book is stolen property. It was reported as "unsold and destroyed" to the publisher, and neither the author nor the publisher has received any payment for this "stripped book."

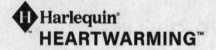

ISBN-13: 978-1-335-46012-7

Her Colorado Cowboy

Copyright © 2025 by Liz Colter

All rights reserved. No part of this book may be used or reproduced in any manner whatsoever without written permission.

Without limiting the author's and publisher's exclusive rights, any unauthorized use of this publication to train generative artificial intelligence (AI) technologies is expressly prohibited.

This is a work of fiction. Names, characters, places and incidents are either the product of the author's imagination or are used fictitiously. Any resemblance to actual persons, living or dead, businesses, companies, events or locales is entirely coincidental.

For questions and comments about the quality of this book, please contact us at CustomerService@Harlequin.com.

TM and ® are trademarks of Harlequin Enterprises ULC.

 Harlequin Enterprises ULC
22 Adelaide St. West, 41st Floor
Toronto, Ontario M5H 4E3, Canada
www.Harlequin.com

Printed in U.S.A.

Award-winning author **Eliza D. Collins** writes heartfelt and heartwarming romance with characters you'll want to fall in love with. She shares plenty in common with her Tillacos Creek Ranch characters, living in rural southern Colorado with her West Texas cowboy husband and their menagerie of horses, dogs, chickens and various strays who adopt them. Look for news of her Tillacos Ranch Romance series on Instagram @elizadcollins or sign up for her newsletter at her website, elizadcollins.com.

Visit the Author Profile page at Harlequin.com.

To my mother, who always believed. I wish you'd been able to stay with us just a little longer to see this.

Acknowledgments

There's always an army of supporters behind any book. Many thanks to mine.

First and foremost, a big thank-you to my RAMP mentor, romance author Roxanne Snopek, who gave me much-needed advice on my first draft that led to all the wonderful things that followed. Thank you to the staff and judges of The Emily contest and the New Jersey Romance Writers Put Your Heart in a Book contest for awarding first place to this book and getting it in front of editors and agents, leading to me signing with my agent.

Thanks to Stephany Evans of Ayesha Pande Literary for believing in my storytelling, and to my editor, Dana Grimaldi, for championing this book and taking the chance on signing it for a four-book series. Thank you also to my support groups and beta readers, all great authors in their own right: my Elementals group—especially Sandy Parsons and Harrison for multiple passes—and my fellow year-one RAMPers. Your feedback and your ongoing support have meant so much to me!

Lastly, thank you to Dr. Charlie Mizushima for the veterinarian advice (though any additions or deviations from his suggestions for plot reasons or from errors I've made are entirely my own doing) and to his wife, author Margaret Mizushima, for putting us in touch.

And of course, as always, love to my husband, Greg, for his support and understanding of all the things that come with being married to a writer.

CHAPTER ONE

KELLI'S TRUCK BARRELED down the county road, zipping beneath the tall log arch and decorative metal sign that proclaimed the entrance to Tillacos Creek Ranch. Her GPS had predicted a sixteen-minute drive to the address Cole Tyler gave her, but the estimated arrival time steadily ticked down with her increasing speed. Her truck rattled in protest and dust plumed in her rearview mirror. The GPS map showed the house not far ahead, down a road to her right, and she could already see a high-roofed barn in the distance.

When he'd called, Cole said the cow had been in labor longer than normal. A single foot of the calf finally presented, and then all progress had stopped. Kelli had asked Cole to feel the first two joints of the leg to determine the direction they bent, as front and hind legs flexed differently. He'd thought he felt a hind leg, meaning the calf was breech. Usually, the cord breaking was nature's cue for the calf to begin breathing air, but its hind leg pinching off the cord could have the

8 HER COLORADO COWBOY

same effect. The unborn calf would try to breathe and suffocate instead. Every second counted.

Kelli had grown up in this valley and Cole had been her closest friend in grade school, but being back on the Tylers' vast thirty-six-hundred-acre ranch for the first time in fifteen years felt strange. It seemed almost like she was driving back in time to Cole's second-grade birthday party where she'd been the shy boy's only guest. Or her last time here, at the seventh-grade party with his new junior high friends, where Andy Sanchez started an impromptu boys-only football game and she'd barely talked to Cole.

The outer edges of the ranch looked much the same as the rest of the county, dry sage and even drier rabbitbrush poking up thickly out of the beige, sandy soils of the high prairie. But speeding now between thousands of acres of cultivated pastures, the difference was dramatic. With much of the land under irrigation, the weeds and brush vanished, giving way to a lush carpet of grass just beginning to green in the lengthening days of early spring.

Blanca Peak loomed large on her right. The peak was a local landmark, but she usually saw it from a distance of a few miles away. Now she'd have to duck her head almost to the truck seat to see the nearly fourteen-thousand-foot snow-capped summit out the passenger window. Ahead of her, more of the Sangre de Cristo Range stretched out of sight to the northwest, the snowy heads and purple peaks vanishing in the distance as they merged with the puffy white clouds and blue skies of Southern Colorado.

She turned right onto the dirt road leading to the house, then left onto a short gravel driveway to the barn. Cole must have heard her truck. Before she'd turned the engine off, he emerged from the open barn doors with a handsome black-and-white Border collie at his heels.

The dog wasn't the only handsome one. At just over six feet, Cole was broad-shouldered, narrow-waisted and had a jawline any Hollywood leading man would envy. It didn't seem fair that Cole kept getting better-looking year after year. Not that she was in the market for a guy, good-looking or not. She'd broken up with Allen two months ago for cheating, and frankly didn't care if she ever dated again.

She got out and took her first good look around. The log home was as she remembered, large and beautiful but not ostentatious, and the property well maintained and tidy. With Blanca Peak behind and green pastures all around, the setting was as picturesque as a postcard.

"Thanks for getting here so quick, Kelli." Cole's voice sounded deeper in person and more resonant than on the phone. "Or should I say, Dr. Hinton?" His words were warm, but his stance seemed a bit stiff, as if he was unsure whether to shake her hand, hug her or leave things at the verbal greeting.

Kelli was equally unsure about the protocol for greeting a childhood best friend all these years later, but he'd asked her here as a professional. She extended her arm and they shook. His large hand, warm and calloused, enveloped hers.

"It worked out well. I'd just finished up my last small animal patient for the day when you called."

In truth, she'd been overjoyed to hear from him. After passing her veterinary certification boards last summer with a specialty in cattle, she'd moved back to Burgess with the goal of joining a large-animal practice. Small towns meant fewer opportunities, though, and there had been no positions for a livestock veterinarian anywhere within commuting distance. She'd ended up opening a solo clinic for the flexibility to work with both large and small animals, though start-up costs had nearly swamped her. Still, it had been worth it to stay in Burgess, because no way would she abandon her goal of moving back to be near her aging parents.

She'd rapidly gained clients with dogs, cats, rabbits, turtles and the occasional goat, pig or horse, but still found acceptance with the local cattle ranchers an uphill battle. Of all the cattle outfits in the San Luis Valley, Tillacos Creek was the largest working ranch by a wide margin. In the summer, the Tylers sold semitruck loads of hay throughout Colorado, and in the fall, their herd of fifteen-hundred cattle could set beef prices from the New Mexico border to Wyoming. If Cole Tyler decided to start using her as his ranch vet, it could be a game changer for her.

"How's she doing?" Kelli asked.

"Same as when I called you. She laid down on her left side when we got her in the barn, so we snubbed her up to a post to keep her in that position."

We probably meant him and one of his ranch hands. Cole and his brother, Troy, were the last remaining family living on the ranch, but Troy had turned his back on ranching years ago to work as a firefighter.

"Perfect," she said. Not that anything about this would be easy, but lying on her left was the best position for both the cow and unborn calf.

She unlocked two long tool compartments on her custom truck bed topper. Cole lifted down her heavy med-kit box while she gathered a few extra supplies. He wore no jacket, despite the cool day, and standing side by side with him for the first time in years, she realized just how brawny he'd become. She guessed him at about six foot one, shorter than his two adoptive older brothers but broader through the chest and shoulders. The most striking differences between Cole and his brothers, though, were his black hair and dark eyes, along with his ruddy skin. A look that contrasted sharply with Troy's and Lane's blond hair, blue eyes and light complexions.

"I have a calf puller in there already," he said, as she reached for her bars and ropes.

"Great. Then unless it comes to a C-section, this should be all we need."

He led her down the alleyway of the large well-lit barn, a building probably more costly than most homes in the county. His dog trotted between them.

"Who's this fella?" she asked.

"This is Baxter. He's the real boss around here." He glanced down with obvious affection.

Despite Cole's palpable worry for the cow, his smile was so easy and genuine that it stole her breath for a second. Sure, she'd encountered him once or twice in the three months since he'd moved back after grad school but walking next to him now was different than seeing him at the far end of a grocery store aisle. It would be easy to get lost in those dark eyes beneath his black Stetson hat.

She tried to shift her focus back to the job ahead as she followed him along a series of narrow horse stalls. It wasn't easy. Cole was everything that drew her like a compass needle to north—and exactly the opposite of what she needed. Her sorry string of boyfriends from high school onward had driven that lesson home. Every one of them athletic and good-looking, and every one of them willing and able to weaponize those looks to attract women into relationships peppered with machismo landmines: Strength that led to swagger. Protectiveness that morphed into possessiveness. Collecting women like notches on a belt. Using their looks to obtain favors or money. And, of course, cheating…because they could.

In the past fourteen years, she'd dated the classics. Everything from a junior high baseball pitcher to a frat house president to an amateur stock car racer. They'd all been trapped in their own clichés like flies in amber. Now she could add Allen to the list. The martial artist. The man who'd moved from Denver to Burgess rather than lose her. The one she'd felt more certain about than all the others put together. The one she'd broken off with two months ago after discovering his infidelity. If she ever did date again, it certainly wouldn't be with a testosterone-laden muscle head. She was done with them for good.

The natural smells in the barn concentrated as they moved away from the large doors: hay and clean cedar shavings, animal dander, and the faint odor of mulch and fresh manure. They reached the first of six roomy box stalls. She could see before entering that the animal was in distress. The pretty white-faced and copper-coated cow was lying on her side, straining weakly.

Kelli breathed a small sigh of relief on seeing that the hoof of the calf was still the only thing showing. A very small sigh. There was still plenty that could go wrong.

"She's a heifer, right?"

Cole nodded. "I'm still familiarizing myself with the herd, but the logbook says this is her first pregnancy."

It struck her what an adjustment this must all be for him, taking over the responsibility of the huge family ranch years before he would have expected to. She'd read Ben Tyler's obituary after his fatal heart attack in January and heard around town that Cole had moved back from Texas to run the ranch.

She pulled on a jumpsuit and unpacked a Betadine sponge, gloves and mineral oil, setting them next to the pulling ropes and bars Cole had laid out for her.

"What can I do to help?" he asked.

"Nothing at the moment." He looked at loose ends and she added, "Maybe the proverbial hot water isn't a bad idea, though."

"Got it," Cole said. "Be right back."

Kelli smiled to herself. Women had been sending fretting men for hot water at births for centuries, getting them out of the way while they took care of the hard work. Besides, she really would need it for cleaning the calf's mouth and nostrils and for washing up afterward.

While Cole was occupied, she pulled on a plastic glove that came up to her shoulder and got down on her knees in the straw to do her exam. The cow looked in nice shape. A young mother, which usually meant good health but sometimes a difficult first birth.

She stroked the cow's flank. Petting a cow wasn't exactly in the veterinary how-to handbook, but nearly all mammals were licked by their mamas as babies and found the similar sensation of petting soothing. The cow held her gaze, her big brown eyes soft, as if she knew Kelli was there to help.

"Okay, sweetie. Here we go."

She followed the calf's foot up into the birth canal. The baby appeared to be right side up with its other hind leg tucked forward, beneath the belly. As breech births went, it was one of the less troublesome positions. She squeezed the leg and the calf moved slightly, reassuring her that they were dealing with a viable fetus. Finished with the exam, she opened the med box and drew up some lidocaine.

She could hear Cole moving about at the front of the building because, of course, a barn like this would be plumbed with hot and cold running water. A moment later Baxter's pattering trot and panting breath approached. Next, Cole reappeared, holding a bowl of water for her between his hands and a bucket for the calf dangling from his fingers, both steaming in the chill air.

He set the bucket and bowl against the bottom rail of the stall.

She filled him in on her findings. "I'm about to give mama a tail block to numb her and then I'll reposition the calf."

She drew up the medication. Baxter looked at Cole, awaiting orders.

"Go lie down," he said in the quiet, gentle voice she remembered from childhood. He inclined his head toward the wall behind him and the dog obediently trotted across the barn aisle and flopped down.

"He's a good boy. A working dog?"

He nodded. "I got him as a pup in Texas. Picked him from a box of free puppies outside a grocery store. I didn't even know he was pure collie. I was just trying to make sure at least one of the puppies got a good home. I didn't expect anything more than a companion, but he took to training like he'd come from champion lines."

"He might have. There are a lot of good herding dogs in Texas."

She recapped the used needle and tossed it in a biohazard bag, keenly aware of how much she missed the unconditional love and loyalty of a dog. Getting a dog had been pushed to the background for so many years that it surprised her recently to realize she no longer had the barriers of college life or Allen's allergies and pet-hair hangups standing in her way.

"Okay. The shot should take effect in a minute or two."

Cole shifted restlessly, as if looking for something to do. He was acting more like a new father at a baby's birth than a rancher, but she knew better. All three Tyler brothers were tough, and Cole was no stranger to calving. He'd been the only one of the three boys to major in ranch management and get his masters in agricultural business to follow in his adoptive father's footsteps.

"Worried about the calf?" she asked.

"A bit." He must have picked up on the fact that he was acting strangely and fessed up to the real reason. "I guess I also feel a little awkward that I've never called you out here and then ask you to come out when I have an emergency."

"Oh, that. Don't worry about it. Vets are plenty used to covering for each other. Who's your regular vet?"

"Bill Salem. He's been the ranch vet for as far back as I can remember."

Kelli's hopes rose. Maybe Cole was acting funny because he was thinking of switching. Bill had been treating cattle and horses in the Burgess area for decades. He must be well into his sixties now and had been progressively cutting back his hours over the past year. She'd inherited two of his horse clients recently—one who spoke well of him but wanted someone more available, and one who was less complimentary. It sounded like the closer he got to retirement, the less effort he'd been putting into his practice.

"Was Bill tied up on another call?"

"He's out of town. His service said he took off early for the weekend and won't be available for ten days."

"Ah. Good to know." She mentally shuffled her schedule to prepare for an uptick in business next week. She lifted and dropped the cow's tail, meeting no resistance. "Looks like she's numbed up. Time to get to work. Would you hold the tail out of the way?" She prepped the cow with the Betadine sponge and liberally applied mineral oil.

Cole said nothing more about Bill, and a new and far less optimistic thought struck her. Ranchers were worse gossips than knitting circles— chatting in diners or through open truck windows on dirt roads. Cole had probably heard through the grapevine that she was trying to build her cattle clientele. He might be acting odd because he had no intention of throwing her regular business and felt guilty about it. The more she thought about it, the more that scenario seemed the likely one. Not that it changed anything. She'd still do the best job she could, same as always, and hope she left him impressed.

Now came the hard part. Even her male counterparts had war stories about their physical battles while trying to reposition a seventy-five-pound fetus inside the mom. And if the repositioning went well, there were still dangers to both the cow and the calf once the pulling started. She scooted into the best of the awkward positions on the ground. Cole tried to give her as much room as possible, but he took up a sizeable amount of space himself. Even with him down on one knee and tucked into the corner of the stall, her shoulder rubbed against his leg and hip.

With a bit of sweat and one-armed gymnastics, she finally shifted the baby enough to pull the bent limb toward her. Once the calf was in a "diving position," she was able to fix the ropes above the hind hooves. She pulled with the next contraction and the legs came forward a few inches.

"Almost there, Mama," she said.

A new contraction began on the heels of the previous one and she pulled again. The calf's rump and hips slid free. Mom pushed once more and Kelli gave a final hard tug. In a sudden rush, the calf slipped out almost onto her lap.

Cole brought the bucket of water to her. She cleaned the little head, washing the baby's nostrils and mouth, and sighed with relief when she saw it take its first breath. She and Cole shared a happy grin until his thousand-watt smile nearly melted something inside her chest and she turned self-consciously back to the calf.

She sterilized the end of the umbilical cord that had broken during the birth, then did a quick check for twins.

"Just the one," she said, removing her glove. "Looks like she's all set."

She untied the cow from the post and removed her lead rope. Mama heaved to her feet and investigated the newcomer, licking circulation and vigor into her baby. The little guy must have been as tired as mom. He still hadn't gotten to his feet.

"Let's help him start nursing," she said.

Shoulder to shoulder, they lifted the calf. Still rattled from his smile and that old sense of kinship and connection, Kelli felt acutely aware of Cole's well-muscled arm against her body. He'd always been one of the taller boys at her grade school, and strong in his high school years from football and wrestling. But dang if he hadn't gotten seriously buff during his college years; his left triceps against her ribs might as well have been warm iron.

After a moment, the calf had its balance and was suckling steadily. Cole stood and held out a hand to help her up. She took it, aware of his strong grip and the individual callouses marching across his palm below each finger.

She removed her soiled jumpsuit while reminding him to watch for the placenta and call her back out if it hadn't delivered in an hour or two. She gave him her cell number as the clinic would be closing soon. He picked up her med kit and opened the stall gate, waiting for her to go first, but she hesitated. Time had suddenly run short to say the difficult thing that had been on her mind since arriving.

"I was sorry to hear about your father, Cole. He was a good man."

Cole nodded and looked down at his boots. "Thank you, he was. The best man I've ever known."

She couldn't imagine how deeply Ben's death must have affected him. His mother had died nearly five years ago from cancer and now he'd lost his father before his time as well. It would be hard enough on anybody, but Cole hadn't just lost his parents; they had been his lifeline. Ben and Cora had fostered him when social services removed Cole from his birth parents at seven years old and charged both parents with criminal neglect. They'd adopted him as their own son and shown him a level of love and care he'd never known.

"Has it been hard taking over the ranch?" she asked as they walked back to her truck.

"I'm settling into it. I'd planned to stay in Texas until June. I took work with a ranching outfit I interned with a couple of years ago, when I was in between getting my bachelor's degree and starting my master's program. They were doing some really innovative things and I'm hoping to implement some of their ideas here."

"Like what?" she asked, happy to let the conversation flow to something less painful.

Together, they loaded her equipment into her truck and stood by the driver's side door as he told her with increasing animation about his cross-breeding plans and the Texas outfit's electronic tracking and data management. They'd also compiled economic data on natural beef production. He said he was hoping to certify as a natural beef supplier, and they shared thoughts about cutting out antibiotics and chemical fertilizers, then progressed to a lively discussion on breed weights and medical advances.

It felt like nothing had changed since grade school, when they'd shared a closeness unusual in children so young. Except that now he was twenty-seven, same as her, buff as a grizzly bear, oozing charisma, and probably her worst nightmare incarnate. Her last lesson had been two months ago. Two. Freaking. Months. She conjured a memory of the pain to remind herself what men like him did to her.

Her phone rang. The home screen showed it was after 5:30 p.m. Rikki was calling more than half an hour past closing time and guilt flooded Kelli for not checking in with her hard-working vet tech.

"Hey, Rikki, sorry I haven't called."

"Oh, that's fine. Jean was running late and only picked up her cat a few minutes ago. That was the last of the hospital patients to go home, so I was wondering if you need anything else at the clinic before I leave for the day?"

Kelli said she didn't and they signed off, but the momentum of her conversation with Cole had broken. "I didn't realize it was so late. Sorry, I'd better get going. I can talk about this stuff all day." She squatted down and patted Baxter goodbye. He wagged his tail at the attention.

Cole opened her truck door for her. "I enjoyed the talk. It was nice to bounce my ideas off someone who's up on the recent studies." He pulled his wallet out of his back pocket and fished through his business cards. "Here's my accountant's email address for the invoice."

She took the card from him and put her hand out to shake.

"How 'bout this?" he said, opening his arms and inviting her to hug. Glad to rekindle their old friendship, she didn't hesitate.

He wasn't one of those men who gave a self-conscious A-frame hug. He wrapped his arms around her and pulled her in close. A proper embrace for two old friends who'd spent far too long apart.

"Thank you for all your help," he said.

His deep voice resonated in his torso. When he let go, she could still feel his warm handprints on her back.

"My pleasure. Feel free to call me if you need anything else while Bill's away."

24 HER COLORADO COWBOY

And, hopefully, after he got back too. Even if Cole continued to use Bill Salem, maybe he'd think of her instead of Bill's partners when Bill was unavailable. Maybe she could jockey into position to replace him when he retired.

She closed the door and started the truck, still a little breathless from the hug. "Get a grip, Kelli," she mumbled aloud as she spun the wheel and U-turned away from the barn with a wave goodbye.

Kelli would always have a place in her heart for the boy she'd known; a sad child those initial few months in second grade, confused by his first time in school and all the changes in his life. And she'd been the girl drawn to anything that suffered; the girl who moved worms out of rain puddles and brought home injured birds or frogs, a squirrel hit on the road. They'd been close friends for years, right up until he'd transferred at the start of junior high to a larger school with more sports opportunities.

And now they were adults, and they were different people. Cole had turned into a chick-magnet cattle rancher with enough leftover testosterone to rodeo for a hobby—something she'd heard about from her friend, Sienna. On top of that, rumor had it—Sienna, again, always up to date on the town gossip—he'd been seen on a dating site connecting with chic women who wore lots of makeup and had the twiggy figures of magazine models. And with Kelli's last breakup still fresh and raw, she had learned her lesson, *finally*. Her penchant for broad-shouldered tough guys had only ever led to heartache.

She drove back to the highway and turned right, toward town, breathing easier the farther away from Cole she got. Blanca Peak receded behind her and prairie stretched out ahead, dotted with a few newer ranch homes but far more single-wide trailers, homemade, off-the-grid shacks and tiny, mostly unrenovated, depression-era homes. Silos, water cisterns, hay sheds and old tractors sat in yards like battered sentries.

Daylight savings had started a couple of weeks ago and sunset was still a way off, but she kept a close eye out for deer on the road until she slowed at the Burgess town sign. The same as all Colorado town markers, it listed the elevation of 7,780 instead of the population of four hundred and thirty. She turned left and wove her way out the other side of town in less than two minutes.

Her stomach growled in a Pavlovian response to approaching the house at dinnertime. Allen had been a better cook than her—not that it took much to beat her culinary skills—and she'd never minded doing dishes. It had been one of so many little things about the two of them that seemed to fit right. But there'd be no dinner on the stove for her tonight. Not even a couch to sit on to watch

TV since most of their furniture had belonged to Allen.

The nearest discount furniture store was a two-hour drive each way and she hadn't dared take a weekend off emergency call or spend extra money until she'd been sure her solo finances could cover all the bills. Not that she'd needed a weekend off. The thought of entering the dating scene again held all the appeal of donning a swimsuit midwinter and plunging into an ice hole in a mountain lake.

Parking in the driveway of her small circa 1960s house on five acres, she walked inside to a dark and silent home. Yes, definitely time to get a dog.

CHAPTER TWO

COLE SAT ON a hay bale across from the box stall with Baxter at his feet. He could have kept working and checked back occasionally for the afterbirth, but he enjoyed watching the new mother and calf. No matter how busy he was, he would always make time to witness that natural bond between mother and offspring: a litter of puppies romping with their dam, a hatch of goslings paddling behind a protective goose in the ranch pond, a raccoon checking for grain in the barn after dark with an assembly of youngsters waddling behind.

The rumble of a four-wheeler's engine grew loud outside, then shut off. Baxter lifted his head at the soft footsteps approaching and, a moment later, Dustin appeared. His ranch foreman reached into his shirt pocket, drew out the antique watch he always kept there and popped the front open. Only a few years Cole's senior, the lean cowboy had always seemed to be an old soul, and the pocket watch amplified the impression.

"The fence out by the cabin's repaired," Dustin said in his soft Oklahoma drawl, "and there's still an hour or so till sunset." He snapped the watch closed. "Anything else you want done before the evening feeding?"

"No. Go ahead and load up the hay and get the herd fed. It'll be good for everyone to knock off early for once."

"Yes, sir."

Three months as Dustin's boss and it still jarred Cole to be called "sir." He'd been seventeen when twenty-three-year-old Dustin Bradford was hired on by his father. Dustin, who'd been the first person to take Cole fly-fishing and spent hours of his free time refining his skill with bucking horses. A quiet man who'd been promoted to ranch foreman at twenty-nine and commanded the respect of wranglers more than twice his age. The man who had called his father "sir" and seamlessly shifted the title on Cole's first day back home.

Dustin moved to the stall gate and leaned his forearms on the top, one booted foot on a rail. He watched the newborn calf wobble around the stall, testing its new legs. "Looks like they're both doing well."

"They are, thanks to Kelli. We'll keep them in the stall through the weekend, but I expect they'll be out on pasture by Monday."

Dustin watched the pair in silence a moment longer, then nodded to Cole and left to see to the evening feeding. He was a man of few words, but Cole had always suspected that still waters ran deep in his foreman. The sounds of the four-wheeler diminished.

The mama cow started contractions for the afterbirth. The calf tried to run, fell, then popped back up. An hour ago, it probably would have died without Kelli's help. Cole's thoughts drifted back to her. She was even more beautiful now than in her early twenties when he'd seen her on rare occasions at school breaks. Gorgeous without looking artificial, her wheat-blond hair parted crookedly off-center, tousled from work and pulled back in a practical ponytail. No makeup that he noticed and a figure like a professional athlete. On top of all that, he'd enjoyed the most intellectual ranching conversation he'd had since Texas. Too bad she was with someone. Cole had only seen Allen once, in the grocery store shopping with Kelli, right after he'd moved back from Texas. Fortunately, Troy had been with him and let him know they were together; otherwise, Cole might have been tempted to ask her out today.

As if thinking of Troy invoked him, he heard his brother's truck rumbling up the road. The cow delivered her placenta just before the truck pulled into the driveway. Cole threw a little extra hay in the stall, checked the water and wandered out of the barn to give Troy the news about the new calf.

"You've been busy," he said, as his brother

30 HER COLORADO COWBOY

climbed out of his truck with half a dozen bags from different stores.

"I had to take care of some errands before I start my run of days on."

The fire department's twenty-four-hour schedule was so convoluted that even the firefighters had to carry a color-coded calendar of shift days in their wallets. "Days on" meant that Troy's C shift was coming up on their four twenty-four-hour work shifts, each separated by a twenty-four-hour day off, then followed at the end of the round by either four or six consecutive days off.

All through high school, Troy had boasted about his plans to go to New York or Chicago or Los Angeles, talking on and on about getting into a college that had fire science as a major, maybe working as an arson investigator. In the end, he'd attended Adams State College in Alamosa, a town of ten thousand people, twenty minutes from Burgess, and had dropped out less than two years later to take a job with the fire department there. He'd been with them nearly seven years now.

"We have a new calf."

"We have a lot of new calves."

"This one was breech. Kelli just left."

"Kelli Hinton? Why'd you call her?"

"Bill's out of town."

"You didn't call his partners? Sam and Carlos have both been out here plenty."

"Yeah, they have." He let a slight edge slip into

his voice. He'd wanted Troy to be happy about the calf, not argue with him about which vet they used.

In fact, he *had* asked for the partners when he learned Bill was unavailable, but both had been tied up for the afternoon. Now it felt like kismet that Kelli had been free. He'd enjoyed her expertise, her attitude, her fresh take on things and her company more than Bill, Sam and Carlos put together. Not that he had any intention of justifying his decision to Troy.

Their father had wanted all three boys to take part in running the ranch, but Troy and Lane had both been clear about their feelings on the matter. Lane had pursued a civil engineering degree and a master's in international business. And Troy had never taken the slightest interest in anything but being a firefighter. All three of them had inherited the land, but their dad's will had left the ranch management solely to Cole.

He would have loved to share with Troy or Lane that it scared the wits out of him to take the reins at twenty-seven. Or tell them about the pressure he felt now that the success or failure of the ranch—the one their father and grandfather and great- and great-great-grandfather had poured their hearts, souls and blood into—rested with the adopted son. But he couldn't share his stress without worrying them, nor would he expose the fact that he'd discovered their father had been losing money on the ranch the past few years.

Still, Heaven help him if *he* did poorly, because Troy and Lane would draw and quarter him. He didn't plan to do poorly, though. He planned to do everything in his power to bring Tillacos Creek Ranch back to its early glory. Running this ranch was his opportunity to say thank you to his parents in a way that really mattered. He had the education, the drive and a strong vision of the contributions he wanted to make here. If he started giving Troy a say now, he could find himself challenged on every decision from today until forever. So, unless a fire broke out on the property, Troy could keep his opinions to himself.

"How'd Kelli do?" Troy asked, not exactly backing down.

"She did great," he said honestly. "Saved our heifer and new calf." He thought Troy might set his bags down and go see them.

"Oh, by the way," Troy said, heading for the house instead, "I have a date lined up for you tomorrow night."

Cole groaned. "What, from that dating site again?"

Troy had been so sincere about fixing him up after his bad breakup with Amy in Texas a few months ago that Cole had found it hard to say no.

"Yes, from the dating site, but look how awesome that last one was. Too bad she had to go back to Italy. Come on, tell me Alessia wasn't amazing. A rich socialite who looked like a supermodel. Man, she was one in a million."

Alessia had been interesting, for sure. Easily someone you'd expect to see in Vail or Aspen, but a socialite in Burgess? Not in a thousand years. Turned out she'd been skiing in Telluride, then came down to Winter Park for the record snowfall there. She'd seen his profile picture online and, apparently, meeting a "real" cowboy had been worth the hour drive over the pass to Alamosa. They'd had dinner together, but to her disappointment— and Troy's—he hadn't taken things any further.

He hadn't been with a woman since moving back to Colorado months ago, but casual relationships weren't his thing. Far from it. The neglect in his childhood had left him with a near-pathological aversion to feigned affection and emotional game-playing. Troy had been right about one thing, though; he was never going to meet his soulmate if he spent all his time on the ranch, so he'd compromised and allowed Troy to set up a profile and trawl the waters on his behalf. Predictably, the three women he'd agreed to meet had been much more Troy's type than what attracted him.

Kelli was definitely his type, but their timing had always been off. Too young all those years that they were friends in grade school, too separated when they were in different junior high and high

34 HER COLORADO COWBOY

schools, and too late to the party now that she'd moved back from college with a live-in boyfriend. One afternoon with her, though, and he'd lost all interest in seeing the latest of his brother's picks.

Troy struggled to open the screen door with his hands full, then grappled with the front door handle.

"What's tomorrow, Friday?" Cole asked, holding the screen door, stuck behind his six-foot-three brother and his armload of stuff.

The door swung open. Troy wrestled his bags through the doorframe and grunted some affirmative as Cole and Baxter followed him in.

"Sorry. You'll have to cancel. I have a cattleman's association meeting in Alamosa." Cole hung his jacket on the coat rack, then tugged his boots off and set them on the rubber boot mat as their housekeeper mandated.

Troy kicked off his sneakers and flung them haphazardly onto the mat with his toe. "The local yokels' meeting? Dang, Cole, call it what it is. A night out drinking with your buddies." He dropped his packages on the couch.

"We talk business at our meetings," Cole said with mock indignity. "For at least ten minutes during dinner. Then we drink." Truth was, the meetings *were* real business meetings, casual atmosphere or not, but he wasn't going to pass up an opportunity to yank his brother's chain.

"Seriously? Hanging out with those guys is

more important to you than meeting Barb? It's a one-shot deal. She's coming through here tomorrow, headed back up to Denver from a week in Santa Fe. Something to do with a gallery show down there."

Troy pulled out his phone and poked at the screen a few times to open first the dating site, then the woman's profile. He held it face out for Cole to see. From the photo and optional stats she'd listed, Barb Okeke could have been a sister to the other three women Troy had set him up with. Attractive photo, lots of makeup, twenty-five years old. Runway model proportions. Her profile screamed city girl and listed interests in museums, sculpture and travel.

"You like her so much, maybe you should go out with her."

"I'll be at work tomorrow night. Besides, Jan got over her latest beef with me. We're going to a movie Saturday."

Cole shook his head. Troy and Jan had been off and on more times in three years than a kitchen light switch. He didn't know how anybody could stay coworkers through that. Any sane person would at least have put in for a different shift or station.

"Come on," Troy said. "You owe me for blowing it with the last one."

"I think you're more disappointed about that than she was."

36 HER COLORADO COWBOY

Cole actually *had* felt a bit bad about walking Alessia to her car and rather abruptly saying good-night after she'd quite obviously expected an invitation to his ranch. It seemed she wasn't a woman who heard *no* often in her life. She'd been speechless for a moment and her sultry affectations dropped away, giving him a brief glance of the woman behind the heiress mystique. Regaining her composure quickly, she'd wished him a good-night with a wry smile, then gotten in her car to drive more than an hour back over the wintry pass. Not that he worried about her; she probably could have hired a limousine if she hadn't felt like driving.

Cole started up the stairs to shower away the day's dust and dirt before dinner.

"You sure you want to cancel with Barb?" Troy called after him.

He answered without turning. "Alamosa. Cattlemen's association."

He didn't add that if it had been Kelli's profile, he would have bailed on the informal meeting in a hot minute.

CHAPTER THREE

KELLI WAVED GOODBYE to the family, her last appointment at the end of a long day. Lucy, Jack and their mom waved back, each of the children with one hand on their goat's halter and the mother holding a leash to the stray dog they'd found. The mom, the children and almost certainly the goat were all happy that the follow-up exam had shown the udder infection to be completely resolved. The family was also delighted that the dog had checked out healthy and was now fully vaccinated.

Kelli was the only one somewhat disappointed. She'd arrived planning to take the dog. The mother had mentioned on the phone the other day that they'd lured him into a pen with food and were looking for a home for him. With Allen's objections out of the way, Kelli had made up her mind to say yes today if he was still available, but it turned out the family had fallen in love with him and foster-failed.

She started her truck and checked her phone

for any notifications she might have missed and, more importantly, to see the time. Five o'clock on the Friday of her first weekend completely off in two months could seriously not come fast enough. The time display showed 4:52 p.m. and counting. No emergency calls, no messages from Rikki. Excellent. She opened her contacts, thumbed past Allen's with a mental note, *again*, to remember to delete him and tapped the call icon next to Sienna Herrera.

"Hey you," Sienna answered, "what's the word?"

"I'm headed home to shower. I'll be at your place by 6:30."

"Should I prepare iced tea or tequila sunrises to go with dinner?"

"Long Island iced tea, please."

"That bad, huh? Well, hang in there. I'll see you soon."

Next, Kelli recorded a new voicemail stating she was closed for the weekend and providing the number to the twenty-four-hour emergency clinic in Alamosa. The financial downside to owning a solo practice had been huge, but one big advantage was setting her own hours.

An hour and a half later, Kelli drove to the other end of town. Burgess was small enough not to have a single traffic light, and she wove past mom-and-pop stores, two restaurants, the post office and the blend of old ranch houses that had been swallowed by town limits as the area grew.

Most homes were decades old—both the ancient two-story ranch homes from the early 1900s and the tiny single-story homes from the 1950s and '60s. A few newer developments with more stylish family homes lay on the outskirts of town, but Sienna owned one of the little single-story houses just a block off the main street, saying the size was a perfect fit for her.

Kelli let herself in the front door. Mouthwatering smells of the bubbling fish and prawn stew that Sienna had promised wafted from the kitchen, rich with spices, onion, potato, corn and chipotle. It had long been her favorite of Sienna's many recipes. Kelli might hate cooking, but she really, really loved food.

Once in Sienna's immaculate kitchen, the visuals enhanced the smells: crusty bread, a bowl of butter, and a tall glass of amber liquid by her place setting at the small table.

"Don't get excited," Sienna said, noticing her eyeing the glass. "It's plain-old iced tea. I'm looking forward to going dancing tonight and don't need you throwing up on my shoes after one beer at the Longhorn." She turned back to the stove, flipping her curtain of long dark hair over her shoulder.

Kelli had been joking about the Long Island iced tea, anyway. She was a lightweight—unlike her best friend. Drinking something that strong would probably not be pretty.

40 HER COLORADO COWBOY

"Your logic is sound as always. Besides, I wouldn't want to saddle you with a depressed drunk to babysit tonight."

Sienna paused, wooden spoon dripping into the stew pot. "Are you sure you're up for this?" Genuine concern replaced her standard flippant banter. "You know I'm fine with staying in and watching TV if you're not ready for something this social yet."

Kelli shook her head. "No. It's okay. You're right. I can't stay a shut-in the rest of my life." She took a seat at the table. "Dinner here instead of the Longhorn is nice, though."

"You know I would have been happy to provide moral support, alcohol and/or chocolate truffles every evening instead of just that first couple of weeks."

"I know you would have. Honest, though, that was all it took to get my pity party out of my system and figure out that Allen was nothing more than the same guy I've always dated, just in new packaging. I think that's why I've kept putting off doing this—going out and trying again. I just don't recognize the ick factor when I see it. If a guy acts nice, I think he is nice."

"The problem is that *you're* nice, so you assume everyone else is too." Sienna tasted the stew, nodded and turned off the gas. "But the good news is I'm not. I don't trust any of them, and you've got me as your wingman tonight. Better yet, even though I'm back on nights as of today, I now have weekends off until May. I'm all yours Friday, Saturday, Sunday and every other Thursday for the whole month of April."

Kelli occasionally had to respond to nighttime and weekend emergencies, but she couldn't imagine dealing with a 911 dispatcher's schedule. Three months of 7:00 a.m. to 7:00 p.m. alternating with three months of 7:00 p.m. to 7:00 a.m. Working only three or four shifts a week did *not* make up for that.

Sienna ladled up two bowls, handed one to Kelli and took a seat. "So seriously, are you ready to paint the town or not?"

Kelli played with her straw, half wishing her drink really were a Long Island iced tea.

"Gotta start sometime, right?"

"That's the spirit. And can I just say again that you've taken the whole Allen thing a whole lot calmer than I would have."

"I didn't look very calm when I was throwing every scrap of his clothing out the front door while he was in the shower." She took a bite of the stew and moaned in appreciation, then buttered a big slice of bread.

"You have no idea how much I wish I'd seen that."

"I think I came up with a handful of new swear words too."

"Ooh, I'll have to get those from you."

HER COLORADO COWBOY

Kelli scoffed. "Like you need them."

"You can never have too many swear words in your repertoire." Sienna wagged her spoon at her. "You know, I still can't believe that dunderhead was cheating on you. There is no justice in the world if that blowhard, Steven Seagal wannabe could be unfaithful when you were one-hundred percent faithful to him."

There was nothing in the world as comforting as a loyal friend. Sienna had never said a bad word about Allen in the eight months he'd lived in Burgess, but she'd rolled straight into defensive best-friend mode as soon as she heard the news. She had a new slur for Allen every time Kelli mentioned him. And Sienna was right, he *had* been quite the wannabe with his endless talk of Tae Kwon Do, his short stint a decade before as a mixed martial arts fighter and his action-flick obsession.

Sienna was trying to help but bringing up Allen's infidelity again was painful. Not the ugly-cry pain of two months ago; more like death by a thousand paper cuts now. She reexamined their fourteen months together, asking herself for the hundredth time if she should have seen it coming.

When they'd first met, Allen had described his work-from-home "headhunter" job by comparing it to Jerry Maguire. Like the sports agent Tom Cruise portrayed, corporate headhunting was a 24/7 job of wining and dining upper-management prospects, trying to get them to sign with the companies he represented before another headhunter sweet-talked them away. He'd been in the shower one Sunday evening when his phone rang and the contact had shown only as *Steve*, same as the first name of the man he was courting for a VP position at Lockheed Martin. The #3 aerospace company in the world, headquartered in Denver, was offering a big incentive if Allen could bring them the right person for the job.

Kelli had answered his phone for him, trying to be helpful. Before she could swallow the big gulp of water she'd just taken, a woman's voice blurted out, "Babe, I know I'm not supposed to call you in the evening..." It had come as such a surprise that Kelli had nearly inhaled the water, giving the woman ample time to ramble on and leave no room for doubt about her, or Allen, or what the two of them had been up to on his frequent trips to Denver.

"You know, that's the only thing that still stings," Kelli said, already half finished with her stew and reaching for another slice of bread. "He was off messing around with some other woman—or women—while I'd actually convinced myself that this was it. This was the one I'd been looking for. The first guy I'd been serious enough about to move in with. A guy who chose to relocate to the middle of nowhere rather than lose me when I said I had to be near my parents."

44 HER COLORADO COWBOY

"Okay, reality check." Sienna set her spoon down. "Can I tell you something?" Kelli nodded. "I never saw you guys making it. And I mean that in a good way," she amended quickly. "Like a 'good thing you escaped that one' way."

"You're just saying that to make me feel better." Sienna laid a hand on her heart. "Swear."

"Why did you never say it before?"

"Because when you were together you wanted so much to believe it would work. And afterward, it would have sounded like rubbing it in. But even if he'd never cheated on you and the two of you got married, I just never saw him as your soulmate. I mean, he was good-looking, and I get the mutual attraction, but I never saw wild, unbridled love in your eyes, you know? And you're so special and so vibrant. Honey, you are definitely a person who deserves love. The real thing. The whole deal."

"You're sweet," she said, reaching over and briefly squeezing Sienna's hand, "but I'm still not sure I wouldn't be better off just giving up. This whole dating thing is like one of those wood puzzles with pieces that fit together to make a circle that I can never figure out." She gripped the base of her iced tea between thumb and forefinger and rotated the glass slowly, watching the ice cubes bump and swirl. "The guys who make me feel fireworks…or bonfires…wildfires even… for a week or two or ten? They break my heart."

She shook her head and wiped her damp fingers. "They're the worst possible matches for me. You should know. You've picked up the pieces enough times." She sighed. "I finally find one who feels like he's grounded and professional and grown up, someone who looks like he's in it for the long haul, and then that happens. And he's not even the only one who's cheated on me. Remember Rudy from my second year in vet school?"

"You know I don't have the answers," Sienna said. "If I did, I'd be with my guy right now instead of you."

"I wish you were. I wish one of us could win at this stupid game."

She meant it too. She loved Sienna. She had for more than fifteen years. And she would have been as happy for Sienna finding true love as if she'd found it herself.

It had been a good day for Kelli when Sienna's mom moved to Burgess to be near her sister after her divorce. It was the year that Cole transferred to Alamosa Junior High, but Kelli had hardly seen him outside of classes in the previous year anyway while he played Little League and youth football, and got his first quarter horse, and helped out more at the ranch. Sienna had been new in town with no friends, and she and Sienna had glommed together like an atomic bond. Their friendship had remained solid, even long distance. And when

46 HER COLORADO COWBOY

Kelli moved back from college, they'd picked up like they'd never been apart.

Finished with dinner, Sienna carried their bowls to the sink while Kelli cleared the rest. Kelli rinsed and Sienna stacked the dishwasher. They had the pot soaking and the dishes put away in no time.

"So, we gonna sit around here and cry all night over Cheater McPeter or you ready to go to the Longhorn and go dancing with me?" Sienna placed one long-fingered hand on her narrow hip as if daring her to give the wrong answer.

"Dancing," Kelli said. "One hundred and ten percent dancing."

CHAPTER FOUR

THE USUAL SUSPECTS were already present when Cole arrived a little after seven on Friday night. The Longhorn Tavern was one of those rare finds; a nice bar. Quiet on the weeknights and mellow on the weekends until the rowdier crowd started showing up around ten o'clock. They offered all-ages dance lessons a couple nights a week, served good burgers every night and offered an inexpensive but good-quality steak dinner between six and eight on Friday and Saturday to encourage an early drinking crowd.

Cole put his dinner order in at the bar and joined the others at a table in a back corner of the room. He hadn't been far from the truth when he teased Troy that the meetings were short and the socializing long, but over dinner he and the other San Louis Valley Cattleman's Association members shared information about everything from beef prices to pasture issues to nutrient tips.

By the time the eight ranchers pushed their plates away, talk had turned to spring weather,

48 HER COLORADO COWBOY

hiring new hands and the upcoming rodeo. The others were past their prime for competing, but Tim ran the scoreboard, Juan was partnered with a bucking bull breeding program outside Denver, and Lacey, the lone woman in their small group, was an ex-barrel racer with a daughter who was up-and-coming nationally. Cole had never had the time or the talent to compete seriously, but he'd entered bronc riding at Texas rodeos throughout his college years and was signed up for the local event next week.

Their meeting ended a little before eight o'clock, just minutes before the subdued background music was due to switch to the live DJ. They'd ordered a new pitcher for the table when Lacey suddenly stood with a look of thunder on her face.

"I swear, if you think your troubles are over when they turn twenty-one..."

Cole leaned back to see around a post and followed her gaze. He hadn't noticed her daughter, Jenna, here as well, sitting with her own friends halfway across the room. At last month's meeting, Lacey had mentioned planning her birthday party, so he guessed Jenna had been legal drinking age for all of a week or two. The blonde firebrand stood, hands on hips. She wore a short shirt and tight jeans with embroidery and sequins across the back pockets that drew his eyes where they didn't want to go. She looked to be delivering a lecture to a boy wiping liquid and foam from his face. In the background, a muscular man in a Longhorn T-shirt was headed her way. Lacey hurried across the room, holding her hands out to the bouncer and gesturing to her daughter in an "I've got this" way.

Cole shook his head and turned back. Juan Escobar chuckled—he had five daughters.

Lacey returned with a completely unrepentant Jenna at her heels.

"*He* insulted *me*," she was complaining. "You should be defending me."

Lacey walked her to the only open chair, at the end of the table between Cole and Juan. Jenna flopped into it and leaned back with her arms crossed.

"You can thank me later that you didn't get kicked out of here," Lacey said.

"Can I go back to Lori and Cindy?" Jenna asked. "We can get another table."

"May I," Lacey said. "And, no, you may not."

"I promise I won't go near Brody. We're broken up for good. He's sooo immature."

Cole suppressed a smile, guessing the irony wasn't going to catch up to her anytime soon.

"Mind your manners and stay quiet until we're done. You're at the adult's table now."

"I *am* an adult," Jenna said under her breath.

The DJ bellowed a welcome into the microphone and the volume of the music tripled. Lacey returned to her place at the opposite end of the table and shouted a question about who planned to go to the cattle auction in Albuquerque in June. They each gave opinions on the selections and prices and lodging at the auction as if it were the most important subject of the night. When the topic ran out of steam, they adjourned for the second time and she released Jenna from her vow of silence.

"Stay here while I finish my beer and then we're going home." Her gestures filled in the gaps in her words, which were drowned by the music, before she launched into a new conversation with the man next to her.

"Are you entered in the rodeo this weekend?" Cole asked, taking pity on Jenna.

Under his attention, the young woman's demeanor changed instantly from pouting daughter to confident young woman. "I am. It's just for practice, though, since it's only a preseason event."

"How long have you been pro?"

"This is my fourth year in the Women's PRA."

Cole had his Pro Rodeo Association card as well, but she didn't ask.

"How's your season gone?"

"Good. I'm ranked fifty-first and earned nearly six-thousand dollars since November. I'm only living at home because my parents are helping me with the travel expenses for now. Once I earn enough, I'll move out and transfer to Tennessee or Oklahoma University to be closer to more events."

Her parents had probably spent twice what she'd earned in competition. Then again, if she was good—and it sounded like she was—it had the potential to pay off. The top few riders in the country made hundreds of thousands of dollars.

"I'd be doing better already but Wildfire slowed down over the winter. I think he's getting a little arthritis so I'm looking for a new horse."

"A couple of my ranch hands spent the winter training mustangs my father got from the BLM sale last year. I can ask if any of them are showing promise."

The Bureau of Land Management culled mustangs from wild herds to prevent overpopulation and starvation. It had been the first time his father bought mustangs, and Cole had been looking forward to seeing how they worked out.

"Okay. Thanks." She was leaning forward on her elbows now, her face close to his. Her eyes darted to the middle of the room where her freshly dumped boyfriend sat cleaning his face with bar napkins and a glass of water. A new song began.

"Ahh," she said, sounding like someone had just stabbed her with a knife or ripped her soul from her body. She looked down at her hands dramatically, then back at him. He lifted his eyebrows in question.

"This is my favorite song ever. Think I could talk you into one dance?"

Cole was beginning to regret trying to entertain her. Juan must've heard at least part of what she said and gave him a sympathetic smile over her head.

"I better not. Your mom looked pretty mad. I wouldn't want to keep her waiting when she's ready to go."

Jenna glanced pointedly down the table at her mother's glass, still mostly full. "She could nurse that for another half hour." A resolved look crossed her face. "Hey, Mom," Jenna yelled, "I'll be back in a minute." She pointed a finger at Cole's chest, pointed to the dance floor and held the finger in the air to indicate one dance.

Juan shook his head, still smiling. Cole wished he'd talked to Tim on his other side instead of Jenna. Twenty-one and twenty-seven weren't six years apart, they were worlds apart. Beautiful as she was, he had zero interest in her rebounding into him or the rumor mill that could start up in this small town if he danced with her.

Jenna was already standing as if he'd agreed. She grabbed him by the hand and tugged him up out of his chair. He glanced at Lacey, who threw her hands up in a "what can I do?" gesture. A glance at the tables on the other side of the dance floor showed the "ex" boyfriend watching, as Cole felt certain Jenna had planned.

She already had him on his feet and everyone at the table was looking. To pull away from her now would embarrass them both. He was doomed.

CHAPTER FIVE

KELLI PRESENTED HER ID to the Longhorn doorman and received her hand stamp just before the eight o'clock cover kicked in. Not that she and Sienna couldn't afford a cover charge these days, but old college habits died hard. Sienna picked a small table for four near the dance floor. They sat next to each other to hear better and ordered two longneck beers.

"At least *you* take me out," Kelli said when the beers came, tapping the top of her bottle to her friend's. "You know Allen never brought me here. Not once, even though he knew I loved to dance."

"I keep telling you, butthead was no catch."

Kelli tugged at the straps of her borrowed dress and brushed a finger over the unfamiliar feel of mascara on her eyelashes.

"Quit fussing. You'll smudge it."

Before leaving, Sienna had crossed her arms and examined Kelli's choice of long-sleeved shirt and jeans. She'd crooked her finger and walked into her bedroom, pulling a sleeveless denim dress from her closet. With Sienna being three inches taller and naturally slender, Kelli had protested that the dress would never fit. Turned out it had a tie that hit Sienna at the ribs and her at the waist, so it fell to an attractive mid-calf length that just brushed the tops of her dancing boots. Sienna had also pushed makeup products on her. Kelli tried to remember the last time she'd worn either a dress or makeup, much less both.

Canned music played at a background volume and the dance floor was empty. The DJ was in the booth, getting ready. Kelli nursed her beer and tried to inconspicuously people-watch. She recognized three or four clients among the slowly growing crowd but saw no interesting prospects for dance partners.

"So, weekends, you and me," Sienna said. "What do you want to do tomorrow?"

"Not what I want to do, what I have to do. I finally have two days off and I've got to get some furniture of my own. Without the things you loaned me, the house would look like it should have a for-sale sign out front."

When she and Allen met, Kelli had been an impoverished college student with a bunch of mismatched garage-sale furnishings and cinder block bookshelves. He'd been a professional with a nicely decked-out apartment in Denver. She had no idea how he'd gotten a moving truck on a Sunday evening the night she broke up with him, but while she rage-drove halfway through New Mexico with orders for him to be gone when she got back, he'd managed to get completely gone. Him and everything he owned; plus a few minor things they'd bought together.

"Wow. Okay, I was picturing something a bit more fun like hitting the hot springs in Crestone, but furniture shopping it is. After that, though, we're working on getting you back up on that horse before you get gun-shy for real." She fluttered the fingers of one hand. "That's a mixed metaphor, but you know what I mean."

"I'm not sure I do. Which horse is this, exactly?"

"Look, I know how you feel about online dating, but we at least need to get you a profile. I mean dancing is fun, but the odds of you meeting Mr. Perfect tonight are slimmer than the toothpick that guy is chewing." She nodded to the next table. "With an online profile, you can sit at home and weed guys out by whatever you're looking for, starting with a cute profile picture."

"You're right," she said. Sienna stared at her wide-eyed with happy surprise. "I don't want to try online dating."

"Ugg. I should've been ready for that," Sienna murmured into her beer. She seemed lost in thought. "What about Todd McKenzie? Did you know he'd gotten divorced?"

"I didn't know he'd been married or divorced.

Thanks for the thought, but I think this is one of those things that just needs to happen when it happens."

"That's a terrible plan. That's how something like Jimmy Deacon happens."

"Oh, give me a break. That was high school. I've got my eyes wide open this time." She pinched her mouth shut, realizing she'd said the same thing after each disastrous relationship. And Sienna had been there every time.

The DJ suddenly belted out his welcome nearly making her jump. Two men who'd been eyeballing them across the dance floor came over to their table and asked if they could join them. Sienna said yes at the same time Kelli said no, and they ended up leaving.

"You *are* going to dance tonight, aren't you? I mean with somebody besides me?"

"Yes. I promise. If the right guy asks me, I will. I just wasn't ready for on-the-hunt characters like those two to sit down and stake us out for the evening and expect something at the end of it."

"You're right. Good idea. We'll play the field."

About a dozen couples were on the dance floor already. Kelli sat back, tapped her foot to the beat and watched them swirl around the floor. The first people out were usually the regulars, an older crowd that showed up early and left early. Two of the couples were in their sixties or seventies, and it was obvious they'd danced together for de-

58 HER COLORADO COWBOY

cades. The women could anticipate every turn, every spin, every new hold. They glided around the floor like twenty-five-year-olds. No, better, because they had a lifetime of partnership. Kelli couldn't help but wonder if that was something just never meant for her. Maybe she'd end up an old spinster veterinarian.

The next song was a line dance, an upbeat, easy one that she remembered from years ago. Sienna slammed her beer down on the table so hard that foam popped out the top. She grabbed Kelli's hand and half ran for the floor so they wouldn't miss the beginning. Kelli fumbled through the first few bars, but the steps came back to her after a couple of repetitions of the pattern. When the regular music started again, she and Sienna sat down red-faced, sweating and happy. It always amazed Kelli how much moving to music could lift her spirits. Maybe Sienna had been right; this was what she'd needed.

"How come you've never met anybody here?" Kelli asked.

"There was that one guy, James, that I kept posting pictures of a couple of years ago, but it was never something that was going to last."

"What does?" she said, her emotions hurtling over a precipice and onto the downhill section of the never-ending roller-coaster ride.

"Sorry. I didn't mean to invoke Captain Clueless."

"You didn't. I did." Kelli sighed into the beer

she was nursing, about to take a swallow, when she froze. Cole Tyler was being led to the dance floor by a peppy blonde wearing a skimpy top tied above her navel and skinny Western jeans. She looked young enough to be a high school senior. She dragged him by the hand, and Kelli couldn't help but remember the feel of Cole's warm hand in hers when he'd helped her up yesterday. The black Stetson hat he always wore matched his crisp black shirt, black boots and black hair. He looked like confidence and competence incarnate. Kelli turned her head quickly and studied her beer bottle, hoping he hadn't seen her.

"You look like you've seen a ghost," Sienna said, scanning the room.

"It's nothing."

Sienna was on the scent, though, and kept searching. "Oh. Cole Tyler? What's that about?"

"What's what about?"

"That look on your face."

"Really. It's nothing." Sienna continued to stare at her. "I was at his ranch yesterday, helping deliver a calf. It was nice talking to him again is all."

"Oooh. I see. Well, tall, dark and handsome always did trip your trigger."

Yes, it did. And, yes, she *had* thought about Cole today, more than once. But she knew enough to know she wasn't stepping onto the slippery slope of dating a macho dude ever again. She watched as he and his partner faced each other

60   HER COLORADO COWBOY

in dance hold and wondered if they were here on a date. Then she wondered what it would feel like to face him that close, have his arm across her lower back, move with him, rest her hand on that broad shoulder. If there were any justice in the world, his good looks would be counter-balanced by stiff, ungainly, off-beat dancing. Unfortunately, he stepped out perfectly on the downbeat into a smooth two-step. Kelli sighed again.

"Yeah, well, so what if it trips my trigger. Look where it's gotten me." She counted off on her fingers. "Jimmy, Casey, Brad, Mike, Rudy." She held her hand out to Sienna, fingers spread wide. "And now Allen."

Sienna had been there for some of them and Kelli had told her about the rest in long soggy phone conversations. Jimmy Deacon, junior year at her high school, a boy who had encompassed everything she thought she ever wanted. First baseman in the all-county summer boys' team. The boy who had told her he found her beautiful and then mocked her in front of his friends when they didn't find her cool enough.

Casey Barlow, senior year, who lived on another of the ranches in the area and invited her out to see him break one of their horses. Then he'd cajoled and pleaded to kiss her in the barn until she relented. And within a week, he'd moved on to a new girlfriend. Brad Johnston in Fort Collins when she was an undergrad. Twenty years old and so good-looking that all her dorm friends could talk about was how cute he was. He'd asked Kelli to the fall fraternity party and then dated her for four and a half months. He'd also gotten "falling down" drunk at all his frat parties and eventually graduated to a variety of drugs. Next had been Mike Okoro, who'd borrowed money from her on a regular basis with a sob story about how he might have to drop out if he couldn't keep paying for school. Later, she'd found out that his parents paid for school and she'd been his unwitting stock car racing sponsor, rather than Budweiser as he'd claimed. Fast-forward two years later to her next serious relationship. Someone she thought was going to be "the one." Rudy Hightower. A veterinary student like herself, with enough looks and charm for any three guys. By that time, she doubted all men, but he proved himself again and again. He took her nice places, he remembered birthdays and special occasions, and went out of his way to plan a killer Valentine's date. He was suave and debonair right up until she caught him in a friend's dorm room. With her friend.

"Those were all 'flash in the pan' guys. Well, except for Allen, and even he wasn't in your life all that long. Girl, you've carried a torch for Cole Tyler for years."

"Have not," she said, indignantly. "We were just little kids when we were friends. We were too young to even think like that."

"I know that, but something about that friendship stuck with you both. I saw it every time we went to a football game or wrestling match he was in. If he'd stayed on at our school, you guys would have been high school sweethearts for sure."

It was true. Some part of their old friendship had lodged in her heart. As she'd grown up and understood his past more, she'd thought many times about the childhood Cole had survived and the quiet and sensitive boy he'd been. Knowing his traumas had shaped her opinions on drugs in high school and helped her say no to peer pressure. His history had played a part again in her summer before college, influencing her to volunteer with the local Head Start program. And when she'd talked with him yesterday, their conversation had been so easy and comfortable, it was like they'd never spent all those years apart.

"Well, he didn't stay on, and we weren't sweethearts, and, no, I'm not looking to date a male model, rodeo-head rancher of a cowboy."

Unable to help herself, Kelli glanced to the dance floor again just as the pair glided along the rail not twenty feet from her. Cole smoothly turned from dancing forward to dancing backward without missing a beat. His gaze swept her way. She twisted in her chair till her knees bumped Sienna's hip and she was nearly facing the opposite side of the room. "Besides, you're supposed to be looking out for me here. It's your job to keep me away from men like him."

"Then why were you looking at him that way just now?"

"Because I'm weak and stupid."

"Easy there. Nobody gets to talk about my best friend that way." A man approached their table, but Sienna shook her head before he got close. "Seriously, Kelli, you're one of the smartest and most centered people I know."

"Apparently not when it comes to men. And anyway, you were the one gossiping about him dating all those model wannabes since he moved back. Sounds like a player to me. Looks like one too."

"It wasn't *all* those women. It was two or three of them, according to Lisa at work who watches the dating sites and eats like five times a week at the only good restaurant in town. And what? You're going to hold it against him that he's been dating other women while you were with Allen?"

"What I'm saying is that I need to keep from going down this road yet again."

"And that road is?"

"That kind of guy." She snuck another look his direction.

"Big, strong and good-looking? Right. Yeah, let's avoid that at all costs."

"No, you ding-dong." She turned back to sit more naturally. "I need to avoid what comes with

64 HER COLORADO COWBOY

big, strong and good-looking. The 'tudes. The attitude that comes with the package. Like 'worry more about looking cool with a woman than being genuine with her.' Or 'women are disposable because there'll always be another one who'll fall for your charms.' Or 'the grass is greener…'"

"Uh-huh, but this is me you're talking to. I *know* the reason you gravitate toward men like Cole. Remember? And I don't see that going away."

"Well, help me get over it, then. Geez, it was only like twenty years ago."

"I think there are some things we don't get over, Kelli." Sienna locked gazes with her and, for once in her life, looked serious. "They're the things that make us, us, you know?" Kelli guessed that Sienna included herself in that statement. Her party girl of a mom and judgmental father influenced more of Sienna's choices than she cared to admit. "You will always gravitate toward a big, strong, manly man. That break-in affected you. How could it not? And your dad saved you and your mom."

Just speaking of it invoked emotions from that summer before second grade, when two drifters had broken into their house during the night; practically unheard of in Burgess. Her older sister had been at a sleepover, but her dad had been home, thank heavens, and not away working nights. She hated to think what might have happened otherwise. Kelli could still remember her mother's fear-filled eyes, waking Kelli and pulling her into the closet. Her mother's hand over her mouth. Her father's voice tight with adrenaline when reporting the incident once the men ran off after encountering an armed homeowner declaring himself to be law enforcement.

Kelli's father wasn't a big man, barely taller than she was now. But he'd seemed big when she was young, and he'd been a state patrol officer and a protector to the family when they'd needed it. Kelli was a capable and confident adult who could take care of herself these days, but the incident had definitely wormed its way into her psyche in such a way that nothing attracted her quite like a big manly man.

"Yeah, well it's past time I get over it. I swear, I'm dating nothing but accountants and symphony musicians from here on out. And your job is to make sure I don't slip and fall into some good-looking testosterone overdose like Cole Tyler."

"You sure are protesting a lot there, lady. What if he's actually one of the good ones? And in case you've forgotten, I'm not the only one who remembers your big secret fear, or the fact that Cole has had plenty of his own. You're the one who told me you two stayed so close all those years because you'd shared your nightmares with each other."

"I know. I was there. So?"

HER COLORADO COWBOY

"What I'm trying to say is, maybe he still has that big ol' sensitive heart except now it's wrapped in hunky wrapping paper. Besides, a vet and a rancher. Seriously. Does it get any better?"

Kelli flung her hands in the air. "I don't know why you're still on about Cole. He's with someone. See?" She held up one hand as a shield and stabbed a finger his direction.

She tried not to look again, but she did anyway. The song had ended. Cole and the young woman were leaving the dance floor, heading for a shadowy corner behind a post at the back of the room. She watched for a minute to see if he returned alone. It was standard etiquette to escort a woman back to her seat, after all. But no. He didn't reappear.

"Seriously, Sienna," she said, turning back, "if you're my friend, you'll help me find a young version of Mister Rogers. I don't care anymore about big and strong. I don't even care about good-looking. The thing I want more than anything in the world is a sweet guy with a heart of gold who'll treat me right."

Kelli folded her arms on the table and dropped her head into them. She felt Sienna rubbing her back.

"It's okay. You'll find the right one. If nothing else, there's always the process of elimination. Just go through them all."

Kelli couldn't help laughing. Thank goodness for Sienna.

Seeing Cole dancing with someone else made her want to drown her sorrows in a vat of tequila, but this was exactly the sort of behavior she had to unlearn. Men who looked like him had women lined up, and most of those men would discard one for the next in a heartbeat. No, thank you. She'd been discarded enough for one lifetime.

The next song was an upbeat two-step. She was bobbing her head to the music and watching the growing crowd of dancers on the floor when she noticed someone standing at her elbow. She looked up to see a man in his fifties who'd been among the first couples on the floor.

"Would you like to dance?"

He looked safe. Sienna, who knew most of the regulars on sight, nodded discreetly and Kelli accepted. As he walked her to the dance floor, the man introduced himself as Matt. With his tan hat and heavy-boned face, she couldn't help thinking of a short Matt Dillon.

He led her confidently around the floor and when the song ended and another began, he lifted his brows in question. She nodded "yes." They were halfway around when Sienna passed her, dancing with one of those men who spin women around and around like a top. Kelli could never have managed it, but Sienna kept up impressively well. At the end of the second dance, Matt walked her back to her chair, thanked her and approached an older woman at a nearby table.

Sienna returned breathless and plopped down. "That was a workout." She used her napkin to dab sweat from her brow, careful not to smear her makeup. "How was yours?"

"Very gentlemanly."

"Matt's here every weekend. I've danced with him a few times. I think he's a widower, but I've never gotten the feeling he was on the prowl."

It had been a good way to break the ice, and after seeing her accepting offers, other men tried their luck. She danced the next couple of songs with different partners but, unfortunately, none of them "tripped her trigger" like Cole. While dancing with a guy who emitted beer fumes with every breath, despite the early hour, she began to search the recesses of the bar with a growing fear Cole would return to the dance floor with the young woman. She might be subjected to watching them flirt or kiss or who knew what. Worse, he might notice her and come say hi; him with his young thing on his arm and her with who knew what guy. Matt, maybe.

The music grew louder, the dance floor fuller and, though it was probably not even nine o'clock, she suddenly hit her limit of "fake it till you make it" for the night. Her reaction to seeing Cole and his date had turned the heat up on her two-month surplus of emotions and they were beginning to boil over. By the time she returned to the table, all she wanted was to leave.

CHAPTER SIX

COLE WALKED JENNA back to their table, then excused himself, planning to go say hi to Kelli. He'd been surprised when he first spotted her sitting with her friend—Sierra? He'd even done a half turn while dancing to get a better look. There'd been two beers on Kelli's table, not three or four, so it looked like she and her friend were having a girls' night out.

Lacey reached out and grabbed his shirtsleeve as he passed.

"Thank you for dancing with her," she said. "That was good of you. It probably saved a lot of angst tonight. She'd only gone out a couple of times with that boy, but she liked him."

"I'm sure they'll patch it up."

"Oh, no they won't. She doesn't get over insults well, even if it's teasing."

"She looks plenty tough to me," he said, glancing to Jenna, who had gone back to her chair and looked surprised to see him talking to her mother.

"She can be. On the outside. Inside, she's all

marshmallow. She was bullied pretty bad in junior high before we spent a new car's worth of money on dental bills. Now she thinks the best defense is a strong offense. She's got a chip on her shoulder and a giant target on her heart. On top of that, she's got a heck of a competitive streak too." Lacey shook her head. "It's a rough combo."

"I'm sure she'll find her footing in time."

"I hope so. Anyway, it was nice of you not to turn her down on the heels of whatever that was." The boy and his friends had left during the dance, but she waved in the direction he'd been sitting. "Okay, she'll be miffed if she figures out what we're talking about. Cows. There, now you can say I was talking about cows."

"Actually, I was just headed over to see a friend." Cole turned to make his way to Kelli's table but saw that a man twice her age had just taken her out to the dance floor. He stood and watched them. She danced well; something he hadn't known about her.

He returned to his seat. Jenna looked curious but didn't ask what her mother had said to him. When the next song started, she mentioned, pointedly, it was another one she especially liked. He was glad if one dance helped reboot her self-esteem but knew better than to let this get out of hand.

Fortunately, Tim and Juan took pity on him and intervened before she could push her agenda. Tim asked if he had any experience with bovine respiratory disease, then launched into an intense discussion, which Juan joined. Cole glanced over his shoulder. Kelli was back at her table, but she and her friend were deep in conversation. The next time he looked, her friend was there but Kelli wasn't. He finally spotted her dancing with a different guy, this one younger, holding her a little closer. No law against someone in a relationship dancing with other people, but it made him wonder if she and her boyfriend were still together.

Jenna had been right about her mother. Lacey nursed her beer for another twenty minutes and Juan and Tim kept him safely engaged the whole time. Finally, Lacey stood, said her good-nights and collected her daughter. Cole looked again for Kelli and saw her returning from the dance floor with yet another partner. He got up, strangely nervous at the thought of going over to chat, and if the signals felt right, maybe asking her to dance.

Kelli didn't sit, though. She came around to her friend's chair, spoke briefly in her ear and they both grabbed their purses. Standing at the top of the steps that led down to the main floor, he watched them both leave.

"She's outside in the greenhouse, checking on her seedlings."

Her mom was sixty and still worked full-time as an office manager for a medical group in Alamosa, but Kelli had noticed her slowing down too. One leg had always been a half-inch shorter, and she limped more now on a hip that would need a total replacement soon.

"What are you up to today?" he asked.

"Sienna and I are headed out soon to go furniture shopping."

"You know I meant it when I said we'd be fine with the two recliners if you want the couch. We probably haven't sat on it in six months."

"You need it for company. I don't think Mom's book club ladies are quite bohemian enough to sit on the floor."

"The amount of wine they go through, I doubt any of them would notice."

"Thanks, but honestly, I'm looking forward to fixing my place up with my own things finally." She was also looking forward to returning the card table and plastic folding chairs she'd borrowed from them as a makeshift dinette set.

"Do you need money?"

"No. I'm fine." She said it very convincingly, she thought.

Looking around at her parents' twenty-year-old furniture, she wished she could buy some for them too. Someday she would. They'd been doing okay when they were both working, but then medical co-pays had mounted up and they discovered that early social security and early pension benefits barely made up half her father's old salary.

"Anything you or Mom need from Pueblo while I'm there?"

He pursed his lips and shook his head. "Nothing I can think of." The patio door slid open and her mother came in pulling off her gardening gloves. "Momma," he said, "anything you need from Pueblo? Kelli's headed up there."

"Hi, sweetie. I didn't know you were coming over today. No, I can't think of anything we need that I can't get in town."

If Kelli worried about her father getting overweight, she worried just as much about her mother looking thin.

"Call me when you get back," her dad said, "and I'll help you move things inside." He made his way to his well-worn recliner and sat with the sigh of someone eighty-two rather than sixty-two. Her mother perched on the arm of the chair, and he placed a hand on her back.

"The furniture store will deliver it and set it up for her," her mother said, with a pat on his knee and a poignant look in her eye. Whether he'd said it sincerely or knowing the store would take care of it, he could hardly lift a grocery bag anymore, much less a couch.

"I'm glad to see you finally have some time

off," her mother continued. "Are you doing anything fun this weekend?"

"Sienna and I went out for a drink last night."

She didn't mention dancing. Neither her father's *or* mother's heart could take that. They were more anxious for her to find a new boyfriend than she could ever possibly be. Her older sister had been married five years and given them three grandchildren already, with another on the way. Apparently, that wasn't enough to satiate the needs of whatever alien presence possessed parents when unattached children neared the age of thirty.

Probably they just wanted her to find what they had for themselves. She'd been helping her mother clean out a closet a few months ago and discovered a shoebox holding hundreds of little notes and candy hearts and tiny trinkets. It turned out that every time her father had worked a night shift, he'd stuck some surprise under the bed covers for her mother to discover when she went to bed alone. The fact he'd done that was cute. The fact she'd saved them, cute squared.

Her parents' alien possessors' needs aside, they'd both been supportive when she'd broken up with Allen. In fact, her father's reaction had been he *never liked that little punk, anyway*. Her mother had waited a whole month to admit she hadn't liked him either. Was Kelli really the only person who'd never seen Allen for what he was until he rubbed her face in it? And if she couldn't see men through a non-distorting lens, how would she ever find a good one?

As if summoned, Cole sprang to mind again. Then Cole dancing with Miss Tight Jeans.

Kelli checked the time. "I'd better get going. Mom, if you still have potting to do, I'll come back tomorrow and help out." She kissed them both goodbye and heard her mother squeal like a schoolgirl as her father pulled her into his lap before she closed the front door.

CHAPTER EIGHT

COLE'S PHONE RANG midday on Saturday, just as he finished catching up on paperwork. It was Dustin.

"Sorry to bother you," his foreman said in a voice even more quiet than usual. "That kid, Billy, showed up again. I'm keeping him busy helping me with the irrigation, but I thought you should know."

"Is he still asking for a job?"

"He is. He's also been asking how many bunks are in the wranglers' cabin."

"What is he? Fifteen? Explain to him I can't even legally hire him full-time unless he's over sixteen, and that would mean leaving school, which I don't want to see him do. And I'll bet his parents don't either."

"Yes, sir." Dustin hesitated, which was unlike him. He usually said what needed to be said, then got back to work. "You might want to know he's sporting a pretty colorful black eye. Says his friend's llama kicked out when they were checking a cut on its leg."

80 HER COLORADO COWBOY

Cole wondered if the llama wore steel-toed boots. "I'll be there in a few minutes."

THE FOUR-WHEELER BOUNCED across the third and largest of the hay pastures as Cole aimed at the huge metal wheels standing framed against Blanca Peak. Baxter balanced on the back platform, tail wagging, bright eyes searching for cows to herd or any other work awaiting them.

Cole parked near the small motor unit responsible for turning the giant wheels that carried hundreds of yards of heavy pipe and impact sprayers across the field. Crouched on one knee over the metal box, Dustin levered at something with a wrench while Billy Wilson looked on at his side. The boy's attention locked on Cole once he realized the person parked near them wasn't another ranch hand.

"How do they look?" Cole asked.

Dustin walked over, Billy at his heels. The boy had his cowboy hat pulled low, putting his face in shadow, but Cole could see the dark smudge of purple under his left eye. The boy's dad was right-handed as he recalled. And a mean drunk if rumors were true.

"Most of the motors are in good shape but this one has a frozen gear." Dustin gestured with the wrench. "I'll get it replaced tomorrow. We have a spare in the shed. And one motor in the northwest pasture has something going on that I haven't figured out yet."

"We can take a look at it together tomorrow. Anything else?"

"Dale and Tansy checked the water troughs for ice just after sunrise. You have a heater out in one of the stock tanks."

Cole nodded, making a mental note to pick up a new submersible tank heater in town. They could still get freezing temperatures for up to another six weeks. "How about the cattle? Any signs of labor from those last few?"

"Not this morning. My money would be on 260 to be next, though."

Cole only knew a couple dozen cows by number, but that was one of them. A heifer, and one his father predicted would throw large calves. They'd have to watch her once she went into labor.

"Billy, isn't it?" Cole said, turning his attention to the boy who had listened quietly and attentively to the conversation.

"Yes, sir."

"You live in Burgess?"

"Yes, sir."

He looked down at the boy's sneakers.

"You walk here?"

"I hitched a ride on the highway and walked the rest."

About a three-mile walk from the highway to the ranch. The boy had initiative.

"Ever worked cows?"

"No, sir. But I'd sure like to."

"Why is that?"

He hesitated only a moment. "I like being outdoors, I guess, and working with animals. I can ride a horse too. And I don't mind hard work."

"What do your parents think of you getting a job during the school year?"

"They won't mind," he said too quickly. "If you want, I could move into the bunkhouse. That way I'd be here whenever you need me."

The boy's father, Donny Wilson, worked at the gravel pit Monday through Friday and had held steady work there for years. Cole guessed that weekends were when he cut loose. If Billy wanted to say that a llama kicked him, Cole wouldn't get anywhere confronting the story or the family issues; likely, neither would the police. But if he could do something to help keep the boy out of harm's way, he would.

"One thing at a time," he said. "First, I'd need written permission from your parents for you to work here. Second, the law says you can only work limited hours. If your folks agree, it would be weekends only, and only if you can prove to me you're keeping your grades up at school. Are your folks home now?"

"Yes, sir. I think so."

"Well, get on." He thrust his chin toward the four-wheeler. "Let's go talk to them."

ELIZA D. COLLINS

THEY TOOK THE four-wheeler to Cole's truck, left Baxter at the house, then drove to the Wilsons'. Cole had never been to their home before. It was small and in bad repair. The front yard held three old cars. Like a lot of folks with mechanical skills, Donny probably bought junkers to resell.

Cole held Billy back at the door and knocked to avoid barging in on the Wilsons or sending Billy inside alone to explain why he was here. His mother answered, surprise widening her eyes followed by concern. She glanced quickly to her son's black eye and back to Cole.

"Hi, Em. Sorry to drop in on you like this. I was wondering if you and Donny had a minute to talk about me using Billy for some weekend help at the ranch."

"Sure," she said, seeming to relax. "Come on in." She slurred the invitation into one word in her West Texas drawl. The television was on with what looked like an '80s movie playing. A vacuum sat in the middle of the room. She moved it and offered him a place to sit and coffee or a beer to drink.

"No, thank you," he said to both. "I have to get back to work. Still a lot to do today."

"Let me tell Donny you're here." She vanished into a back room.

He and Billy waited in silence, Billy telegraphing his nervous excitement in his fidgeting hands and hopeful eyes. When Donny emerged following Em, Billy's hands stilled and his eyes held only the nervousness.

Donny was an average-sized man, in his forties, Cole guessed. He hadn't shaved today, and his hair looked bed-rough. He wore jeans and a rumpled long-sleeved work shirt he might've slept in.

"Cole," he said, reaching out to shake hands. "You got coffee on?" he said over his shoulder to his wife.

"There's still some warm."

"You offer some to our guest?"

"Of course I did."

"Well go get me a cup, would you?"

She went through the narrow door into the kitchen. Cole could see the large cabinets painted cream yellow that looked to be original from when the house had been built.

"Have a sit." Donny gestured to the couch and took the recliner for himself.

Donny leaned back in a manner that was both relaxed and challenging: chest out, head tilted back. A lion in his own den. Unlike his wife, he never glanced at his son's eye. If Cole dared to ask, he'd be given the llama story or one about the boy being clumsy or maybe just told to mind his own business. Cole had no doubt he could beat Donny right through the living room floorboards if he'd wanted to, and had half a mind to do it. One hard right to that stubbled, arrogant jaw and he could drop him like a sack of grain. It wouldn't do any good, though. In fact, just the opposite. Billy would be the one to pay for it.

Em returned and handed Donny a mug of coffee old enough that it didn't steam.

"Em said you got some work for Billy?" Donny said, taking a large sip.

"I do. I've got all the full-time ranch hands I can hire, but it would help me out to have someone willing to work Saturdays and Sundays. The work doesn't stop on the weekends, and I get spread thin giving days off. I told Billy he could have the position as long as he kept his grades up and the two of you approved."

"I got no problem," Donny answered for them both. "Bit of hard work would do him good. See what it's like to work for a livin'."

"Since he's a minor, I'd need it in writing for my records." He produced a sheet of paper and pen from his shirt pocket. He could feel Billy's eyes boring into him anxiously, waiting for the rest. Cole ignored him.

Donny read the boilerplate permission Cole had scratched out at the ranch, signed the paper and pushed it back across the scuffed pine coffee table.

"Great," Cole said, tucking it back in his pocket with the pen. "I can start him today if he wants. I'll pay three an hour over minimum wage to start, sixteen hours a week." Cole imagined the extra income would be a help to them all. Billy squirmed next to him. Cole continued to ignore him.

"Sounds good to me," Donny said, standing when Cole did and putting out his hand to shake again.

Cole gave him a firmer than strictly necessary shake and said, "Good. We'll be done by sunset tonight, if you want to come get him then." Billy's gaze nearly bored a hole in the side of his skull. "Tomorrow he can start his normal hours. We feed at sunrise, so he'll need to be there half an hour before."

Donny paled a bit. It was nearly noon now and he was still looking rough from the night before. He glanced to his wife.

"I can pick him up in the afternoons," she said, "but you know I can't go in the mornings." Cole had known that Em worked an early nurse's aide shift at an assisted living facility in Alamosa. He'd banked on her still having weekend shifts.

"Hmm. You don't drive yet, do you?" Cole asked Billy. The boy shook his head. He looked to Donny and paused, just a heartbeat for pressure, before offering, "I suppose he could come over Friday evenings and stay in the wranglers' cabin for the weekend. They're a good crew and we have an extra bunk in there. He can eat meals with the other ranch hands."

Em looked from Billy to Cole again, under-

standing dawning on her face. Whether Donny
had caught on or not, he showed only relief.

"Sure. Why not. It'll be a few meals a week we
don't have to feed that bottomless pit."

"Well, what are you waiting for," Cole said to
Billy. "Go get your gear."

Billy sprinted off and was back in five minutes
with a packed duffel. Em Wilson saw them out.
Blocked from her husband's view by the door,
she laid one slender hand on Cole's forearm and
mouthed a thank-you.

SITTING AT THE stop sign, waiting to get on the
highway, Cole had a thought. "You ever been to
the sand dunes?" he asked Billy.

The boy looked perplexed at the unexpected
question. "Just once, on a school field trip."

"There'll be plenty of time for work later. What
do you say we have lunch out there?"

"Sure," Billy agreed, with a smile that nearly
hid his black eye.

The kid might as well have fun now if he was
going to be working every weekend for the rest
of the school year. More importantly, though, it
would be a bit of uninterrupted time to get to
know the boy.

Cole drove around the block and headed back
into town. Options for food were limited in Burgess, but Blake's Place—a tiny privately owned
grocers on Main Street—made sandwiches with

88 HER COLORADO COWBOY

local meats, good cheeses and homemade breads. It was best known for the old-fashioned ice-cream soda fountain bar along the front wall, but ice cream wouldn't survive a drive and a hike, so they ordered sandwiches and grabbed some potato chips and a couple bottles of water.

"You know anything about ranching?" he asked once they were back on the highway.

"Not much, I guess." Billy plucked self-consciously at a speck of lint on the hat in his lap.

"That's okay. You'll pick it up. Spring is busy. Calving, branding, tagging, taking care of the fields, castrations. In the summertime, we move most of the cows onto the Forest Service land we lease up the mountain. We check on them about once a week plus cut hay and take care of the rest of the stock here at the ranch. In the fall, we move the cows back down and keep them either at the ranch or on the other federal land we lease from the BLM. Winter is the hardest season with feeding twice a day and keeping everyone healthy until spring."

The sand dunes were only a few miles north of the ranch, about the same distance that the town lay to the south. They passed Blanca Peak again, standing majestically in the midday sun, as Cole filled him in on the details of what would be expected of him. Topping a final rise a few minutes later, the dunes came into sight on the left, undulating for miles.

"It's weird how you can't see them until you're close," Billy said.

Cole agreed. It *was* odd that thirty square miles of tall dunes could be so well hidden, but the mountains encircled them nearly 180 degrees and the rolling terrain of prairie and high desert concealed the rest. Cole had been here on school trips, like Billy and every other kid in the area, plus he'd brought plenty of visiting friends and family. He could have recited the brochure information verbatim about the dunes being the tallest in North America, and how they'd formed over the eons due to the height and shape of the mountains and the high winds in the area.

They reached the entrance and Cole paid their fee. A minute later, they rounded the visitor's center and turned left into the nearly empty parking lot. Sand rose up directly in front of them, dune after dune, trapped by the same mountains that created them.

He reached over the seat and grabbed a dusty daypack, an equally dusty baseball cap and a pair of hiking boots he kept on the back seat floorboards for weather too icy or muddy for cowboy boots. He changed his shoes and tossed their lunches and water into the pack.

Within a couple of minutes, they'd crossed a shallow stream and started up the first dune. It didn't take long for his calves to ache from the deep, soft sand. Billy, on the other hand, appeared to have the endless stamina of any teenage boy. Cole finally cried uncle after more than half an hour of long uphills with only short downhills between dunes. They sat down partway up the summit of their third dune. More dunes lay beyond them, steeper than the ones they had already summited, but they were high enough now to see the green valley below and white-tipped mountains in the background.

It wasn't only the solitude that had led Cole to bring Billy out here for a talk. This was where his father had brought him the day after he and his wife began fostering Cole; maybe because real life and all its problems felt remote and far away in this surreal landscape.

He took a water bottle out of the daypack and drank deeply, saving his sandwich for the highest dune.

"I don't know if you've heard anything about my past," he said, pushing open an old door that felt rusted shut, "but I had a pretty rough childhood. The Tylers adopted me. My birth parents were drug addicts."

Starting was the hard part; for both of them. Billy, who'd left his hat in the truck and given up trying to hide his black eye, had to know where this was going. Fortunately, he didn't shut down. Surprise appeared to win out.

"How'd you end up with Mr. and Mrs. Tyler?"

"I was removed from my home in Alamosa

when I was seven. It isn't something that happens often, both parents permanently losing their rights to raise their child. Mine was a pretty extreme case." He didn't want Billy thinking, for better or worse, that he was suggesting the same might happen to him.

Billy doodled in the sand with one finger, saying nothing. "Did they hit you?" he asked at last, looking away from Cole.

"No. It was strictly neglect. They were functional addicts when I was little. Later, not so much. As I got older, I knew that sometimes life would be loud and scary for a while but there'd be food and other people would come around. And sometimes they'd be as animated as two corpses till they ran out of drugs. I wouldn't get to eat when they weren't hungry, and I wasn't old enough to be able to fix myself much." He looked out at the mountains and took a deep breath of fresh, cool air before continuing.

"Even when they were in a bad way, there'd be times they were straight and then they'd try to make everything up to me all at once. They'd take me out for my favorite food, play my favorite games, buy me things. And when they disappeared back into their drug haze again, it felt worse than if they'd never cleaned up at all."

He removed his baseball cap and ran a hand through his hair, then looked down, studying the stitching on his cap, rubbing at the brim with his thumbs.

"The last year or so was the worst. Their addictions had them by the throat and they were high all the time. Sometimes they'd leave and not come back for a couple of days. A neighbor took me in if she noticed them gone too long. She had her own issues, but she'd feed me, and she taught me to read. I've always wondered if it was her who turned them in. Or maybe one of their suppliers cut a deal with the police when they got busted."

Billy said nothing, but Cole knew he understood the subtext. He got that a "rough" childhood meant surviving more than the physical challenges. That it encompassed more than could be summed up in words. And that just because it was in the past, it didn't mean it ever went away. Whether Donny Wilson was a decent man when sober or whether he was a hard man all the time, Cole knew the effects on Billy would branch into tangles that would affect myriad emotions and experiences throughout his life.

"Child welfare came with four duffel bags to pack my stuff. The things I owned worth taking didn't even fill one. The lady asked me how long I'd been without a toothbrush, and I couldn't tell her. There were stories about me in the local TV and newspaper when my parents got arrested. It's why a lot of folks in Burgess know about my early childhood."

Or thought they knew, anyway. People acted as if they understood his whole life because they'd read a news story or two twenty years ago or heard about it from someone else. They knew nothing about him. Kelli knew, though. He'd shared more with her through months of passed notes and recess whispers and nightmare retellings than he'd ever told social services, or the police, or even his new family.

Cole wrapped his forearms around his upraised knees.

"I'm not asking what your folks are doing or not doing and I'm not asking what your life at home is like," he continued. "It's none of my business. But I want you to know that you can come to me anytime. I understand what it's like to be in a situation you can't control. I also know the things I felt inside back then weren't black-and-white, like other folks imagined. I guess they still aren't. If you ever want to talk, about anything, I'll listen to whatever you want to say."

Billy didn't meet his gaze. His body was stiff, like a nervous colt. "Yeah. Okay." He pulled off one sneaker and poured out about two cups of sand, then did the same with his other shoe. He put his shoes back on without unlacing them, the soft scrape of his cotton socks against the canvas the only sound in their world.

Cole drew breath to change the subject, but

Billy surprised him by asking, "So, what happened to your parents?"

"I don't know. They were prosecuted for the neglect and the drugs. I don't know how much time they served. They were sent out of state. As far as we know, they stayed gone."

"Oh. I meant your real parents. You own the ranch now, right? Did they move away?"

Billy said it so sincerely that Cole's breath stuck in his chest, jarred by the emotional shift from the pain he'd walled off to the pain he hadn't. He scooped a handful of sand and watched it run from his fist.

"Mom died about five years ago. Bone cancer. Very painful." He dusted off his hand. "Dad died about three months ago now. He'd only just turned sixty-three. He had a heart attack in the barn. My brother Troy found him."

"Oh. Sorry."

"Ben and Cora meant everything to me. They were the best parents I could have asked for and I can't imagine what my life would be now if they hadn't taken me in. It's been a hard thing to come to terms with, but you accept what you can't change, right?"

Billy considered this as the two of them stared out over the millions of tons of sand. "Did you?" he asked. "Accept it?"

Cole knew he meant more than Ben's and Cora's deaths. It was a fair question. He sighed.

"I've tried to."

They sat in silence again, letting the vast expanse of sky and sand and valleys and mountains wash over them. When he was sure Billy had no more to say, Cole tossed their water bottles back into the daypack.

"Ready to tackle the last two summits?"

"Yeah," Billy said with a smile.

They set off for the highest dune.

CHAPTER NINE

THE GIANT FURNITURE shopping extravaganza ended with the acquisition of a new couch, table and chairs, TV stand, dresser and bed. They went to three different stores, plus driving to Pueblo and back. By the time Kelli dropped Sienna off, she wanted nothing more than to go home, flop down on a comfortable bed for the remainder of her Saturday afternoon and really rest for the first time all week. Only problem, she didn't have a bed. The bed and all the rest had been paid for, but delivery was set for some nebulous time on Monday morning. Flopping down on a lumpy futon in an otherwise bare room just didn't have the same appeal.

Kelli decided if she couldn't have her relaxing Saturday afternoon nap, she'd try for some quality time to herself. A hike sounded perfect—if she could think of a place she'd be alone. It would be just her luck to be followed all the way up some narrow mountain trail by a clown-car-sized family outing. Then inspiration hit. With the entrance fee at Sand Dunes National Park, locals often opted for the myriad free trails nearby if they didn't have a parks pass like she did. And even if other people were there, the dunes had plenty of room to spread out. She headed for the highway and turned right.

HER INTUITION HAD been good. There was only one other truck in the parking lot and no one in sight on the dunes. She felt her energy and spirits lift as she started walking. It felt good to expand her lungs, to be on her own to walk or push herself, to hike hard or just stop and enjoy the quiet.

She'd never been one of those people who always had to be with someone, so it wasn't exactly loneliness she felt out there in that big expanse. It got her thinking again, though. It all felt so disheartening to wonder if there even was a "right one" for anyone. Maybe the whole concept was just a marketing spin. But then she thought of her parents.

She arrived at the top of the first dune and looked up to see two guys hauling butt down the slope in front of her. They were plunging through the deep sand at a skidding scree-slope run. The smaller of the two looked to be a teenager who began moon-jumping so enthusiastically that he fell and rolled. The other reached down to help him up and it slowly dawned on Kelli that she recognized the man, though it took her a minute

98 HER COLORADO COWBOY

to peg Cole in a baseball cap instead of his trademark black Stetson.

She considered heading a different direction, but the boy was on his feet again. They were walking instead of running now, but there was no chance of hightailing it out of sight before Cole noticed her. Sure enough, he looked up just then and did a double take. His face split into a handsome grin.

They met at the valley between the two dunes.

Kelli the Veterinarian put on her happy face at the chance to ask after his cattle. Kelli the Heart-Stomped Woman who'd sworn off macho men, cringed at the thought of making small talk with the best-looking rancher in Colorado right after seeing him out dancing with that young woman. Oh well, at least he was here with this boy, and not Miss Tight Jeans.

"Hey, Kelli. Didn't expect to run into you out here," he said.

Accountants and symphony musicians, she recited in her head like a mantra. She was only interested in accountants and symphony musicians from here on out.

"I know, right?" she said, working to keep the irony out of her tone. "How're your cow and calf doing?"

"Great. Strong and healthy, both of them." He slapped a hand on the boy's shoulder. "Billy, this is my friend Dr. Hinton. She delivered a breech calf at our ranch a couple of days ago. Kelli, this is Billy Wilson, my newest ranch hand."

"Pleased to meet you, Dr. Hinton." He extended his hand and they shook.

She tried to focus on the boy's green eyes and not the brush marks of pink across his cheekbone, or the palette of black, purple and red beneath his left eye.

"So, what are you and your new boss doing out here? Chasing a few really athletic stray cows?"

Billy laughed. "No, ma'am."

"I thought I'd give him a few final hours of freedom before becoming a wrangler," Cole said. "A last chance to change his mind."

They all smiled but she knew very well what Cole was doing. Seeing him with the bruised boy brought back a flood of memories from their shared childhood. He might not have carried marks on his body, but his scars had been evident in his eyes and silence. She couldn't help but think about what Sienna had said last night. *Maybe he still has that big ol' sensitive heart except now it's wrapped in hunky wrapping paper.*

"Do you hike here often?" Cole asked her.

"No. I haven't been here in ages. Years. It just seemed like a nice way to spend a Saturday off." He looked ready to keep the conversation going, but she'd had about all she could take of those dark eyes on her, that strong, lightly stubbled jaw. "Well, I'd better not keep you two."

100 HER COLORADO COWBOY

He swallowed whatever he'd been about to say and touched the brim of his baseball cap in a symbolic hat tip. Billy said it had been nice to meet her. A quick farewell and they were on their separate ways, them striding down, her plowing up the next dune.

Perfect. Now she just needed the love of her life to materialize on the next dune and take her mind off Cole Tyler.

"Mister Rogers," she recited. "Accountants and symphony musicians."

Why did he rattle her so much? She'd talked to him easily enough at his ranch. But, of course, that was part of it. There had been the shared goal of a successful birth, the mutual love of ranching and cattle and a lifestyle most people knew nothing about. On top of that, their conversation had been so natural that it tugged her heartstrings for the closeness they'd once shared. So easygoing that yesterday she'd woken up thinking about him. Remembering his comfortable smiles, his full-body hug.

She'd been through this enough to recognize things for what they were, soothing the hurt that Allen had caused by projecting her affection onto the next big hunk whose orbit she'd entered. And a man like Cole had a heck of a gravitational pull. She shouldn't feel upset that she'd seen him dancing with Miss Tight Jeans, she should be grateful.

"Men like that have women lined up," she muttered to herself "and go through them like a fox through a hen house."

CHAPTER TEN

COLE WOKE SUNDAY morning before his alarm went off. He lay in the dark trying to recall the dreams that had left him feeling oddly calm and comforted. An impression of talking with Kelli emerged but, when he tried to examine it, slipped away like reaching for a handful of mist. Still groggy, he shifted and stretched. Baxter, lying against his hip, sprang up and licked his face enthusiastically then jumped off the bed, eager for their day to start.

"You'd better conserve your energy, buddy. We've got a busy day ahead. You get to herd bulls today."

Until Billy had overheard, his plan had been to move them on Monday. The boy hadn't complained, but Cole had seen his disappointment at missing out on a real cattle drive. He and Dustin ended up testing the boy's riding skills before dinner last night and changed moving the bulls to today instead.

Rolling out of bed, he pulled on yesterday's

jeans and headed downstairs barefoot and shirt-less to start a pot of coffee brewing. His stomach growled when he opened the fridge but instead of eggs and bacon, he removed a Tupperware tub of fat and gristle meat scraps. Baxter wagged his tail and followed him in bouncy steps to the laundry and mudroom where a plastic bin of dog kibble stood on the counter. He dumped and refilled the water bowl there and measured out kibble into the food bowl, then topped it with the meat scraps from his dinner last night. He set it down for a very excited Baxter, knowing that Dustin and the ranch hands would be taking care of the cows and horses by now. Cole had never eaten a meal without making sure his animals were fed and watered first. After living in a home where his own needs had been met at irregular and unpredictable intervals, nothing in his care would ever wait on what it needed to survive, worrying it had been forgotten.

With Baxter seen to, he foraged in the refrigerator for his breakfast, realizing the last of the bacon and the eggs were gone. Judging by the aromas lingering in the kitchen, Troy had polished off both before leaving for work half an hour ago. Sundays could be slim pickings since Sally, the family's weekday cook and house cleaner for the past ten years, shopped for them on her way in on Monday mornings.

Cole scrounged up some oatmeal, then finished

dressing and grabbed a heavy jacket against the cold morning air. He saddled his bay gelding, Jet, and rode past the barn and corrals to the cabins beyond. The smells of cows and grass and alfalfa filled the air, and a light fresh wind chilled his face. There was a storm possibly due late tomorrow, but today had rolled out bright sunshine for their task along with the cloudless cobalt blue skies so iconic to Colorado. Baxter trotted at Cole's side, eyes shining with excitement.

The cabins had been built in Cole's grandfather's day. With modern technology, the need for wranglers had dropped from eight or ten men in his grandfather's time to three men and one woman under Dustin's supervision now. Dustin lived in the nearest cabin, the wranglers lived in the farthest one and the center cabin had been remodeled years ago by his mother for guests.

Dustin sat mounted in front of his cabin. The four full-time wranglers, Dale, Jake, Heath and Tansy ranged nearby. Tansy had been the newest addition, a feisty woman in her forties who'd worked for outfits from Canada to Texas and hadn't blinked at the bunkhouse sleeping arrangements. Near Tansy, Billy sat comfortably on the quarter horse Dustin had found for him.

The seven of them rode for the BLM land. Crossing the field beyond the cabins, Cole searched for the last few pregnant cows among the growing herd of new mothers. New calves ran and bounced like rocking horses, playing while building muscle and agility.

They crossed three pastures, four gates and the dirt road that bisected the ranch.

"Hopefully those new kids won't come hot-rodding by when we bring the bulls back," Dustin said, reining close to him.

"What kids?"

"They're either new here or visiting. I've seen them driving around the last few days."

"Have they been harassing the cattle?"

"No. They don't seem the least bit interested in the cows. They just like to speed down the dirt roads and fishtail around the corners. They probably do doughnuts in the Family Dollar parking lot at night too."

Cole had done the same as a kid. Troy and Lane, too, probably. Kids being kids.

His thoughts changed track as he noticed the increase in the cowboy cactus growing along the western edge of the ranch. "We need to take care of that soon. That stuff spreads faster than a prairie fire with a tailwind."

"Have you seen Jim Stand's property lately?"

"No. I haven't been out that way in ages. Is it bad?"

Dustin nodded. "A couple of years ago, he said he was too old to fight it. Now it's taken over a forty-acre field."

They crossed the small stretch of open country in front of the BLM lands he leased from November to May. The bulls were scattered widely across the three hundred acres of public lands, but in short order they'd culled twenty of the fifty-eight and started moving them back to the ranch. The hurdle would be getting them across the road and through the gates, then slowing them down as they got closer to the breeding pastures they remembered. They moved calmly at first but once across the road and through the second gate, the bulls began walking faster, heads lifted, eyes rolling. Some vocalized, and the cows ahead answered.

"Keep them in check," Cole said. He gave a piercing whistle and shouted, "Away to me." Baxter stopped zigzagging behind the rearmost bulls and took off like an arrow from a bowstring, making a quarter circle counterclockwise to flank the bulls on the right and slow the ones in the lead. Heath shouted, "Come by," to his Australian cattle dog, who performed the same maneuver on the left. Baxter slowed the outside bulls, but one or two in the front began to push faster.

"Billy," Cole shouted to the boy riding on the right. "Watch those bulls in the front. If they break, stay back out of the way." Billy nodded, acknowledging he'd heard. "Dustin, you'd better get up there with him."

The riders and horses worked as a team with the riders sitting back in the saddle and using leg signals and loose reins while the horses pivoted sharply to force the bulls back in the desired direction. They were on Tillacos land again and fenced in but, out of control, the bulls could charge the cow pasture ahead, tearing up the fencing and injuring themselves in the process.

Cole saw the wreck an instant before it happened.

A large bull at the front broke free and charged to the right. Two more followed. Dustin kicked his horse to a gallop but hadn't yet caught up to Billy. The remaining bulls were trotting, ready to split every direction like racked pool balls on a hard break shot. The wranglers were riding three to each side. The lead riders moved to the front to control the speed of the remaining seventeen bulls while trying not to spook the entire herd into stampeding. Cole headed up the right side, gaining on Dustin and Billy while keeping an eye on the bulls at his side. When he next spared a glance, he saw Billy far to the right, trying to pull level with the lead runaway bull. A large patch of Christmas cactus was directly in front of him. "Don't get hemmed in!" he shouted. "Baxter, away to me!" he said again, encouraging the dog to get in front of the lead bull.

Smaller and more nimble than Billy's horse, Baxter found a new gear and came level with Billy. It looked like he was going to turn the bull back toward the herd, but Billy had reined away from the cactus patch ahead and was now on the bull's left side, inadvertently pushing it forward and to the right, where it already wanted to go. The adrenaline-charged bull, faced with the horse gaining on his left, the dog coming up on his right and a broad patch of cactus in front, planted both feet and kicked out hard. Seventeen-hundred pounds of muscle went into that kick, and Cole held his breath for Billy. The horse reared, but the boy kept his seat and the sharp hooves missed them both.

Coming down, the bull twisted, like the athlete it was, hind feet landing three feet to the right of the still planted front feet. The massive body of the bull blocked Cole's view but he heard Baxter's sharp yelp. It pierced him like a sword.

The fight had been taken out of the lead bull and it cut back to the safety of the herd. The wranglers had the rest slowed down. Billy and Dustin got the other two runaways turned back and the entire herd calmed. Dustin wheeled back toward the cactus patch as Cole galloped up from the other direction.

Baxter was lying on his side, unmoving.

"Take the bulls on in," Cole shouted to the wranglers as he guided Jet beside Baxter. In a steer-wrestling move, he dismounted on the off-side of his still-moving horse. Jet stopped as soon as he left the saddle. Dustin dismounted and took one knee silently beside him. Baxter's eyes were open, but he hadn't tried to move.

"Help get the bulls into the corrals, then come back with the four-wheeler."

Dustin mounted up again while Cole wrestled his phone out of its holder. There was no bleeding he could see, but he knew that internal hemorrhage was a bigger risk. Baxter whined softly.

Cole thumbed through his recent calls until he found Kelli's cell phone number. With one hand resting on Baxter's shoulder, he hit redial, hoping he would be able to reach her on a Sunday.

CHAPTER ELEVEN

KELLI GLANCED AT her ringing cell phone, expecting it to be either Sienna or her parents. It was neither and she didn't recognize the incoming number. The clinic number went to voicemail outside of business hours, but plenty of clients had her cell number.

"Hello?"

"Kelli." It was Cole. His tone was anxious and overly loud. "It's Baxter."

"What happened?"

"I didn't see it. We were moving bulls. I think he got kicked."

"Is he conscious?"

"Yes."

"Where did he get kicked?"

"There's a hoof mark on his chest, but I don't see any bleeding. He's not getting up. Dustin's gone for the four-wheeler, but it'll take a few minutes for him to get back here and then a few more to get Baxter from here to my truck. I was hoping you were taking emergency calls today."

"Of course I'll see him. Sounds like it'll be quickest if I meet you at the ranch. I could be there in about fifteen minutes. Where are you?"

"I should be at the barn by the time you get here."

"Okay. Be careful moving him. I'll see you soon." Kelli's heart went out to Cole. He sounded on the edge of panic, and she'd seen how bonded he and Baxter were when she delivered the calf.

Her business was 50 percent mobile, and everything she might need was probably already in her truck. She mentally ticked off the most likely possibilities. She had a portable X-ray machine in case of fractures—an old one-foot-square cube she'd bought used from the university's veterinary hospital when she graduated. She also had plenty of casting and splinting supplies in the truck. If there was internal injury—a likely scenario, unfortunately—she had an ultrasound machine, but if the bull had damaged the liver, heart or lung, Baxter might not even make it until she got there.

She drove as fast as she dared, arriving at the barn in a cloud of dust. Baxter lay, unmoving, on the back of the four-wheeler. Her heart sank, fearing the worst. Cole looked as vulnerable as he had on that first day of second grade, his face tight with anxiety, his emotional pain expressed in every line of his body.

"He's just the same," Cole said as she grabbed

her med-kit and walked to him. "He doesn't seem to be getting worse but he's not moving."

Kelli chewed her lip. She wanted to reassure him, tell him everything was going to be fine, but vets learned fast not to make promises they couldn't keep. Not whining or moving could be a sign of deep shock. She asked Cole to fill her in on the details of the accident.

"Hey there, Baxter," she said, petting the dog gently on his hip to put him at ease for the examination.

Cole stroked Baxter's face, standing so close to her that she smelled the dust on his jeans and the sweat on his shirt. Like Cole, she saw no obvious signs of blood. She checked the color of Baxter's gums and took his temperature and respirations, then did a head-to-toe exam. The dog looked concerned when she pressed on his chest, but he didn't whine. Going down the body, she found no acute injury.

"He's such a good boy." A thought struck her. "Did you tell him to stay still?"

Cole had to think about it. "I suppose I did. Probably a bunch of times."

"Let's see if he'll stand."

Cole snapped his fingers above his dog's head. "Baxter, up." Baxter rolled to his stomach and stood. His right front leg seemed unable to hold weight.

"Dogs are stoic, but it's a good sign that he's

willing to get up. I'd like to x-ray his sternum and his front leg."

Cole helped while she took the X-rays she needed. She powered on the digital tablet that she used for patient notes and sending bills to the printer in her truck. Opening the X-ray app, she found the new files and viewed the images she'd just taken.

"I'm not seeing any obvious fractures. My X-ray machine isn't exactly cutting edge and viewing the results on my tablet isn't ideal, but I'll be sending these to a radiologist for a proper reading. As far as internal injury, I can't rule it out yet, but the color in his gums is good and I'm not seeing any of the usual signs."

"That's great." Cole's entire body relaxed with relief.

"There are still a lot of things that could be going on with him. I'm concerned about this front leg. The dirt from the hoof mark is near the antebrachial nerve plexus." She touched just to the inside of Baxter's shoulder. She didn't want to tell him at this point that a bad injury there could mean permanent loss of use of the leg. "I'm a little hesitant to give him anything for pain or swelling right now since I don't want to mask any symptoms."

She stroked Baxter's head and ears. He still stood on the four-wheeler, his tail slowly wagging. He didn't look as bright-eyed as usual, but

114 HER COLORADO COWBOY

for getting kicked or trampled by one of those big bulls, it was amazing he was standing at all.

"I think the best thing would be for me to take him back to the clinic and observe him overnight. Maybe longer. I want to watch that leg and also make sure we're not missing something more serious. I'll probably give him a light sedative to manipulate his shoulder and maybe take a better X-ray while he's under sedation. If I see any signs of internal injury, I'll let you know. At that point, I'd want to do an ultrasound."

"Of course. Do any tests you think he ought to have." Cole lifted Baxter and placed him on the front seat of Kelli's truck. "I don't know what I'll do without the little guy. He's been my shadow for the last five years."

"I'll touch base with you tonight," she promised him before getting in on the driver's side.

"Well, I guess this is goodbye for a bit, buddy." Cole leaned into the open passenger door, rubbed Baxter's ears and gave him a kiss on the top of the head.

Kelli left the ranch, feeling like she was taking a piece of Cole with her. Baxter watched out the passenger window as the ranch receded in the distance. It was sweet and unexpected how close the two of them were. It made her think again how ready she was to have a dog of her own. The downside, of course, was experiencing the kind of heartache Cole must feel now—or worse, the inevitable loss at the end of their too-short lives. And she was mighty vulnerable to loss these days.

At home, Kelli followed the gravel track around the side of the house and parked in front of the clinic. The property she'd bought had been perfect: zoned for agriculture with no covenants and possessing a shed that she'd turned into indoor/outdoor kennels with large heated dog houses for longer recovery, as well as a livestock loafing shed with two stalls and a corral, and an old but solid detached garage. On the downside, converting the garage into a clinic had required a substantial business loan. And the loan was on top of the money she owed her sister for the down payment on the property. And that one on top of her school loans and mortgage payment. Frankly, she'd been astounded yesterday when the furniture store approved her credit line.

She lifted Baxter out of the truck. The front leg still wasn't moving or holding weight, so she carried the sturdy boy—probably forty pounds of dog—into the clinic and over to her surgery table. She administered a light sedative and did another full-body exam, including shaving the sore area by his shoulder and probing at the bruise forming there. She felt his belly again for any blood pooling and checked his gums to make sure they had remained healthy and pink, indicating proper circulation. Lastly, she took one final X-ray with the

116 HER COLORADO COWBOY

shoulder in a better position, then administered an anti-inflammatory drug and something for pain.

While Baxter slept off his sedative in one of the post-op crates, she transferred the X-rays from her tablet to her digital wall viewer. She still felt certain she wasn't seeing any fractures. As promised, she emailed the files to the radiologist, though the report wouldn't come back for a couple of days.

"I'm worried about that shoulder of yours," she told her groggy patient as she opened the crate door. Baxter thumped his tail. During her clinic rotation, she'd seen one dog permanently lose use of both front legs from a similar injury. She couldn't imagine how Cole might take the news if this turned out to be a badly damaged nerve.

"You're a good boy, Baxter. Would you like to come stay in the house with me?" The answer was another thump of his tail. She moved one of her portable crates to the house and returned. Lifting the big fuzz ball again, she carried him to her living room.

She told herself that the main reason for keeping Baxter in the house instead of the clinic was because she had no other hospital patients, and it would be easier to keep an eye on him. Secondly, she could darn well get dog hair all over the house now if she wanted to. But there was a third reason. One she didn't want to admit to herself. She liked having Cole's dog in her home because, in a way, it felt like having Cole there without the emotional danger of actually having him there. Sort of like wearing a new boyfriend's T-shirt, something personal and intimate of theirs to keep for a while.

Baxter settled so well that she left him uncrated for the time being and sat on the floor with him in front of what had been her spare TV. *What a weird week*, she thought. After not running into Cole Tyler for who knew how many years, now she'd been around him four times in as many days. Her heart wanted to read signs and portents and fate into it so badly that it tried every angle, but her brain was having none of it. If seeing Cole everywhere she went had anything to do with fate, then fate was testing her resolve to resist the manly charms of macho men.

She waited until after dinner to make sure there was no change for the worse in Baxter, then gave Cole a call. He picked up on the second ring.

"Hey, Kelli. How's my boy?"

Baxter was staring up at her, probably hearing Cole's voice on the other end. She rubbed one of his soft ears.

"The good news is that I'm not seeing any issues outside of that shoulder but, unfortunately, he's still not moving that leg. I gave him a shot of anti-inflammatory medication that I hope will help. We should probably touch base again in the morning and go from there."

118 HER COLORADO COWBOY

"Got it." He paused, like he might have been debating signing off, but launched into a new topic instead. "I didn't really talk to you much the day you helped me with that calf. Well, other than about cattle ranching, anyway. I saw you at the Longhorn the other night and was headed over to ask how you've been doing, but you were just leaving. But maybe this isn't a good time either," he said hurriedly. "Maybe you and Allen are in the middle of dinner or something."

The statement took Kelli by surprise—first that the knitting circle of rancher gossips hadn't picked this tidbit up yet, then a brief flash of panic over his less-than-subtle probe. Here she was, sitting on her floor, petting his dog and chatting with him on the phone. Did she really want him to know she was single again? Cole, of all people. But she had never been any good at lying; she could barely manage evasive. She fingered a lock of soft hair between Baxter's ears. Burgess was too small—he'd find out sooner or later, anyway. Truth was, she wanted him to know.

"No, it's fine. Allen moved back to Denver. We broke up a couple of months ago."

"Oh, I'm sorry," he said. He sounded genuine.

"It's okay. It was for the best."

"I'm still sorry. It's never an easy thing to go through." Something in his voice said he'd had some personal experience with that. "Change of subject then," he said more cheerfully. "How do you like being back in Burgess?"

"I love it. It was always my plan after I graduated. Mom and Dad are getting older and my sister lives in Connecticut. She only makes it out here once or twice a year to see them."

"I didn't know Sissy moved to the East Coast. What's she doing there?"

Kelli smiled. She hadn't heard her older sister's nickname in a hundred years. She'd been Blair before Kelli's birth, then dubbed Sissy once she had a little sister—the same way her dad always called their mom Momma. Blair had finally put her foot down and reclaimed her real name in high school. "Her business is kids."

"Like day care or teaching or something?"

"No like three of them already and a fourth on the way."

Cole laughed. It was a deep, throaty laugh that gave her goose bumps. "Really? Wow."

"I know. Wow is right. I never saw her as a stay-at-home mom. I always thought she'd be an astronaut or deep-sea diver or something." They both laughed. "How about Lane? Where is he these days?"

"Dubai. At least, last I heard."

"Seriously? What's he doing out there?"

"He graduated from School of Mines in Golden with a civil engineering degree, and then got a degree in international business in Denver. He became some kind of hotshot city development consultant. He travels all over the world."

It felt wonderful talking to Cole like this. Almost as comfortable as talking with Sienna, except that the sound of Sienna's voice didn't give her goose bumps.

"How about you?" she asked, stretching out on the floor, as comfortable as she could get without a couch. Baxter laid his head against her knee. "What's it like for you being back?"

"Like you, I'd always planned to come back. I was finished with school. I just stayed on for that job I was telling you about. I'd planned to work there until June."

There was a pregnant pause. They both knew what had brought him back six months earlier than he'd expected.

"I know I said it already," she said, filling the silence, "but I really was sorry to hear about your father. I never got to know him all that well, but I remember both your folks from the football games. My dad and I sat with them pretty often. They were always there for your games."

She heard him shift. Soft sounds; maybe a pillow. She imagined him in his bedroom, stretching his tall strong body out on the bed to settle into their conversation like she had.

"Yeah, they were."

"Has it been weird taking over the ranch?"

It was a personal question, multilayered. Having said it out loud, she wondered if their old friendship was a solid enough foundation for such a weighty question. She was about to withdraw it and ask something lighter when he answered.

"It has been," he said, softly. "I majored in ranching so I could help Dad as he got older, but I sure never expected it to all fall on my shoulders so soon. He had so much still to teach me. And even though we expected that I was going to be the one to take over, I don't think it really sank in until they read his will. It was probably just as weird for my brothers."

"You're going to do great, Cole. I loved your ideas for the future of the ranch, and there's no one in the family better for the job."

"Thanks. I appreciate that. I really do." There was another pause. "Hey," he said, suddenly sounding self-conscious, "it's getting late. I should let you go."

"Well, you probably still have stuff to do," she said at the same time.

They both chuckled, breaking the heavy tension.

"Okay," she said. "I'll call you tomorrow morning and let you know how Baxter is doing."

"Have a good night, Kelli."

"You too, Cole."

After they hung up the house seemed twice as quiet. For a while, she tried to go back to her paperwork, but her focus was shot and her thoughts kept migrating back to Cole. To the sound of his voice and the timbre of his laugh. To the fact that he'd apparently wanted to come over and talk to her at the Longhorn, and so maybe he hadn't been there with Miss Tight Jeans. And, most especially, to what he might do now that he knew about Allen.

CHAPTER TWELVE

COLE WOKE ON MONDAY, predawn, as usual. It took him a second to orient to the fact that Baxter wasn't lying beside him. Next came a stab of worry as he wondered how the little guy had done through the night. Surely, Kelli would have called him if he'd taken a turn for the worse.

It had been nice talking to her last night. Comfortable in a way he hadn't been with a woman since Amy in Texas. He'd always thought Kelli pretty in high school when he saw her around town, but he'd dated pretty girls at his own school. Something about Kelli had always tugged at him when he saw her, though, like a fishhook in his gut.

Truth was, she'd saved him as a child every bit as much as Ben and Cora Tyler had. She'd eased him into school life, helped him learn the routines and guided him through the foreign social structures. Most importantly, she'd trusted him enough to share her night terrors with him that stemmed from her home invasion in the summer, allowing him to share his ordeals with her as well. Together, they'd exposed their traumas to the light of day.

Swinging his legs out of bed, he lifted his cell phone from the charger and checked for messages. Dustin had sent him a text twenty minutes ago with new numbers on the fertilizer inventory for the hay fields. Another thing to order. Past time to get up and get going. In the summers, he liked to shower after work, rinsing off the day's sweat and dust, but this early in April, the mornings were still cold, twenties or thirties usually. He turned on the water to let it warm and stepped into the shower. His thoughts swirled with his plans for the livestock auction in Wyoming next week; the older cows that hadn't calved this year and needed to be sold; the crossbreeding program he wanted to start to get the weight up on the steers going to market. Focusing on work helped him rein in his worries about Baxter...and keep his thoughts from drifting to Kelli.

AFTER LUNCH WAS Cole's usual time to ride or drive the property, check in with Dustin and attend to any field duties, but today Baxter took precedence. Kelli called mid-morning to say Baxter was improving and she thought he could finish his recuperation at home.

Cole followed Kelli's directions through Burgess, then out the other side, where most of the properties came with acreage. He turned left down a dirt road and then right onto an unmarked road. Half a mile later, he came to an older single-story rancher with a large outbuilding in back, small lean-to and corral.

He knocked on the front door and Kelli appeared a moment later. She wore a button-down blouse tucked into jeans and a pair of work boots. Her blond hair was pulled back in a simple ponytail and her bangs framed her hazel eyes and mascara-darkened lashes.

His chest tightened unexpectedly at the sight of her, like the air had squeezed from his lungs, or his heart had just doubled in size. He found he wanted an excuse to reach out and touch her: to run a finger along the fringe of bangs where it caught against one eyebrow; brush his knuckles under the thin gold chain to slide the clasp up off her collarbone and to the back of her neck.

"Come on in," she said, pulling the door wider. She had Baxter on a leash at her side.

Baxter spun in excitement. He favored his right front leg but seemed to be putting a bit of weight on it. Cole squatted down to keep him from bouncing around too much in his enthusiasm. It had been a surprisingly long twenty-four hours without him. He'd found himself thinking about feeding him at dinner and again at breakfast, checking his water, and looking for him reflexively at bedtime. He scratched his fuzzy head and neck while Baxter whined.

"Have a seat," Kelli said.

She waved to a couch that looked brand-new. The small table he could see through the arch to the kitchen had a sales tag hanging underneath. The slight chemical smell he'd noticed when he walked in registered now as plastic, perhaps lingering from some recently removed protective wrap.

"This is nice," he said, taking a seat and feeling he should say something.

"Oh, uh, yeah. Thanks." Kelli took a seat at the other end of the short couch. She seemed flustered, as if she wasn't sure whether to elaborate on the newness or not, then bent to Baxter and touched his shoulder instead. "As you can see, he isn't fully recovered but he responded so well to his first two doses of anti-inflammatories that I'm optimistic the nerve injury is temporary. It's kind of like hitting your funny bone really, really hard. Hard enough that the nerve swells and makes your hand useless for a while."

"Ouch, buddy," he said, wincing at Baxter in sympathy.

"I was prepared to try cortisone, but he seems to have turned the corner with the nonsteroidal drug, which is good. It's important to keep him on the medicine I'm going to send home with you until he's completely better. And make sure

ELIZA D. COLLINS

127

he rests that leg. I'd expect recovery in a week or two, but you're going to need to restrict his movement for a few days more at least. I'll get his medicines for you."

She hopped up and grabbed two bottles from the kitchen counter. He watched her, lithe as a cat but tense somehow as well. He'd hoped she'd be more off-duty with him today after their conversation last night.

"This is his anti-inflammatory. Twice a day for ten days, including yesterday. It'll help with pain as well, but if he still seems sore, he can have this one up to three times a day." She handed the anti-inflammatory to him and held up the second bottle. "This one's strictly for nerve pain, so give it as needed up to the dosing listed on the label." She handed the second bottle to him and sat again.

"I'm just relieved it wasn't a worse wreck than it was."

"You two dodged a bullet, for sure. Anything could have happened. And I've seen an avulsion— a tear—in that nerve. It's bad news. We still don't know for certain about fractures, but I should have that report back from radiology in another day or so. I'll call you and let you know what I hear. Do you have a crate at home?"

"No, but I can rig something."

"It's okay. I have half a dozen. Best to make sure he's secure."

128   HER COLORADO COWBOY

She vanished into the bedroom and returned with a crate.

"Did you buy this place?" Cole asked, looking around the neat house.

"I did. There was no way I could set up a clinic at a rental. You want to see it?"

He was pleased she asked, and he didn't mind spending a little extra time with her.

"Sure."

"Go to bed," he told Baxter, giving him the same command to get in the crate that he used for the dog bed at home. Baxter loaded up like a pro and waited while he secured the door. "Good boy. We'll be right back."

He followed Kelli out the back door and to the outbuilding he'd seen when he parked. The clinic had a neat waiting room with two doors leading deeper into the building, one to an exam room with a raised table and the other into a small surgery with metal operating table, instruments and medications.

"I can't handle major trauma here, but routine surgeries and noncritical trauma or illness are no problem."

They continued out the back door from the surgery to the corral and a stable with two stalls and a livestock sling rigged to the roof.

"What do you think of being a vet?" He knew that getting the degree wasn't a guarantee that one would enjoy the job. He'd stayed in touch with a friend from high school who'd been nine-tenths of the way through med school when he decided he didn't want to be a doctor and opened a restaurant in Denver instead.

"I love it," she said. "There are downsides, for sure. Putting animals down that could be saved, abuse, things like that. But hopefully I'll see less of those here than in a city. And the good parts are really good. Helping people who care about their animals. Most of all, I love the large animal side of it. I guess growing up around farms and ranches and livestock, I've always felt connected to them."

Cole watched her as she talked, entranced by everything about her. Her features were such a small part of what made her truly beautiful. Her energy and compassion and enthusiasm shone out from her like a small sun. She understood and cared deeply for some of the things in life that meant the most to him.

"I'm really impressed, Kelli. You've done a lot here in a little time. It can't have been easy straight out of school." Ben and Cora had put him through college, just like his brothers, but Kelli's parents were less well-off. She'd probably done most everything on her own or through scholarships and loans.

"Thanks, Cole," she said as they headed back to the house. "It's been challenging but it should start getting better now the practice is growing."

130 HER COLORADO COWBOY

"I always knew you'd excel at whatever you chose. You went all-in about everything you did. Remember that Play-Doh project? Your elephant was so big it was three different colors."

Kelli laughed out loud, snorted and covered her mouth with her hand, still laughing. "Oh, my, you remember that? I thought Miss Solkey was going to explode over the amount I used. It was so big the trunk fell off." She laughed, then snorted again, making him laugh too.

Maybe he'd been flooded with too many emotions lately—his breakup with Amy, his father dying, the burden of responsibility he'd shouldered—but Kelli seemed the answer to all the things he'd looked for without finding. Down-to-earth, compassionate, hardworking, smart, a deep sense of family. He wanted to ask her out, right then and there. They were already back at the house, though, and the shift felt too abrupt. Not the right opening, and he didn't want to risk getting turned down.

Oblivious to his swirl of emotions, she let Baxter out of the crate and put a generic nylon leash over his head to keep him from running.

"He was an excellent houseguest. I'm going to miss him." She sounded like she meant it. "Well, I guess that's it. I'll let you know in the next day or so if the radiologist sees anything on the X-rays but call me in the meantime if there are any problems." She handed the leash to him.

"Will do," he said. "I'll be talking to you soon."

He doffed his cowboy hat and gave her a big smile that he hoped conveyed a little of his future intentions.

CHAPTER THIRTEEN

KELLI CLOSED THE DOOR, feeling more than a little giddy. Dang. Those shoulders, those eyes, that smile. Her knees felt like Jell-O.

"Stay strong," she muttered. The same thing she'd told herself before she went ahead and changed into a new shirt and jeans before he came over. And then she'd gone a step further and put on makeup just because she'd felt like it.

It was like Cole embodied everything she had ever found attractive in a man. The kind of man that drew her like bugs to a bug zapper—and ended about as well for her as things did for the bugs. She wondered if it was just a rebound phenomenon, but the truth was, with the way things had ended between her and Allen, she didn't even miss him.

MONDAY AND TUESDAY kept her every bit as busy as she'd expected to be. Tuesday afternoon, Baxter's radiology report came in, confirming what she'd hoped to see. She called Cole right away.

"Hi, Kelli."

That deep voice saying her name made butterflies dance in her stomach.

"Hi, Cole. Great news. The radiology report confirms that Baxter doesn't have any fractures."

"That *is* great news."

"How's he doing?"

"Raring to go but I'm keeping him quiet except for mealtimes and going outside to do his business. He's walking stronger, but still has a bit of a limp."

"He might for a while," she said, "but it sounds like everything is going really well. That injury site is still vulnerable, so don't cave in to him wanting to do more than he should."

"I'll make sure he follows doctor's orders."

She was about to sign off when he blurted out, "Hey, I've got a rodeo in Alamosa this weekend. It's just a preseason event. Nothing major, but I'll be competing in saddle bronc and bareback riding. I was wondering if you'd like to come. I can put you on the guest list."

He'd caught her so completely off guard that she fell into a stunned silence.

"It was just a thought," he said hurriedly. "You know. A thank-you for all you've done."

He was backpedaling; she could hear it in his voice. He'd definitely meant it as more than a thank-you. Panic bloomed in her chest. She'd promised herself no more studly guys with their

134 HER COLORADO COWBOY

manly roles and their macho mentality. *But did Cole have a macho mentality?* She'd never met a man that good-looking who didn't. Besides, it was her fatal flaw in the tragedy of her relationships to never recognize that arrogance and all it came with until it was too late. For pity's sake, he was inviting her to come see him ride broncs in a rodeo. How big a sign did she need? Seriously, she had to nip this in the bud.

"That's really nice of you, but I'm on call this weekend."

"Oh, sure. Well, if you don't get called out, maybe I'll see you there?"

"I, it's just, well…" Gads. How old was she, fourteen? *Spit it out, Kelli.* "I haven't been going out with anyone since Allen left. I mean, it's okay. I'm not all broken up about it or anything. We weren't a great match anyway. I just don't know that I'm quite ready to, you know." She chewed her lip and forged ahead. "And besides, I thought at the Longhorn that maybe you were there with someone?"

"No." He sounded perplexed.

"I saw you dancing with someone and you seemed to be sitting together, so I thought…"

"Oh, Jenna? No. No," he said again with more force. "I was there at a cattleman's association meeting and totally got railroaded into dancing one dance with Lacey Overton's daughter."

Her bullcrap meter had always been faulty, but he sounded sincere.

"Look, tell you what," he continued. "Just think of this as a no-pressure thank-you. You can show up if you happen to be free and if you want to come. I'll hold two spots on the guest list. You can bring a friend. It's scheduled one to four and my events should fall pretty much in the middle, but I'll be there from about noon till four or four thirty."

"Okay," she said. "Sorry," she added, aware that, like too many women, she was apologizing when she wasn't quite sure what for, except that now bringing up Allen and Jenna felt like a bit of an overreaction. "Maybe I'll see you there," she said, meaning it.

They hung up and Kelli nearly vibrated with nerves. Men like him always rattled her brain. She'd probably get an emergency call anyway and then she wouldn't have to worry about whether to go or what the invitation meant.

Later in the afternoon, she was called out for a calf delivery at a three-cow operation north of town. The birthing went well, but she couldn't help thinking about her recent delivery at Cole's ranch. Him kneeling next to her, and the hug he gave her when she left. Which led her to thoughts of yesterday and the feeling it had given her to invite him into her home, talk with him sitting on the couch. And today, him trying to ask her out.

136   HER COLORADO COWBOY

But had he really asked her out? He'd said it was a thank-you. A free pass to the rodeo. It wasn't like she'd be there *with* him. Not like getting asked out to dinner or something. What was the harm in going to watch him ride? She could change her voicemail for a couple of hours and refer calls to the Alamosa emergency clinic. And Sienna liked rodeos. She'd probably be up for it.

By the end of the day, she'd talked herself into it.

"When's the last time you went to a rodeo?" she said, as soon as Sienna picked up the phone.

"What? I don't know. Years, I think."

"There's one out at the fairgrounds in Alamosa this Saturday. Want to go?"

"What's up? You sound weird."

Rats. They'd known each other too long. "Cole Tyler is competing in saddle bronc and bareback riding." She sighed.

"Did he ask you?" Sienna nearly shrieked. "Wait, what about that other gal?"

"He said he was there at a meeting and got railroaded into one dance with someone's daughter. So how about it? Do you want to go or not?"

Saturday afternoon, Kelli changed her voicemail recording and referred incoming calls out for the rest of the night. She needed the break, anyway. Next, she tried on four different shirts before finally settling on the first one. Then came three different hairstyles. In the end, she just left it loose.

She drove over to Sienna's at 1:00 p.m., still wondering if she was making a huge mistake. Sienna was ready on time, as always, and they headed out in Sienna's Kia.

"How many times you going to button and unbutton your shirt?" Sienna asked as she pulled onto the highway.

"What?" Kelli looked down, catching her hands in the act of undoing the top button. She'd been thinking all week about seeing Cole today and her nerves were getting in the way of just being herself. She clasped her hands in her lap. "Am not."

Sienna laughed. "Yeah, right. Just like you didn't fuss with your hair at all either."

"Why am I so bad at this?"

"You're too hard on yourself, Kelli. You've never been bad at it, just unlucky."

"No. I suck at dating. That's why the bad luck. And why I keep choosing losers."

"You think Cole is a loser?" Sienna sounded mockingly incredulous.

"No. That's the problem. I never do, at first. Until they turn out to be awful. He rodeos, Sienna!" She heard herself getting a little high-pitched and toned it back down. "It doesn't get more manly man than that. Cole Tyler is my kryptonite."

"Then why are we doing this again?"

"Oh, just pay attention to the traffic." There

138 HER COLORADO COWBOY

were only two other cars on the road as far as Kelli could see in either direction.

"Right."

It was early in the season but a warm and sunny day, and the large dirt parking lot was nearly half-full. They gave their names at the gate and followed the tunnel to the stands. The rodeo grounds were nothing elaborate, just an arena for local events, stock shows and the small county fair. They'd arrived after the calf roping and near the end of the steer wrestling, which was perfect. She understood the origins of the rodeo events, but team roping was her least favorite as they used such young calves. She always rooted for the first cowboy to miss, which meant the calf ran free. Kelli was headed up the steps when Sienna pulled her by the hand down to the second row.

"If we're here to watch him ride, we might as well be where we can see him."

The speakers were turned up to eleven, like every rodeo she'd ever attended. The announcer boomed out that Cody Sanders would be competing today, a pro-rodeo cowboy out of nearby Raton, New Mexico. Kelli remembered him from the huge Cheyenne Frontier Days in Wyoming, when she'd been in school in nearby Fort Collins. He'd stood out not because he was top among the rising number of Black pro-rodeo cowboys, but because he'd been tied for first when he got thrown from a horse that hung up in the gate in the second round. He'd crashed shoulder-first into the gate but had taken the re-ride option anyway and, injured, rode to the buzzer for the high score of the day. Cole had stiff competition today, for sure.

The rodeo clown did a short bit when the steer wrestling ended, followed by a gift-certificate giveaway from one of the sponsors. Next, the saddle bronc competition began. There were nine riders, with Cole fourth in the lineup.

The first rider had trouble keeping his horse settled in the chute and the announcer improvised for an extra couple of minutes. Finally, the gate swung open. Like bull riding, the riders had to make it to the eight-second buzzer to qualify. If they made the buzzer, the animal and the rider both received scores, which were combined for the total. The horse blasted out of the gate and the rider came off at just over four seconds. By the time Cole's turn came up, only one competitor had made it the full eight seconds for a score of eighty-two.

Kelli spotted Cole in the chute and felt those butterflies dancing in her stomach again, watching him from across the arena as he gripped the bronc rein and adjusted his balance on the horse. She had to wonder if her butterflies were more for his safety or because he'd invited her or because she'd accepted. He nodded his head sharply and she held her breath.

The gate flew open, and his horse exploded out. His form was good and he made it through those first few treacherous moves, trying to synchronize to the rhythm of the horse. His body jerked forward and back, held to the saddle by the strength of his arm, his core muscles, his balance and sheer willpower.

"Rank horse," Sienna said, leaning toward her. Like most people in the county, she'd grown up on summer rodeo events and knew a hard-bucking horse when she saw one.

Watching him, Kelli felt all the things she hadn't wanted to feel. His black hat, the crisp navy blue shirt with his entry number pinned to his back, and the blue fringes on his chaps flying with each buck caused a flush deep inside her chest.

Halfway through the ride, the horse changed direction and Cole pitched off-balance. Her heart skipped a beat; her worry blatantly higher for him than the previous riders. Buckoffs could mean anything from a hard landing in the dirt to catastrophic injury. On the next jump, he regained his balance and she breathed easier.

The buzzer sounded, loud and harsh. The pickup riders came to either side of him. With the horse still bucking, Cole let go of the rope, leaned out and wrapped his arms around the waist of the pickup man on his right. He slipped off the saddle, then let go and dropped athletically to his feet. The second pickup rider paced the bronc and released the bucking strap. The speakers were blaring out praise for both the horse and Cole's performance. Kelli applauded with the rest of the crowd.

He stood in the arena to watch the scoreboard. His score flashed in yellow lights at the same moment the announcer shouted it out. Eighty-seven. An excellent score out of one hundred possible points. Maybe good enough to win.

Cole scanned the stands. Hoping he was looking for her, Kelli gave an enthusiastic Forest Gump wave when he glanced her direction. He didn't spot her, though, and vanished behind the metal gates where the livestock and competitors staged. Relieved, after the fact, that her effusive display had gone unnoticed, she turned to Sienna, who gave her a "you are so busted" look.

CHAPTER FOURTEEN

THE OTHER COMPETITORS fist-bumped Cole and slapped him on the back as he walked through the livestock holding area. Staying on till the buzzer was at least partially luck but getting a qualified ride and a high score always felt good. He climbed the rails of one of the metal panels and watched as his good friend Derek Anderson gave the nod to the gateman. The horse came out well but spun on the first jump. Derek went flying and landed on his back in the soft sand.

Last up was Cody Sanders, the only rider in today's event who competed on the national circuit. He'd drawn Legend, a horse worthy of a pro. Blasting out of the chute, the horse kicked its hind legs straight out, landing hard, full of energy and fire. The horse lived up to his reputation, but so did Cody. He rocked hard to the left but recovered his balance and rode to the buzzer. His score came in a moment later. Ninety-two. A high mark for a rider at a small event like this, and one that easily beat Cole's score. The crowd cheered wildly.

There was another short break while the clown did a little bullfighting. The clown being Joe Fitzpatrick, the bullfighting mainly consisted of jumping into a barrel and letting the bull head-butt him around the arena. Probably the safest option, as Joe was getting a little old for all this. Cole scanned the arena once again for Kelli while Joe did his shtick, but there were too many faces too far away and he gave up.

Barrel racing was next. There were only six women competing but three of them were national competitors. He'd spotted Jenna earlier, but they hadn't spoken as they'd both been occupied with their individual event preparations. After barrel racing came the bareback bronc event and he headed for his chute.

The organizers did a good job of keeping things moving and it wasn't long before Cole's turn came up. He eased down onto Bramble's back just before the competitor ahead of him began his ride. Bramble chuffed and pawed the sand, then gave a bucking hop in the narrow chute, scraping Cole's leg into the railing. A couple of minutes later, the arena was clear and he was up. He tightened his grip on the handhold of the narrow rigging and gave a sharp nod. Bramble burst out of the gate, wild-eyed and fast.

Cole hung on for about four good jumps, but

144 HER COLORADO COWBOY

the horse suddenly paused, changing its rhythm mid-buck. It landed hard and he pitched to the right. When the horse kicked its hind feet high, he couldn't shift his weight fast enough and got launched headfirst over its right shoulder, coming down hard on his hips and back.

The horse bucked again, hooves landing too close to his shoulder for comfort, and he scrambled to his hands and feet. He scuttled two steps before the pickup riders rode between him and the horse, turning it away from him. One rider pulled the bucking strap and together they herded it into the tunnel.

Cole dusted off, picked his hat up out of the sand and waved to the crowd. A woman popped up and gave a big overhead wave. Kelli. He didn't care anymore that he hadn't ridden to the buzzer or that he hadn't won the saddle bronc round. His face split into a wide grin and he lifted his hat in the air in a return wave.

As Cole walked back to the staging grounds, he heard the crowd and the announcement when Cody rode to the buzzer for the second time today, winning the competition. Bull riding was up next. Always a crowd favorite.

"Hey, Cole." He turned, hoping to see Kelli, but found Jenna there instead. Her wide smile was nearly as white as her hat. "Congratulations on placing second in the saddle bronc riding."

"Thanks, and congratulations on your win."

"I wish it counted toward national standings, but thank you. So, you going to the Longhorn tonight?"

There was always an informal after-party at the bar following an event. He planned to go but tried to think of something honest to say that wouldn't raise her hopes or hurt her too much. She was going to have a bumpy road in life if she took things as personally as her mom made it sound.

He heard his name and looked up to see Bud Silverton, who'd been posted at the gate to prevent spectators' access to the livestock and competitors' area. "You have a visitor. Doc Hinton."

"Let her back, would you?"

Bud waved Kelli through the open gate and pointed Cole out to her, down the fence and half-hidden by the rumps of a couple of horses. Her friend Sienna followed her.

Jenna studied his face with a piercing scrutiny and shoved her arm through his. He remembered Lacey's other comment; the one about her competitive nature.

"You didn't answer me," she said playfully.

Kelli circled the horses and spotted him. He tried to extract himself, but Jenna had a lock on his arm.

"Uh. I'm not sure," he said, pulling away. When he looked up, Kelli had turned and was headed back toward the gate.

146 HER COLORADO COWBOY

"Save a dance for me if you do," Jenna called after him as he jogged to catch up with Kelli.

"Hey," Cole said to get Kelli's attention.

She turned back to him with a stiff smile on her face. Sienna's expression was as dark as an afternoon thunderhead.

"Hi, Cole," Kelli said.

"I'm really glad to see you here. I wasn't sure you'd come."

"How's Baxter doing?"

Her redirection threw him. "Uh, good. Better every day. Limping a lot less. Thanks."

"I didn't mean to interrupt you and your friend. I just came back to say thanks for the tickets and to congratulate you on taking second in saddle bronc."

Cole's mouth tightened in frustration. He wished he could roll the clock back a few minutes and have been anywhere except next to Jenna.

"You weren't interrupting anything. At all. Seriously, I'm done with events for the day, and I was thinking about coming out to join you in the stands."

"Yeah. That's exactly what it looked like you were doing," Sienna said. Cole shot her an exasperated look that said she wasn't helping.

He gently cupped Kelli's elbow and led her to the other side of the horses next to them. Sienna followed closely, not giving him a chance to get Kelli alone. "Look, maybe it's more awkward to talk about this than let it go, but I don't want there to be any misunderstanding. There's nothing between Jenna and me. She's young, and she just went through a breakup that she's not dealing with very well."

Kelli shrugged unconvincingly. "It's none of my concern."

"I'd like it to be," he said. She looked up at him, surprise on her face at his frankness. "Are you sure you have to leave? If you can stay, I'd still like to come out and join you."

"No. I'm sorry. I really should go."

He nodded, disappointed. "Oh, hey, a bunch of folks are going to the Longhorn tonight. The rodeo organizers hired a live band out of Pueblo. I thought I'd show up early, maybe around eight." Kelli opened her mouth but the expression in her eyes said she was going to say no, and he didn't want her to. "Just think about it. I'd really like it if you could come."

"Maybe," she said, "if I don't get called out this evening." She turned, and Sienna followed.

"I hope I see you tonight," he said to her back.

CHAPTER FIFTEEN

THAT'S WHAT THEY were so good at, these kinds of men. Reeling women in with their looks and their words and their charisma, then spinning whatever story suited their needs until they got what they wanted. She'd been there before. Too often. So when Cole pulled her aside and told her about Miss Tight Jeans—Jenna Overton according to their phone conversation the other night and the rodeo program today—she'd looked straight into his dark eyes, expecting to see that same cagey, manipulative "please believe me" look she'd fallen for in the past. Instead, he looked genuinely worried. Heartbreakingly hopeful.

That, or he was even better at this than the others.

Sienna started her car and pulled out of the parking lot. "You okay?" she asked.

Kelli stared out the windshield. "Wow. I mean, wow. Seriously, why would he even invite me here if he's hanging out with her?"

"Well," Sienna said in a far too calm and reasonable tone, "that's a good question. So, do you really think that's what happened?"

Kelli turned and stared at Sienna's profile. "Oh, come on. You're taking his side? I was the one being diplomatic and reserved back there. You were the one ready to take him out."

"I'm not taking his side. I'm on your side, always. And yes, I was ready to flay him on your behalf...until he turned all up-front and explainy. I saw the look on her face when she had her mitts on him, and I saw the look on his. He also said she'd cornered him into that dance last Friday. Isn't that what you told me? Maybe she's got him in her sights, you know? And I'd hate to see you pass up a good thing if that's all it is."

"He really did sound like he wanted me to go to the Longhorn tonight."

"Yes. He really did."

"So what exactly do you suggest I do, oh wise one?"

Sienna took her eyes off the road to look at Kelli. "The more important question is what do *you* want to do?"

Kelli gave a deep sigh and dropped her head back against the headrest.

"I want to feel important to a man for once in my life. Like, 'center of his world' important. I want to meet one guy who won't turn out to be a giant jerk and hurt me. And I guess I want to reconnect with my grade school best friend and find out if he's still the same person inside."

She thought about the list that had tumbled out. It hadn't been a frivolous answer; those three yearnings had roots that went all the way to her heart.

"Listen," Sienna said, "let's go together. If he turns on the Prince Charming act and you lose your cool, I'll be there with a fire extinguisher. If he starts flirting with rodeo girl, you'll be with a bunch of other people and maybe you'll find somebody better."

"That's true. Right," she said, the idea taking hold. "It's not like he'll be the only man there."

"Okay, but we'd better have a signal in case I see you turning to jelly."

"Like what?"

"Stranger danger?" Sienna suggested. Kelli laughed. "Your pants are on fire, here let me put that out for you?"

Kelli laughed harder. "Quit it. I didn't stop to pee before we left."

"Tell you what. You forwarded your emergency calls for the rest of the day, didn't you?"

"Yes," Kelli mumbled. It hadn't exactly been a lie to tell Cole she might come tonight "if she didn't get called out." She wouldn't get called out, but she still might or might not go.

"Okay. You give me your phone to keep in my purse and I'll tell you that you have an emergency."

"Done."

SIENNA MENTIONED SHE needed to go shopping for some new clothes and they decided to stay in town, go to dinner and generally hang out until heading over to the bar. Kelli found a cute sleeveless shirt at a strip mall clothing store and changed into it for the evening.

Cole had said he planned to be there around 8:00 p.m., so they arrived fashionably late a little past 8:30 p.m. The live band—loud, energetic and seriously talented—was already playing. She and Sienna were headed for a small booth along the wall when Cole appeared at her elbow. He'd changed into a crisp white shirt that stood out strikingly against his black hat and ruddy complexion.

"I'm glad you could make it." He smiled that thousand-watt smile of his. "If you'd like to join us, we have a few tables over there." He nodded toward the right side of the room where Kelli saw a large knot of people, some with sponsor or event patches sewn onto the sleeves of their shirts. There were about twenty of them spread across four tables pulled close together, and she guessed there'd be more coming.

"Okay. Thanks," Kelli said while Sienna avidly scanned the large group of athletic young men.

Even without the patches, Kelli could've picked them out. Real cowboys and cowgirls always stood out from the crowd of weekend-hat-wearing office workers and line-dance enthusiasts.

152 HER COLORADO COWBOY

Cole pulled out a stool for her, then took the next seat. Sienna sat on her other side. His strong voice carried over the music as he introduced everyone by name. When Cole mentioned she was a livestock vet, a new look of respect entered the eyes of the men who didn't know her.

Yep. Not just another pretty face. How about that, boys? she thought.

"Can I get you something to drink?" Cole asked, looking also to Sienna.

They both ordered beers.

"Have you eaten?"

"We stopped on the way here."

Cody Sanders was sitting on Sienna's other side and the two of them quickly struck up a conversation. The man across from Kelli asked her a question about bovine foot rot in cattle pastured near a river, and her answer started a lively conversation about herd management.

A couple of barrel racers were in the group, though thankfully not Jenna Overton. There were also a couple of girlfriends and wives, and more people were pulling extra tables and chairs over. People drifted in and out of the group, going up to the bar for drinks and food or heading out to the floor in pairs to dance. When yet another question about cattle disease came up, Cole saved her. "Give her a break, guys. She's off-duty tonight." He turned to her. "Would you like to dance?"

Kelli felt her palms go sweaty. She'd been hoping he would ask and dreading it at the same time.

"Sure."

They both stood and she saw the questioning look that Sienna shot her. She flashed her friend a subtle thumbs-up to let her know she hadn't lost her marbles yet. On the way to the dance floor, she covered her nerves by telling Cole that the older upbeat two-step song was one she'd always liked and mentioning how much she was enjoying the band. It surprised her when he said the lead singer was friends with his brother Troy.

Cole took her by the hand as they stepped up onto the wooden dance floor and she melted just a little at the feel of him when he pulled her in a half circle to face him. He lifted her right hand into a nice dance frame and placed his other hand on the small of her back. "Texas triple-two or regular two-step?"

"I'm a Colorado girl. Regular two-step, please." He flashed her a smile, waited for the beat and started them on the quick, quick steps.

Kelli had seen him dance but, moving with him now, she could tell in the first half-dozen steps that he was a natural. They glided smoothly across the floor with him turning them often to give her a break from dancing backward. After two laps around the rail, he began spinning her occasionally, which she followed comfortably. Daddy's little dancer. She may not have had what it took to be great, but she was passably good, and she still loved to dance every bit as much as she had as a child.

Kelli's palms quit sweating and his large calloused hand felt good in hers. With them both in boots, her eyes still only came to the notch of his neck. His shirt was only open at the top button, just enough to see the inner edges of his collarbones and the corded muscles of his neck.

The song ended too soon, but they stayed on the floor until the first notes of the next song began. He quirked an eyebrow at her under that dark hat brim, and she nodded. After one lap around the floor, she saw Sienna and Cody join the dancers. Sienna may have come along to support Kelli, but Kelli was glad to see her friend having a good time too.

Sienna was dancing backward and Kelli forward. Sienna shot her an "everything okay?" look. Kelli smiled and gave another thumbs-up behind Cole's back. After two dances, Cole led her off the floor, hand in hand, back to the table, a perfect gentleman.

But then, weren't they all at the start?

Back at the table, Kelli sipped her beer, nursing it along. Getting tipsy would be the worst thing she could do tonight. One of the other cowboys who'd shown up alone asked Cole if he could dance with Kelli. *Derek*, she thought. She ruffled slightly at someone asking Cole's permission, like she was his possession. Then again, if she was a guy, she wouldn't want to tick Cole off either.

Cole won more points by telling Derek to ask her, and she nodded yes, keeping her promise to herself to go slow and keep things casual. Tonight was a test to see if she could spend time with a handsome man who rang all her bells and still keep her head. Go slow, dip her toe in the waters and look for the "no diving" warning signs, instead of doing her usual cannonball leap off a cliff.

Sienna danced with multiple partners and, after Derek, Kelli danced with Cody. Even Matt, the Longhorn regular, dropped by the table and took her out for a dance. When Matt escorted her back, she saw that her table had filled to capacity, the tall stools scooted leg to leg. Even her chair was occupied.

By Jenna. Sitting on her barstool. Chatting with Cole. Kelli felt like she'd just bitten into a slice of lemon.

As Kelli approached, Cole said something to Jenna. The annoyingly well-proportioned blonde stood, shot a weighing glance toward Kelli, then flashed a smile full of promise at Cole before sauntering to one of the group tables with some open chairs. Kelli had worked up a light sweat from dancing and reclaimed her seat, fanning herself with a cardboard coaster, glad she'd chosen a sleeveless shirt for tonight. The band was

156 HER COLORADO COWBOY

playing a little louder, the bar was filling up and a side door had been propped open, letting in the cool night air.

She and Cole talked as best they could over the band, which wasn't much. Jenna didn't come back but Cole eventually danced with a couple of women who asked him, though Kelli noticed he asked no one out to the dance floor but her. When Kelli asked Sienna to check her phone for the time, she was surprised to find it was nearly 11:30 p.m. She didn't care one bit. She and Allen had been so work-oriented that she'd nearly forgotten what it was like to have a late night out. It felt good to act twenty-seven again instead of fifty-seven.

Another of the rodeo cowboys was headed her way when Cole took her by the hand and said, "My turn, boys," with a note of finality. He glanced at Kelli for her reaction. "If that's all right with you?"

She nodded, trying to keep her cool as they went back out to the crowded dance floor. The music had grown louder with each set so now they had to talk mouth to ear. The song ended a few bars later and the lead singer announced they'd be taking a short break after one more.

The music started and it was a slow two-step; a love song. Cole took her right hand gently and pulled it against his chest. He moved close and wrapped his left hand around her back. By now, their body language was well in sync and she knew what he wanted. With a little flutter in her heart, she pressed into him. He moved them in a dreamily slow and romantic dance, their feet barely shuffling while others lapped them. After a minute, she laid her head against his shoulder. He let go of her hand to wrap both of his around her back and she slid both of her arms up around his neck, bringing them even closer together. She felt the rise and fall of his breath and the steady pulse of his heart.

The song ended like the breaking of a spell. The chime of midnight for Cinderella. Kelli stepped back, her heart rate elevated. Struggling to regain her equilibrium, she straightened her shoulders and smiled a casual smile, like there hadn't just been a moment between them. Cole placed a hand on her back but didn't take her hand walking back to the table. She wasn't sure if he felt awkward as well, or if he was just reading her, picking up on her need to establish a bit of personal space again.

She thought about suggesting to Sienna that they leave, but recorded music started for the break; a line dance. Sienna popped up from her stool and grabbed Kelli's hand. She shook her head and Sienna took off without her. It was probably for the best if they stayed a bit longer, anyway. It would seem weird if she left now, and besides, she wanted that balance back. The feel-

158   HER COLORADO COWBOY

ing she'd had just before the dance, that she was in charge of her night and her emotions.

She sipped at her beer to cool off while conversation around the table grew livelier during the break. The set of three line dances ended. Sienna came back flushed and wiped her brow with a bar napkin, shoving it under her shirt to dab her armpits. *Sooo* Sienna. She looked at Kelli while Cole was talking to the man next to him and mouthed, *"Do you want to go?"* Kelli gave her a little shake of the head. Sienna made comically big eyes at her and turned back to Cody.

Kelli could sense Cole waiting for a signal from her that it was okay to dance together again, but she wanted a little more time. He began a conversation with Jim Hammond, another bronc rider, about the draws today for the horses they rode. She made a trip to the bathroom, and when she came back to the table, Cole was gone. Her heart stopped for a moment, and she wondered if she'd botched everything, not only whatever was happening between them tonight, but also the reconnection to their friendship. Maybe dancing with him had been a bad idea. Maybe she should have just talked shop with the people here to help add to her livestock clientele and worked on rebuilding her friendship with Cole.

Sienna came back from the dance floor and Kelli looked at her in panic.

"Did you see Cole? Did he leave?"

"I don't know. He wasn't on the dance floor."

Kelli played with the label on her beer and answered Cody's question about hock injuries in horses. A couple of minutes later, she nearly sighed out loud when Cole returned to the table with a fresh pitcher for everyone.

She was getting emotional. Could three beers spread out over four hours be affecting her? Maybe. She hardly drank these days. More likely, it was just the whole relationship game. The intricacies were beginning to overwhelm her. She found them exhausting at the best of times. Deep breaths.

She quit playing with her beer label and glanced at Cole to discover he was studying her. What *did* she want from him? Honestly, she couldn't answer that right now, except that she wanted them to be comfortable with each other.

"Would you like to dance?" she asked him sincerely. No overtones. No games.

His face relaxed into a grin. "Yes."

The song was a slow waltz. He didn't hold her as closely as during that slow dance, but it felt sweet, and moving together to the rise and fall of the song was both elegant and romantic.

"I'm really glad you came tonight," he breathed into her ear.

She looked up at him and smiled. "I am too." She meant it.

He held her hand all the way back to their table.

160   HER COLORADO COWBOY

They sat down, and he took her hand again, in front of everyone. He watched for her response, allowing it to be anything. She left her palm in his. Cole squeezed her fingers gently once.

Being attracted to another person was its own kind of dance, one with myriad steps and mis-steps. Nonchalantly, she slipped her hand out of his to take a cold gulp of her beer. She could feel her emotions ramping up again, starting to spin all directions like a gyroscope, and knew it was time to leave.

The song ended and she turned to Sienna only to see that Cody had scooted closer to her and things were starting to look intimate. She hated to pull her friend away when she was having a good time. Sienna felt her staring and glanced over, easily recognizing *the look*. Kelli saw the war in her friend's face for just a moment, but friendship trumped personal interest.

"I promised my mom I'd drive her down to Trinidad early tomorrow to see my aunt," Sienna said, loudly enough that both Cody and Cole could hear. "I'd better get going."

"Right," Kelli said to Cole. "Well, that's my ride. Besides, I've had a pretty busy work week. I'm beat."

He looked at her with those big dark eyes. She could see the question in them, asking if he'd done something wrong.

"I had a really good time tonight. Thank you for asking me."

Cole stood. "I'll walk you out."

He took his jacket and said his good-nights, meaning he was taking off as well. She wouldn't have to wonder if Jenna, or someone else, would be hitting on him the minute she was gone.

"I'm glad you showed up," he said, speaking to them both as he held the front door open and the cool night air hit them. "Sorry it was so loud. Kind of hard to catch up as much as I'd hoped."

They reached Sienna's Kia and all three of them stood there for an awkward moment.

"Well, I'll just get in the car now," Sienna said louder than necessary, choosing to be obvious. She unlocked the car and slipped in. "No hurry, Kelli." She closed the door.

Cole and Kelli both smiled.

He stood close, holding both her hands lightly and looking like he wanted to kiss her good-night. "Maybe we could get together again?" he suggested. "Somewhere quieter and less crowded."

There it was. Ball in her court. Her heart fluttered and she hoped her fingers weren't trembling.

"I'd like that."

"Maybe we could go for a ride?" For a moment, she processed it as a car ride, then realized he meant horses. "I could show you some of the ranch."

"That would be nice."

"I have to go out of town this week for an auction in Wyoming. How about next Saturday?"

"Saturday would be good." She didn't move to get in the car.

He was looking into her eyes, reading her face.

Leaning in, he touched his lips to hers. His mouth was warm and soft, and his kiss was gentle and brief. He didn't push for anything more.

The winning field goal.

He stepped back and opened her door for her.

"Noon, Saturday? I can pack us a lunch."

"Sounds great." She tried for an elegant Sophia Loren smile that probably looked like a bubbly Goldie Hawn grin. At least her voice had stayed steady.

"I get back from Wyoming on Thursday. I've got your number so I'll call you when I get home."

"Okay. I'll talk to you then." She slipped into her seat.

"Good night," he said and closed her door.

Oh, yes. He most certainly did have her number.

CHAPTER SIXTEEN

TUESDAY MORNING, COLE DOUBLE-CHECKED the hitch and connections to the stock trailer and started up the semi to warm the engine. The biggest outfits in the nation owned multiple semis and stock trailers, and small ranches usually had pickup trucks and one pull-behind trailer. Tillacos Creek Ranch fell between the two extremes. Cole had inherited one semitruck with a sleeping berth above the cab and a forty-six-foot livestock trailer that could handle about seventeen thousand pounds of liveweight. Cole, Dustin and Jake all held commercial driver's licenses, but with a handful of cows still waiting to deliver calves, Dustin was staying behind to keep an eye on the day-to-day operations.

Cole and Jake were on the road by 7:00 a.m. They reached the Wyoming state line in the afternoon, and arrived in Riverton, Wyoming, by early evening. He'd booked two rooms at a motel near the Riverton Livestock Auction yard in walking distance of a decent restaurant his dad had liked.

Back in his room after dinner, Cole found himself alone for the first time all day. He took off his hat, moved his duffel bag to the corner, kicked off his boots and lay down on the bed. He wanted to call Kelli but he'd told her he'd call when he got back. She'd acted spooked after their slow dance, so it seemed better not to rush anything with her and just call Thursday as he'd promised. Instead, he relived that slow dance in his head. Memories of them swaying together on the dance floor came back vividly, her arms stretched up around his neck. Rocking in time to the gentle ballad, barely moving around the floor. The smell of lavender in her hair. It made him wish she were here with him right now.

THE WHOLE OF Wednesday was spent in the auction barn, inhaling the scent of cattle and cedar shavings, and sitting on aluminum stadium benches that wore ridges into his butt by evening. He had six years of ranch-specific education under his belt plus on-the-job training: risk mediation, percentage of income to spend on new livestock, optimal herd size per acreage for health and more. Putting it into practice, though, taking over for his father, was a whole world removed from academic theory. This was his family's money and legacy he gambled with. His brothers might not be involved in the ranch, but there was no doubt they'd nail him to a wall if he didn't run it well.

He'd come to this auction specifically to buy Angus cattle for his breeding plan; well-bred animals from a ranch he'd been following for months that was liquidating. The first lot came out and a number of people kicked off the bidding. He held off joining in until the less serious folks dropped out so he wouldn't just be pushing up the bids. By that time, the dozen cows were up near his budget limit. He raised his card with his bidder's number and the auctioneer's spotter pointed him out. He was in the game, but the two other ranchers were as serious as he was, and both quickly bid again.

The auctioneer's chant pulled him in, that rapid, unintelligible ramble punctuated by the punch of the current bid and tease of the next amount so close in reach. He bid again, slightly over his budget. Both the others bid again as well. With a grimace, he dropped out. He had to budget for the bull as well. Two hours later, the whole situation repeated itself with one of his old opponents and two new ones. Again, bidding went too high, and again he pulled out. He poured over the catalogue in the afternoon and debated whether to wait until the final lot late in the day—which risked him going home empty-handed—or bid on other Angus he hadn't checked out as thoroughly. In the end, he decided that driving an empty trailer home was better than risking his money on cows from an outfit he hadn't researched.

The final lot of cows from the ranch he'd se-

166   HER COLORADO COWBOY

lected were herded into the barn at 6:30 p.m. Bids climbed again, but slower this time and he jumped in sooner. The dinnertime slot had lessened the competition and the two bidders who'd won earlier in the day hadn't stayed on to buy more stock. The bidding slowed. The auctioneer stopped on Cole's last bid, then tried to entice someone to go two hundred dollars higher, then one hundred. He called the final bid once, twice...sold.

Cole kept his poker face but celebrated with an inner fist pump. Sweeter still was that due to the lighter bidding, he'd won the cattle for substantially less than the other two lots of animals had sold for earlier in the day. Bidding on the bulls began next and went high, but with what he'd saved on the cows, he was able to get the winning bid again on the bull he wanted most. He paid for both lots and collected the brand inspection paperwork, vet health certificates, interstate transport papers and receipts. Back in his room, he had an overwhelming urge to call Kelli and share the good news, but he talked himself out of it for the second time that day. Like the auction, maybe slow and patient was the way to go.

Thursday morning, he and Jake got the animals loaded early and headed back to Colorado, traveling south the entire length of the state. They arrived home around 9:00 p.m., where Dustin and Baxter met him at the barn. Baxter danced at his feet for a full two minutes.

"Hey, you're moving that leg pretty good now, buddy," he said, squatting down to pet him. "Thanks for taking care of him," he said to Dustin.

"I think he kinda liked camping out in the cabin," he said in his slow Oklahoma drawl.

Dustin had two corrals ready with water and feed; one for the cows and one for the bull. They'd keep the new animals quarantined for the first week. After that, he'd turn them out in their own pasture for another four or five weeks before he'd allow them to mingle with the established herd.

It was ten o'clock at night by the time he latched the gates and Dustin and Jake headed for their cabins. He hadn't wanted to call Kelli from the road with Jake listening in but debated now if it had gotten too late and he should wait until morning. In the end, it seemed only right to keep his promise.

She picked up after two rings.

"Hey," he said.

"Hey, yourself." He heard a smile in her voice.

"Sorry for calling so late."

"It's fine. I'm glad to hear from you. How did your trip go?"

"Good. I came home with everything I set out to get. Remember those Angus I talked about that day you delivered the calf? I just got them unloaded."

"That's terrific, Cole. Congratulations. You

must be excited to be taking your breeding program in a new direction."

"I am, yeah. Thanks. So, we still on for Saturday?"

"I've been wanting to go riding ever since I moved back here. No way I'm letting you out of that."

"Noon still good?"

"That sounds great."

They signed off. Cole slipped his phone into his jacket pocket, feeling a thrill of anticipation for the weekend and a deep sense of relief that he'd heard no hesitation in her voice. Hot and cold affection was the one thing he had no defenses against. The battering ram that could shatter his heart. He'd experienced enough of it in his childhood for two lifetimes, and Amy had torn all those old scars open again before he'd moved back from Texas. It was something he'd promised himself he'd never put up with again.

CHAPTER SEVENTEEN

KELLI ARRIVED AT the ranch just before noon on Saturday. Cole must have heard her pull in and he emerged from the barn leading two saddled and bridled quarter horses. Baxter trotted at his feet. The whole image was so perfect, so "everything her heart desired," that she experienced an unexpected flutter of nerves. Allen letting her down had hurt, but Cole had the potential to wedge much deeper into her heart. So deep he might shatter it.

"Hey, Baxter's looking great," she said by way of greeting. Baxter ran up to her and she squatted down and gave him a quick check, falling back on the life skill where she felt comfortable and confident rather than her dating skills, which felt rusty as all get-out. "The leg feels good. No atrophy. I think he's out of the woods. You aren't planning on taking him with us, are you?"

Cole tied the horses to a rail in front of the barn. "No way. He's following the doctor's or-

HER COLORADO COWBOY

ders for R & R. This is the farthest he's been from the house."

"And who are these guys?" Still fighting to corral her butterflies, she went to meet the horses: a sleek bay and a chunky blue roan.

"This is my boy, Jet." He tipped his chin to the copper-coated gelding with a silky black mane and tail. "I wasn't sure of your riding ability, so I got Willie ready for you. I thought we'd ride a little way up Blanca Peak if that sounds okay."

"I think I'll make it if Willie goes easy on me."

"He's a sweetheart. He'll treat you right."

She stroked the mix of white and dark gray hairs that gave the roan his steel blue coloring, then breathed long and slow into one of his nostrils, in the same way horses introduced themselves to one another. He returned the greeting.

"He has a soft eye." Always a good sign of a gentle horse. "I think we'll get along just fine." She patted his neck.

"I've got our lunch in the fridge. Come on inside."

Cole was so calm, so natural. Not like the men who'd kept her on her toes; the teasing kind, who pounced on any weakness like sharks scenting blood in the water, then said it was just a joke. And if she didn't find them funny, they made it out to be her fault, not theirs. She could see so clearly now that it had been their own flaws, real or imagined, that drove them to cut everyone around them down in a vain attempt to make themselves look bigger. Cole projected none of that insecurity. Her mind quit racing; her shoulders relaxed.

She and Baxter followed him up the steps to the wide wooden porch that ran the length of the house. Inside the front door, the living room and the kitchen beyond were one open area. She remembered a little of the house from the few times she'd been here as a child, and the layout seemed unchanged. The living area looked to have been updated with contemporary furnishings: two large plush leather-covered sofas and matching recliners around a dark granite coffee table. A huge stone hearth and chimney took up most of the wall to her right. It delighted her to see a ranch home with no sad-eyed elk or deer trophy heads on the walls, or bear rugs on the floor. The kitchen had a lighter granite-topped island and stainless steel appliances. A pan rack hung over the island with glistening copper and sturdy cast-iron pans. She somehow doubted that two bachelors maintained the spotless home.

Looking up, she scanned the high, vaulted ceiling with its round log beams. A natural wood staircase near her climbed to the second-floor balcony and the bedrooms. There was no TV in the living room, but a short hall beyond the kitchen had an open archway to a laundry room and three closed doors: likely an office, family room or spare bedroom, and guest bath.

"It's a beautiful home," she said as he rummaged in the refrigerator. Between the fridge door and his body, she couldn't see what he shoved into the plastic grocery bags he packed. "When was it built?"

He tied the tops of both bags before turning back to her. "My dad had the old turn-of-the-century ranch house pulled down around the early 1990s and built this on the same site." He hefted the bags. "I have food and water. Is there anything you need to bring?"

"I'll grab my coat from the car, just in case."

It was supposed to reach a high of about sixty-five degrees today, not bad for mid-April, but she was a Colorado native. She kept a coat in the car all summer and a T-shirt handy in the winter.

"Good idea. We'll be gaining some elevation and going through a lot of shady areas."

He told Baxter he was sorry to leave him behind and scratched one ear, then vanished into the mudroom/laundry room where she heard a dog-door lock slide into place. When they went back outside to the horses, she noticed he didn't lock the front door behind them. Country living at its best. She wouldn't risk it at her home in town, but the ranch, down its long entry road, felt secluded, safe; its own little island of family and wranglers and livestock.

While she got her coat and tied it on behind her saddle with two long leather thongs, Cole slipped a water bottle into each of the canvas holders clipped near the saddle horns, packed their lunch into the saddlebags behind his saddle and checked the cinches on both horses' girths.

They untied their horses from the rail and mounted up. She'd worked with horses for years in a professional capacity, but it felt amazing putting her boot in a stirrup for the first time in ages and settling into a saddle. Willie hadn't lost his winter coat yet, and she could feel the thick padding of his hair beneath her hands. His warmth spread to her calves, and her legs moved slightly with his bellow-like breath. He shifted his weight from one foot to the other, reminding her that she sat astride twelve-hundred pounds of muscle and speed, and she marveled yet again at the willingness of horses to tolerate riders. She patted Willie on the neck and reined him around to follow Cole toward the mountain.

She soaked in the views, riding in the shadow of Blanca Peak as he led them to the north side of the property and then east. On the way here she'd worried she might not be able to keep a conversation afloat for a few hours straight. She was out of practice at this, and it would be mortifying if they discovered they'd already caught up on everything and said all they had to say.

Of course, talking with Cole turned out to be

HER COLORADO COWBOY

as easy as it had been the day she'd delivered the calf, and felt as natural as when they'd been children. Their topics bounced from animals and ranching to college years in Texas and Fort Collins, to hobbies and travel and music and more.

The day couldn't have been more perfect. A few white clouds drifted against a dome of cobalt sky. The winds, which could be violent this time of year, gusted only to a light breeze. He pointed out property boundaries and old landmarks along the way, mentioned the impressive water rights the ranch owned, and showed her the irrigation ditch his great-great grandfather had dug with a dirt scraper and mules. She told him about her longstanding interest in Colorado history and shared a couple of facts he hadn't known about Fort Massachusetts, built on the south side of Blanca Peak in the mid-1800s, only a couple of miles from where they rode now.

"If you enjoy history, maybe you'll like this," he said, angling toward an old cabin that had just come into view.

It turned out to be the original ranch homestead, a one-room cabin from the late 1800s that the family had lovingly preserved. They dismounted and tied the horses to an old hitching post. He unlatched a door made of wooden slats and it swung inward with a creak. Kelli stepped over the threshold and her breath caught. The inside was all browns and grays: unstained wood, dirt floor, a faded black potbellied stove. It felt like the antithesis to Dorothy stepping into full-color Oz, like she'd stepped back in time into a black-and-white Western.

Clean but stale air drifted out through the open door and dust motes swirled in the low light from the single window. She'd expected the cabin to be empty and was amazed to see some of what must have been the original furnishings filling the room.

"When my father was young, they used this as a guesthouse. My mom converted one of the unused wrangler cabins for guests so they could preserve the homestead in its original condition."

Kelli brushed her fingers across the old metal frame of the single bed on its rack of springs in the corner, the wooden chairs at the rough-hewn table and the oil lamp in the corner.

"I think about it sometimes," she said, "what life was like back then. It's amazing to see this slice of it, touch it."

"Were any of your family pioneers?"

"No. My parents moved to Pueblo when they were first married. They met in college in Pennsylvania, and my dad came out to Pueblo to work as a manager at the steel mill. The mill started laying off the next year and the state highway patrol was hiring. His family wanted him to go into something that would use his business degree, but

176 HER COLORADO COWBOY

he signed on with the highway patrol instead and never looked back."

"I sometimes wish I knew more about my birth parents' families, like what skills they had. What they did for a living." He gripped the back of one of the unvarnished wooden chairs and rocked it once on its rear legs. "It's odd not knowing what I might have become if I hadn't been raised here."

She stepped close to him and laid one hand on his forearm. "I have a feeling you would've gravitated to ranching no matter what. Even if you didn't, I'm sure you would have succeeded at any career you picked."

"I guess I'll never know. But I do know that I'm glad I met you back then." He put a warm hand over hers, then let go of the chair and twined their fingers together. "One of the nicest things about moving back here this year has been reconnecting with you. I've never forgotten how you were there for me when we were young."

It had been debated, she'd learned later, whether Cole should start in first grade or second. Since he was seven and he'd had a little homeschooling with his neighbor, it was decided to be in his best interests to start him with children his own age, to help him adjust. If he'd been a grade behind her, she might hardly have known him.

"We were there for each other. It's funny how kids work out ways to let the bad stuff out." Still holding hands, they returned to the cabin doorway as if drawn to the light. "I don't think I could have talked about my nightmares with my parents or my sister, but I could write down something scary and pass it to you, and you'd read it and crumple it up and then it was gone. Until the next one, and then you'd take care of that one too. You always understood my monsters."

"And you know all of mine," he said, stopping at the open door. "I like that you know things about me. So many people here think they know my past, but they don't really understand it at all. You do."

Her heart swelled to hear him confess that she knew him in a way that felt special and private. He lifted a lock of her hair that had come loose from her fabric hair tie and pulled it into the sunlight streaming between them. The strands looked nearly on fire in the shaft of sunlight coming through the door, as if everything this side of the threshold was just a bit unreal. He let the lock go and stroked two fingers down her cheek. A tingle like a raindrop sliding over her skin followed the path of his touch. She didn't want it to stop.

She looked up into his dark eyes, then down to his lips framed by his dark stubble. She wanted to feel the touch of those lips on her own. A weighted silence stretched between them; a moment that communicated everything without words. A moment where she knew they were sharing the same thoughts, the same feelings. She took a step closer.

His hand slid behind her neck and he dipped his head to kiss her. She tilted her mouth up to meet him, resting one hand over his heart. Their lips met, gently at first, then pressed more firmly.

Breaking the intimacy barrier both excited and frightened her. For the first time in twenty years, they were undeniably moving beyond friendship, and it had the potential to change everything between them. He pulled back, watching for her reaction. She felt no regret and gave him a smile she knew reached her eyes, but inside her heart fluttered and her doubts swirled. Everything about him seemed too good to be true. In her experience, that meant only one thing.

"Ready to see some more country?" he asked.

"You bet." Still a little breathless, she turned and ducked out the small cabin doorway, her hopes and fears waging war inside her.

"Snow and ice in the shady spots will keep us from getting too far up the mountain, but I know a little meadow pretty low down that I hope we can get to."

They mounted up and continued to the eastern edge of the property. Parts of the fence here were old wood and wire. Not even milled 4x4s, just rough and irregular branches for posts. He rode to a section that looked like all the others except the branch wasn't buried in the ground and it had a loop of wire wrapped around the top, holding it against its neighbor. He dismounted, leaning into the post to take the tension off the loop, and pulled the makeshift gate open for her.

Beyond the gate, a narrow trail led up the forested mountain slope. As they rode, he told her about his teen years, camping in summertime at their cow camp up the mountain. Her mercurial emotions over the kiss at the cabin receded quickly, and she relaxed again into the conversation.

The air was cool under the trees and full of the scent of pine. They rode uphill a short way and through a couple of patches of snow, but the ground remained mostly clear this far below the summit. They soon came to a small clearing where sunshine bathed the treeless, grassy oval in gold. Early wild daisies and buttercups had made the most of the sunlight and were just beginning to bloom.

They tied the horses to slender aspen trees, clipping lead ropes to their halters and removing the bridles so the horses could graze. Her knees were stiff and her thighs a bit sore, but overall, she felt better than she'd expected to—until her stomach rumbled so loudly that Cole heard it.

"Hungry?"

There was no point denying it. "Starving."

"I'm sorry. We could have stopped earlier."

"No, I'm glad we waited. I'm always hungry and this is a beautiful spot."

180 HER COLORADO COWBOY

He pulled a flannel blanket out of one saddle-bag and spread it on the ground. From the other side, he pulled the grocery bags and unpacked a mini bottle of champagne, two plastic glasses and some small plastic storage containers. He set those down and rummaged some more in the saddlebags.

"I hope I remembered everything. Oh, there they are." He laid out forks, knives, two small, bent paper plates and napkins. One container he left closed and set off to the side.

They sat knee to knee on the blanket. Opening the largest container, he presented two homemade steak sandwiches with cheese that had been melted in, topped with tomato, local mild-roasted chili pepper strips and chipotle sauce. Another held potato salad that he confessed to having bought at a store deli.

"This is amazing, Cole," she said, her mouth watering and her heart swelling at the thought of him planning and preparing the picnic.

He must have been as hungry as she felt because there was little conversation while they both ate. She breathed in the fresh pine air and cool breeze and watched two squirrels chase each other around a tree. She ate everything he'd brought and even licked her fingers after the messy sandwich.

Sipping the last of her champagne, she said, "That steak was wonderful. Homegrown?"

"You better believe it." He pulled the last con-

ELIZA D. COLLINS 181

tainer into his lap and, with all the drama of an
infomercial said, "But wait, there's more." He
opened it. Inside were two chocolate cupcakes
piled high with chocolate icing and topped with
multicolored sprinkles.

Kelli felt her eyes grow wide. She gasped and
actually clapped her hands together in delight.

"Those are my favorite!" She looked up at him.
"Was that a lucky guess?"

"I was hoping you still liked these. I owe Jake
big-time. I made him wait in the truck while I
stopped at three different stores on the way home
from Wyoming. It's part of why I called you so
late that night." He set the tub down in front of
her and gestured for her to pick one. "Remember
your eighth birthday?"

She stopped midway through peeling the paper
off the bottom and raised an eyebrow at him.

"The teacher brought chocolate cupcakes with
sprinkles for each birthday that year," he continued. "I remember you counting down to your
turn. You were more excited about the cupcakes
than you were about the presents waiting for you
at home." He grinned at her and seemed pleased
with himself for remembering this.

The hazy memory of Miss Solkey and her cupcakes returned. She tipped her head back and
laughed out loud. "I *was* super excited, wasn't I?
I mean, I guess I kind of remember those parties

back then, but I never associated my love of cup-cakes with them."

And she loved what it said about him, that he'd remembered that detail and made this gesture. Would Allen have done something like that? Would any of the others? More proof he was different.

He picked up his cupcake and touched it to hers in a toast. Full as she was, she ate the entire thing with gusto, then wadded up the empty paper and put it in one of the plastic containers where it wouldn't blow away.

He leaned forward across the debris field of their picnic.

"You have a little..." He gestured to the edge of his mouth.

Heat rose in her cheeks, and she lifted her hand to her face.

"Wait. Let me get that for you," he said, capturing her hand before she could wipe it off. He leaned closer. Then closer still. Her eyes widened until he raised a napkin to her face.

He wiped her mouth gently. "Sweet. Like you."

Still leaning close to her, he placed a finger under her chin. She allowed him to tip her head up, and he kissed her gently. He'd surprised her by wiping the chocolate from her face, but she'd been ready for the kiss. At least, she thought so until his rough stubble brushed her cheeks and his lips touched hers. Her pulse thundered like a stampede. When the kiss ended, he remained with his forehead against hers.

"I'm going to have to bring you cupcakes more often," he said.

She laughed so hard she snorted. "The sprinkles nailed it."

Today, he'd been everything she'd always wanted and more. While she'd delivered the calf, they'd talked mostly about ranching. While treating Baxter, she'd seen his sentimental side but they'd both been focused on the dog. At the bar, they'd been in a group of people and talking over the music had been difficult. But today was different. A dozen years of dating, and no man had ever made her feel as special as Cole did. Maybe she hadn't needed to worry about avoiding men like him. Maybe she'd just needed to find the right one.

Cole shifted and stretched out on his side; his head propped on one hand. "You know, I can't remember the last time I took a day off."

"Well, it hasn't been *that* long. I saw you at the sand dunes with Billy just a couple of weeks ago."

He took his hat off and rolled onto his back, crossing his booted feet at the ankles.

"Yeah, but I only took the afternoon off," he said. "I'd worked in the morning. Plus, I spent the whole evening rigging Billy out on a horse and testing his riding skills, so I think I deserve a pass for the sand dunes."

HER COLORADO COWBOY

"You were also off the day of the rodeo, and I saw you at the Longhorn the week before that too."

"Okay. Busted. I'm just a big slacker."

Mentioning the rodeo and the Longhorn awoke her worries again. She chewed her lip, debating not saying anything, then forged ahead anyway.

"So, those two times I saw you with Jenna, it really was nothing?"

He pushed up onto his elbows and met her gaze steadily. "It really and truly was nothing. One dance when she asked me, and then her being more friendly than I wanted when she saw you coming to talk to me at the rodeo."

She plucked at the fuzz on the blanket. "Sienna also said you have a profile on an online dating site. Is there anybody else you're seeing right now?"

She didn't know why she was pursuing this and ruining the mood. She'd been so happy a moment ago, but maybe that was the whole point. If the world was going to come crashing down on her, she wanted to see it coming for once. Their kisses had powered her emotions like rocket fuel in a car, hurtling her feelings and responses to him till they moved faster than her common sense could keep up. She'd broken up with Allen less than three months ago, swearing she'd never date another studly man again. And here she was. And here Cole was. He had an excuse for Jenna, but that didn't mean there weren't others.

"Troy put me on that dating site. I wasn't thrilled about it, but the truth is I didn't fight it either. He thought I needed help getting over Amy, a woman I dated in Texas. Two days after my dad died, I was making plans for both of us to fly back here for the funeral when she told me she was having second thoughts about us."

"How awful. I'm so sorry."

"Well, it's not how I would've chosen for her to handle things, but in the end, it was for the best. Her whole family lived in Texas, and she knew I was getting ready to move back here. I don't know, maybe before Dad died she might've thought she could convince me to stay. She was someone who liked getting her way." He shifted to his side on one elbow, and with his free hand, he reached above the edge of the blanket to pick up a spray of pine needles. He broke them between thumb and finger as he talked. "Anyway, by the time I moved back, Troy could see that between Dad and Amy, I was…well, I wasn't doing great. He thought he was helping by putting me on that site. I didn't feel ready, but it did get me out there on a couple of dates. Three, to be exact, over the past three months. None of them clicked for me, but Troy was right. It did help me get over Amy and move on."

Kelli's breakup with Allen had been bad enough. She couldn't imagine what it would have been like if she'd been grieving her father at the same time.

Now she felt bad about grilling him. Looking out for herself was a good thing, a necessary thing—something she'd promised herself she'd do—but the more time she spent getting to know the man Cole had become, the more she remembered the boy she'd known and trusted.

"I understand. I just wanted a heads-up if anyone else was in the picture, you know?"

"Totally reasonable. No. No one in the picture." He tossed the last of the needles aside and studied her. "So, while we're on the subject, I'm guessing you and Allen aren't working on a reconciliation if you're out here with me."

Kelli shook her head. "Not for anything in the world. I might as well tell you. He was cheating on me. I found out by accident."

The look in his dark eyes was complex. Surprise? Empathy? Anger on her behalf?

"Like you said about Amy. It was for the best. No regrets."

"So, we're both firmly unattached."

"Sounds like."

Kelli didn't think the champagne had anything to do with the lightheadedness she was feeling. Without even touching her, Cole ignited a depth of feeling that Allen never had. She stretched out as well, facing him. Cole wrapped an arm around her waist, pulled her to him, and rolled to his back, taking her with him so that she lay snuggled into the side of his chest and shoulder.

Like the night they'd danced at the Longhorn, he might be leading, but she still felt in charge of saying yes or no. She knew she could push to her feet right then and he would pack the horses and escort her back to the ranch. She was safe with him, emotionally and physically.

Allen had made her feel like she hadn't been enough for him. Cole made her feel like nothing mattered but her.

But what did *she* need? Beneath the din of her emotions, her mind whispered the answer: not to rush.

Kelli pulled back and the cool mountain air drifted between them. Leaning back slightly, his eyes narrowed in a question. She smiled to reassure him and laid her fingers over his.

"This is wonderful, Cole. The picnic. Being here with you. All of it."

She traced a pattern on his hand and followed her finger with her eyes rather than meet his gaze. She wanted him to understand her reasons for her mood shift without ruining this wonderful day by trying to explain them.

She was sorting a speech in her head, but before she could start, he spoke up.

"How about a stroll around the meadow before we head back down to the ranch?" His eyes twinkled as he read her like a book and saved her from her awkward explanations.

"Sounds perfect," she said.

CHAPTER EIGHTEEN

COLE WOKE SUNDAY morning thinking of Kelli, reliving the sensations of holding her in his arms in the meadow yesterday.

He was glad she'd kept things at a pace that made her comfortable. He remembered how she'd retreated emotionally after their slow dance last week. She was like a skittish colt, and her trust and her feelings would come along in their own time. Allen had hurt her in some way that hadn't yet healed, and he wasn't about to make the mistake of losing her by rushing things.

Today was his day to catch up on office work, but for the rest of the week he and his ranch hands would have their hands full with spring vaccinations, tagging the new calves and fertilizing pastures. It was already mid-April, too, a tricky time of year. The temperatures were as likely to be in the twenties as the seventies and some of the biggest snowstorms of the year could hit in the spring. In fact, a storm was predicted to come in toward the end of the week, though the meteorologists weren't committing to snowfall predictions just yet.

Despite his plans for the day, by mid-morning he'd managed to do less than half an hour of real work, and the stack of logbooks, tax forms, inventory sheets and accounting statements stared back at him. This wasn't the way he wanted to spend his Sunday. He wanted to be anywhere but at his desk. No, not anywhere—anywhere as long as it was with Kelli. She was off today and all he could think about was calling to see if she wanted to do something together. What, though?

Not another picnic. When she'd left the ranch yesterday, he'd promised to outdo himself the next time. He tapped his pen on the desk, trying to come up with something special. Tough, when they were both so familiar with everything in the area. Maybe something that wasn't nearby then...though it couldn't be as far away as Santa Fe, or it would mean a commitment to either staying overnight or spending all their time driving.

And then he had it. About an hour and a half drive. The same distance as Taos, but not a destination spot—so with luck, maybe she'd never been to the place he was thinking of. And now that the idea filled his thoughts, he couldn't seem to force his mind back to work. He'd been going to give her a call today anyway just to say hi. Why not now?

He tapped his pencil on the desk again as the phone rang.

"Hey there," she answered. He could hear the smile in her voice. A tension deep inside him—the one anticipating Amy's old "push you/pull you" behavior, or worse, his birth parents'—melted away.

"Hey yourself."

"Wow, I'm impressed. No three-day rule?" Her voice was light and playful, but with just a twinge of a barb.

"What's a three-day rule?"

There was a pause, like she thought he was teasing her. "You know, wait three days before you call a woman after a date, so you look cool. Not overly enthusiastic or smitten."

"That sounds like something only an idiot would do. Besides, I *am* overly enthusiastic. And smitten. In fact, the only reason I waited this long to call is because I was trying to get some work done, but I couldn't because I wanted to hear your voice."

"And what do you want to hear it say?" She tried to sound sultry but snorted a laugh at the end.

"That you'll go out with me again."

"I already said yes, dummy. You asked me when we got back to the ranch yesterday. In fact, you promised me something very vague but quite spectacular."

"Yeah, but we didn't set an actual date." He leaned back in his chair, enjoying the flirty back-and-forth.

"And now you're ready to reveal your spectacular plan? Okay—" she took a loud breath and let it out "—I'm prepared to be wowed."

"Not ready to reveal just yet, but I am ready to set an actual date. How about this afternoon?"

"Oh. You really are smitten. Well, the women's idiot rule is to pretend to be busy today, so I somehow seem more alluring or hard to catch. But since that's stupid too, I'll fess up. I'm working on some billing right now and this evening's big plans were spaghetti and finding a new mystery series to stream on BBC, so I think I can fit you in."

He grinned. "Great. How about I pick you up at five?"

"Sure. Any hints? I don't want to wear a dress if you're taking me riding again."

"No. No riding. But the costume party at the end of the night has an 'aliens from outer space' theme, so whatever works for that is fine. Something from the *Star Wars* bar scene would be perfect."

"Excuse me, what?" She sounded incredulous but not gullible.

Cole laughed. "No? Okay, well how about this? We'll be going for a drive, maybe a walk or a stop along the way, and then on to a 'non-costume party' surprise. Wear something comfortable, I

192   HER COLORADO COWBOY

guess, but a little dressy if you want for the evening."

"That's not much of a hint. You're a sly one, aren't you, Cole Tyler? Okay. Business casual, it is."

"I'll see you soon."

CHAPTER NINETEEN

KELLI WAS LOOKING forward to the evening so much that she hardly knew what to do with herself. Tired of checking the clock, she banged out an overdue housecleaning, then called Sienna, as her friend seldom slept past midafternoon when on night shift. There was no answer, so her unoccupied mind went spinning back to Cole like a boomerang, anticipating their date tonight and reliving their picnic in the meadow.

Looking to distract herself, she showered, then picked out what she thought would be appropriate for the evening, though he hadn't given her much to go on. Driving and maybe a walk—or had he said a hike? Anyway, no heels. She could walk a fair distance in her rubber soled work boots, but they were hardly "business casual." Her dancing boots could work under the right outfit, but she couldn't walk over rough ground in them. And who knew what he had planned for later in the evening.

In the end, she settled for "dressy but warm" slacks she'd gotten from an upscale outdoor cloth-

194 HER COLORADO COWBOY

ing store in Boulder, a lightweight cute sweater appropriate for a date and a pair of light running trainers in a blue mesh that could pass for—well, better than work boots, anyway. She picked out a pair of sparkly earrings, brushed her hair a second time and looked at the clock for the third time that hour. Fifteen minutes to spare.

Cole showed up so precisely at 5:00 p.m. that she wondered if he'd been parked down the block. He was dressed much like he had been that night at the Longhorn: a crisp, clean Western shirt—this one black but with a decorative pattern in subtle black embroidery just below the shoulders—clean unfaded blue jeans, black boots and of course the ever-present black Stetson—the pristine one he'd worn Saturday, not the dusty work one he'd worn when she delivered the calf.

He smelled of soap and aftershave and just a tiny bit of rawhide, as if the smell of his saddle or horses or cattle had bonded inseparably to him. And he must have left that short black stubble for her because he was picking up on just how much she liked it. She grabbed her jacket and phone-sized shoulder bag from her couch and let him guide her out the door to his truck.

"Do I get to find out where we're going now?" she asked as he turned right onto the highway.

"Nope."

"So basically you're abducting me."

"Yep."

THEY DROVE EAST for nearly an hour, and Kelli still didn't know where they were headed. There weren't many options along the way, with little but open landscape to either side between Blanca and Walsenburg. The time passed quickly and comfortably, though, while they chatted about horses and cattle and dogs, the color of the Colorado sky, grade school and high school, and old friends and family. When they got to Walsenburg, he followed the highway through town without stopping, then turned south on I-25, back into open country.

Twenty minutes later—about thirty miles from the state border with New Mexico, and with nothing in any direction except a few antelope and more plains—he slowed and pointed out the Ludlow Memorial highway sign. "Have you ever visited the memorial?"

"No. I've seen the turnoff, but I've never stopped."

He looked pleased and signaled to take the exit just ahead. "And here I thought you were a history buff," he teased.

"Well, in my defense, with going to school in Fort Collins, I drove north on I-25 a lot more often than I ever went south."

"How about the coke ovens at Cokedale. Been there?" he asked as they bumped down the short dirt road to the memorial site.

196 HER COLORADO COWBOY

"Are you trying to destroy my impeccable credentials as a Colorado history buff?"

He grinned, and then, with pursed lips and a short nod, she could see him add Cokedale to a mental list of places to take her.

"Don't feel bad," he said. "You knew things about Fort Massachusetts that I didn't, and that's practically in my backyard. Besides, your family's been here for, what, less than fifty years? Mine's been here for a hundred and fifty. I grew up on stories of this area."

Ludlow turned out to be a mining ghost town. The memorial itself had been erected as a monument to the miners and their families who lost their lives in the war between striking coal miners and the militia sent to quash their demands for fair pay and better working conditions.

He parked in the lot and casually took her hand as they walked to the enclosed site. She experienced a tingling thrill at his touch when their fingers entwined. Around the fenced monument were a series of modern information plaques, and they began reading them in silence.

Partway through, she blew out a sigh. "I haven't heard anyone talk about this. How is it more people don't know about it?"

"It was national news at the time, but that was back in 1914."

Inside the fence, a small monument with a carving of a family stood near the bunker where women, children and infants had been murdered in their hiding place while the miners were gunned down and the tent city of the workers burned. According to the signs, the massacre of the miners by the militia and National Guard had reverberated all the way up past the mine's owner, Rockefeller, Jr., and on to President Woodrow Wilson. The nation's shock at the killings formed a turning point in the status quo of worker-owner labor relations from that point onward.

"I still can't believe I haven't ever heard about it before," she said on the way back to the truck. "I mean, my dad worked a while at the CF&I steel mill in Pueblo, so I knew about Rockefeller owning steel. But wow. Just wow."

"Well, there's plenty of state history I'm sure I've never heard about."

"You know about the mob hideout in Aguilar?" she tried as he opened the passenger door for her.

"Should I say no to make you feel better?" He smiled and closed her door.

"Dang." It had been a good try. Not many people knew that the tiny town of Aguilar just down the road—about the same size now as Burgess— had been a hideout for Al Capone and his men in the 1920s. "Well, it's a long drive home," she said as he got in and started the truck. "I have plenty of time to stump you."

He threw an arm over the seat and twisted to see behind as he backed out and headed for the interstate. "What? You think I drove you all the way out here just to see that? That was a point of interest on the way, silly."

"'But, wait…there's more,'" she said, mimicking him when he'd presented her with the cupcakes. "Really? What now?"

"Getting hungry?" He shot her a playful glance.

She snorted a laugh. "Always."

"Thought so."

Less than twenty minutes later, they came to Trinidad, a town a few miles north of the New Mexico border and about the size of Alamosa. She'd been here, of course, but mainly passing through, and other than gas stations and the grocery store, she knew few of the local businesses.

He navigated into the center of town and parked a moment later. They got out in front of Rino's Italian restaurant and walked across the stamped red brick paving to the steep concrete staircase leading up to the entrance of the historic stone building. Once past the foyer, the restaurant unexpectedly opened into an almost Baroque Italian setting. Chandeliers gave off muted light and heavy crimson drapes framed the windows. There were small tables with crisp, white tablecloths and wineglasses with the settings.

"Oh, Cole, this is wonderful." The sentiment was punctuated by her stomach rumbling at the aromas wafting from the kitchen: meat and pasta, onion and garlic and olive oil. She'd been hungry out of habit before. Now she was suddenly famished.

She declined the bottle of wine he offered once they were seated, but they each chose a glass to go with the antipasto he ordered for them to share, the chicken marsala for him and the wild mushroom ravioli she picked out.

"No steak?" she asked when the waiter left.

"I rarely order steak eating out. It can't compare to what I get at home."

"Makes sense."

She was about to comment on the decor when the older man who'd taken their order returned with a microphone in his hand and stood at the top of a short staircase near their table. The canned music stopped and the first strains of "That's Amore" began. Right on cue, their waiter burst into song, walking about serenading the customers with an unexpectedly strong voice.

Kelli turned to Cole in open-mouthed surprise. The sparkle in his eyes said how much he enjoyed her delight.

"How did you find this place?" she asked after the song ended.

"My mom and dad. My mom loved this restaurant, so my dad always brought her here on their anniversary. A couple times a year, they'd bring the whole family down for a treat."

Dinner came, punctuated by two more of the waitstaff erupting into song at unpredictable intervals, then a dessert of spumoni ice cream for him and cheesecake for her. But as lovely as the meal and the atmosphere were, the best part of the evening had to be Cole seated across from her. His smile captivated her, genuine and easy. It broke like a rising sun through his normally quiet and serious demeanor. The man could just about melt her with that grin, but it was the glimpses of the sweet and sensitive boy she'd known that tugged at her heartstrings. He was everything she'd been searching for. The real deal.

The coffee they'd both had with dessert kept them wide-awake and chatty on the drive back. The closer they came to Blanca, though, the more Kelli practically vibrated with uncertainty over how their night might end.

She'd promised herself she'd go slow this time, stay alert for warning signs. The last thing she needed was another man acting gallant and sensitive, considerate and loving, and then turning selfish or callous—or, worst of all, cruel. She tried to picture Cole changing like that and couldn't. He was different…or was that just what she wanted to believe?

He pulled up in front of her house—and, of course, he didn't kiss her there like some high school boy. He came around the truck and opened her door for her. Walking her to her front door, he took her hand, lacing her fingers into his large grip. The mere touch of his skin against hers sent an electrical pulse arcing through her.

"The stars are so bright tonight," she said, stalling while she struggled to collect her thoughts.

They both paused in the gravel driveway, looking up together.

"They are. One of the worst things about college was living somewhere you couldn't even see the Milky Way. Hey, have you ever been out to the UFO tower?"

She laughed. "Not since high school."

The spot was one of the least light-polluted places in Colorado and some UFO enthusiasts had set up a watchtower there. The dark, remote location near the sand dunes was far more popular with high school couples than UFO buffs, though.

They approached the door and her cheeks flushed hot against the cool air. He reached out gently with both hands and cupped her neck. Her heart launched into double time. He brought his mouth to hers and kissed her softly.

"I had a good time tonight." His voice was rough. He brushed a strand of her hair back from her cheek with his thumb. "Okay if we do it again soon?"

Her heart melted and puddled at her feet at his sweet gentleness. She loved that he'd made no assumptions, wasn't pushing her, just asking her out again. It was more proof that he was everything she believed him to be.

CHAPTER TWENTY

"GOOD MORNING, SLEEPYHEAD," Cole said when Kelli picked up the phone.

"Good morning yourself," she said groggily.

"I'm sorry if I woke you. I just wanted to hear your voice before I start my workday." Dustin would already be at the barn. He needed to call his foreman next and let him know the priorities for the day. "I figured you'd be up since you told me last night you have early clinic hours this morning."

"Oh. Rats."

"What's wrong?"

"No," she said. "Rats. Molly Jenger's daughter is bringing her pet rats in before school. That's why I have clinic early. I told her mom I could meet them here at seven thirty but I turned my alarm off and fell back asleep. Good thing my clinic is out my back door."

He could hear her rummaging through dresser drawers and turning on the shower.

"I'd better let you go, then. I just wanted to tell

you I was thinking of you and that I'd like to see you again soon."

"Me too," she said softly.

His heart ached like it had doubled in size, hearing that she wanted to get together again as much as he did.

"I'm sorry that it won't be as soon as I'd like. We're starting vaccinations this week, plus we've got the new calves to tag, and I have to finish getting the fertilizer down on the fields. I've also got three meetings in the evenings. I can't promise I'll be free during the next few days but how about we plan something at the weekend for us both to look forward to?"

"Like what?"

"You choose, would you rather take the historic steam train from Antonito over the pass to Chama, spend a day at a hot springs pool in Crestone or take an overnight trip to Santa Fe?"

"Did you really come up with all that spur of the moment?"

"Of course not. I started thinking about it over dinner last night."

She gave a soft chuckle. "Well, those are some pretty nice options. Can I think about it and get back to you?"

"Just don't take too long. I'm not giving anybody else an opportunity to slip in and make a date with you."

The sounds of running water grew louder and

her voice echoed against the close walls of the bathroom. "I promise. You have the next spot on my dance card."

"I'm probably going to be running late most evenings, but if you have any calls out near the ranch, I hope you'll stop by. I'm not sure I can go five days without seeing you."

"I'll try and swing by if I'm in the neighborhood… Maybe even if I'm not."

"Anytime you can."

He missed her even before they'd hung up.

AFTER EATING A quick breakfast standing up in the kitchen, Cole packed his logbook and a few extra supplies onto the four-wheeler and headed out.

Today, he'd be starting off by examining the new livestock he'd bought in Wyoming. They'd had three full days to settle in. If everything looked good, he and his ranch hands would start spring vaccinations for lepto and annual respiratory diseases. Next would be checking that the last of the new calves were healthy and sound, then pasture management on the south grazing fields, plus getting the fertilizer down on the hay fields during this good-weather spell. At 6:00 p.m., he had a water commission meeting where they'd be voting on the nomination to elect him to his father's open position on the board.

The next couple of days would be every bit as busy as today while they vaccinated the regular herd and did the calf immunizations and tagging. He'd end tomorrow with another meeting, city council this time, thankfully just as a citizen.

"Morning, Mr. Tyler," Dustin said when Cole arrived at the corrals to find his foreman already finished with feeding the herd.

Cole had given up two months ago on trying to get Dustin to be less formal. He'd run into the same in Texas, where upbringings were filled with even more sirs and ma'ams than his own childhood on the ranch. He suspected Dustin's Oklahoma habits were just as ingrained.

"Morning." Cole rested one foot on the bottom rung of the metal corral panel with his elbows on the top rail.

"The new stock is looking good," Dustin said.

"They are," he agreed.

Together, they surveyed the prize bull and the dozen coal black Angus cows in the next corral.

"That bull's a beauty. What's he run? About eighteen-hundred pounds?"

"Nearly eighteen hundred and fifty."

Dustin whistled. "That ought to bring your market weight up."

The cows were alert and clear-eyed, well filled out and showed no signs of dehydration from their trip. "Have you gotten temperatures?"

"Not yet."

"Let's get them moved over to the squeeze chutes. We'll start with temperatures and record-

206 HER COLORADO COWBOY

ing their brands. If everything looks good, we'll get them wormed, vaccinated and tagged, then start on the calves."

"Yes, sir."

Cole pulled the deworming paste and 7-way vaccines out of the Styrofoam cooler he'd brought with him, then started checking his logbook for the information he'd recorded off each vet certification from the auction. His phone rang. He didn't recognize the number and no contact name showed.

"Hi, Cole," a woman said when he answered.

Dustin was preparing to move the cows and they were growing agitated and loud. Cole struggled to make out the voice. "Who is this?"

"It's Jenna." Cole's brain took a moment to register the fact that somehow Jenna had his phone number. "Overton," Jenna added. Her tone slid from friendly to indignant. "From the rodeo?"

"Right. I remember."

"You didn't get back to me about those mustangs."

He'd forgotten. Twice. He'd told her at the cattlemen's meeting that he'd talk to his wranglers and hadn't. Then at the bar after the rodeo, she'd been trying to make conversation with him while Kelli was dancing with someone else and she'd asked about them again.

"Sorry. I didn't check yet. I imagine they'll all have the agility you're looking for, having been wild, but I don't know if any of them have that love for speed you'll want. Why don't I give you Dustin's number? He and Heath did most of the training."

He rattled off his foreman's cell number and suggested she contact him after dinner.

"Okay. Thanks. Hey, are you planning to go to the Longhorn again this weekend?"

He cringed inwardly that she still hadn't taken the hint that he wasn't interested in her.

"No." He answered Jenna's question as succinctly as possible.

"Mr. Tyler," Dustin said, slipping a walkie-talkie back into a holster at his belt. "Tansy says you've got a calf with a bad hoof you might want to look at."

Cole swore. Hopefully just a stone bruise and not something serious. "I have to go."

As he'd expected, Tuesday was every bit as busy as Monday had been.

Like the previous night, his day ended with yet another meeting, this time with the Burgess City Council. He'd planned on the meeting getting over by eight o'clock, but it was closer to nine o'clock before he left. He hadn't talked to Kelli at all since Monday morning and hoped it wasn't too late to call her. Her number dialed while his truck warmed up. He couldn't help a niggling worry that she might have spooked again. He was trying to ease into things with her; put down a strong foundation to allow the opportunity to build something lasting while still seeing her as often as he could. The last thing he wanted was for this to become a brief rebound fling.

The Bluetooth connected and the ringing continued through his truck's speakers as he pulled out onto the road.

"Hello?"

"Hey there. It's Cole. I'm sorry I didn't have a chance to call you before this."

"You sound like you're driving. Long day?"

"A couple of them, yeah."

"That's okay. You warned me you were going to be tied up this week." Her voice sounded sleepy.

The temperature dropped along with the sun this time of year. The thermometer on his dashboard told him it was already down to the upper thirties, but the sound of her voice warmed him nicely.

"We still on for this weekend?" he asked.

"Are you kidding? With the choices you gave me? No way I'm going to let you out of that."

Just hearing her voice made him want to drive straight to her house and wrap her in his arms. "Okay. Good. What'd you decide on?"

"Argh," she sighed loudly. "I haven't. I mean, I love Santa Fe, but it means a whole weekend away from the ranch for you. The hot springs in Crestone sound like heaven but, on the other

ELIZA D. COLLINS

hand, I've never taken that scenic train trip and I've always wanted to."

"Uh-huh." He waited, smiling, while she made a few more sounds of anguished distress.

"Okay. This is it. Here's my decision. Ready? It's spring and not the best time for you to be out of town for two days in a row. I'd love to take that old steam train over the pass, but again, it's spring and the weather is iffy for this weekend...though it would be beautiful in snow, too, I guess." He thought he heard the click of her chewing a fingernail. "No. Final answer. I'm going with the hot springs."

She was right that being gone for a whole weekend would be hard for him, especially with the new cattle to manage, and if she'd picked the train ride, he would have planned to take her again in the fall anyway, when the aspens were changing color.

"Sounds good. Do you have a favorite?" The area had a number of hot springs to choose from.

"Do you know that one that has that whole series of outdoor pools along nature trails? I haven't been there in years and don't remember the name, but Sienna and I went a couple of times and it was wonderful."

It was the one he would have suggested if she didn't have a preference.

"I know the one. Okay, hot springs date on Sat-

210   HER COLORADO COWBOY

urday. I think they open around 10:00 a.m. but I'll check and let you know."

"You were right, Cole."

"About what?"

"You've given me something to look forward to till the weekend."

CHAPTER TWENTY-ONE

WEDNESDAY AFTERNOON, KELLI FOUND herself east of town with a gap between helping Sadie Hanson's mare deliver a foal and a scheduled appointment for a sow pig with an infected foot. Cole's ranch wasn't exactly on the way from one appointment to the other—it wasn't exactly on the way to anywhere except the sand dunes—but she did have time to kill, and he had invited her to stop and say hi if she had a chance during the week. There was no telling where on the ranch he might be, but no harm in swinging by, whether she found him or not.

Driving under the Tillacos Creek Ranch sign gave her a strange sense of adjacent pride—a "my boyfriend owns all this" warmth. *My boyfriend.* It was the first time she'd thought the words. But after all, there'd been pseudo-dates, a couple of real dates, the exclusivity talk, future plans… So, yeah, boyfriend.

Pulling into the Tillacos Creek Ranch driveway, she checked her face in the rearview mirror for traces of blood—or worse—then pulled her hair tie out, combed her hair with her fingers and threw it back in a slightly neater ponytail.

Finding him in the barn seemed unlikely, but she stuck her head in anyway before walking around to the corrals at the back. Cole wasn't there, either, but one of his ranch hands—a woman, she realized—was watering Cole's new Angus bull.

"I saw him heading that way a few minutes ago," she said, pointing to the front of the barn.

Kelli thanked her and walked back around the large barn, thinking how big the ranch was and how long the odds had been that he'd be nearby. If he'd been out on the pastures, accessible only by four-wheeler, it would've been a wasted trip. If she was lucky enough to find him right here, it would make her decision to swing by seem like fate.

She came around the corner between the barn and the house to see someone leading two horses from the pasture gate, coming toward her down the wide driveway. Kelli shaded her eyes against the late-afternoon sun and made out a cowboy hat. The rest of the silhouette looked wrong, though; the height was too short, the figure... okay, the figure was definitely wrong, and now she could see that the hat was white.

When they reached the shadow of the barn, the silhouette resolved and Kelli did a double take. It was Jenna, the barrel racer from the rodeo. A flush of jealousy slashed through her but she pushed it down, willing herself to calm. Surely, there was a logical explanation why she was here at Cole's ranch.

The distance between them closed.

"Hi, Jenna is it?" Kelli knew her name full well.

"Yes. You're Kay, right?"

"Kelli," she said a little more archly than she intended. "Do you know where Cole is?"

"He just headed inside." She nodded toward the house. "Beautiful ranch, isn't it? We just finished our ride. The mountain's gorgeous from this side."

Kelli felt too shell-shocked to answer. He'd taken her riding? She pictured the two of them in the meadow on the mountain. *Her* meadow.

"Well, I guess I'd better get going," Jenna said, leading the horses past Kelli. "Maybe I'll see you here again." She flipped the reins around the hitching post near the barn and strutted to her truck. Turning with an overdramatic flair, she added, "Though if I do, next time it might be my turn for the evening shift." She got in and drove away, leaving Kelli dumbstruck, staring at the trail of dust as her truck vanished around a curve in the road.

She wondered what Cole's excuse would be this time. Whatever it was, it already felt like one too many. He'd danced with Jenna because he'd been "cornered into it." Jenna had been hanging on Cole's arm at the rodeo because she wasn't "dealing well with a breakup." But now Jenna was at his ranch, riding with him, acting like the two of them shared him?

Forget this! Jenna could have the day shift, the swing shift, and the night shift for all she cared. Kelli couldn't believe this was happening to her again.

Another figure appeared from around the edge of the hay shed and Kelli's heart jumped into double time. She needed to avoid Cole at all costs right now. To think that he could treat her as casually and callously as the other men she'd dated sucked the air right out of her lungs. She felt like a boxer losing after fifteen rounds; there was no fight left in her. She did the only thing she could think to do in her shock and dismay; she hurried to her truck to leave.

The front door of the house opened, and she spun. Cole strode out onto the porch holding a thermos in one hand. He looked surprised at seeing her, then raised the thermos in greeting, smiling like the sun itself. She twisted to look up the road and could see now that the man coming toward her was a lean ranch hand a little older than Cole—his foreman, Dustin.

Kelli twisted back to Cole and his smile faded when he saw her expression. He trotted down the steps but Dustin intercepted him. Her fingers toyed with the latch on her door, but Dustin said only a couple of words before Cole headed toward her again. If she could have made her escape unnoticed, she would have—she'd have driven to her next appointment and tried to process all this somewhere away from here, away from him—but she certainly wasn't going to run.

"Are you okay?" he asked, reaching her.

"Yeah. Great. So, is there anything you need to tell me?"

He hesitated, never a good sign at a time like this. His expression held concern. And maybe hurt. "Dustin just told me Jenna was here. Did something happen between you two?"

Kelli remained silent, honestly not knowing what to say.

"Look," he continued, "I didn't even know she was coming over today. She talked to Dustin a couple of days ago about maybe buying one of our mustangs as a barrel horse." He waved his free hand to the horses tied at the hitching post. Kelli examined the two more closely; a paint and a bay. The bay had a mustang brand on its neck. Neither was Cole's horse, Jet.

"If Jenna said something to you, I'm sorry but I'm not surprised. Apparently, she wanted to see me when she got here. Dustin had my back and told her I was busy. I wouldn't even have come back to the house for more coffee if I'd realized she was still here."

His story was plausible. But so was the sce-

216 HER COLORADO COWBOY

nario where Cole had gone riding with Jenna. Maybe to the meadow. All while planning to spend Saturday at the hot springs with her. She'd known men who wouldn't bat an eye at trying it. She'd dated them.

This was a roller coaster she'd ridden one too many times and she had a long history of being too naive. She'd been lied to so convincingly in the past that she'd never doubted until proof had been shoved in her face like some "vaudeville cream pie" joke. Allen had lied. Even though it had been more than two months, her emotions were obviously still running high over his infidelity. The calm and collected her would have verbally shredded Jenna, then stayed to talk to Cole. But her calm and collected self was so far away right now it might as well have been on another planet.

Her voice didn't even shake when she said, "It doesn't matter, Cole."

"What… What do you mean it doesn't matter?"

"I mean, live your life however you want. If Jenna *was* here to see you, it's okay. We've only been out a couple of times. If she wasn't hanging out with you, then okay, even though that's not how she made it sound. If it helps, between believing her and believing you, I really do want to believe you." She realized as she said it that it was the truth.

"I don't understand the problem then." He sounded so lost that it made her heart hurt.

The problem was that she couldn't play the good girl anymore; the one who didn't make a fuss, the one who repressed her sorrow and confusion just to keep a man happy, regardless of how she felt. How could she tell Cole everything was okay and smile and pretend that things were fine when she didn't know yet what she believed? Three excuses in a row about Jenna was at least one too many and definitely stretching credibility.

And even if everything he'd just said proved to be true, the day had still been ruined. Jenna was a glaring reminder that if Kelli wanted to date handsome, macho chick magnets, then she had to expect other women to be attracted to them. And studly dudes with women to choose from weren't exactly renowned for their fidelity.

She took a deep breath and tried hard not to project other men's failings onto him. This was about her choice, her feelings. "What I mean is, that I've been moving faster than I'd promised myself I would."

"So what do you want to do now?"

Her mind swirled with all the consequences from the past and her new resolutions for the future. She needed to be smart for once.

"I think I need for us to go a little slower. You know, dial it back a bit."

"If that's really what you want."

His voice had taken on a frightening distance and deadness that made her want to recant everything she'd just said. No, it wasn't what she wanted. But it was what she needed.

"It is."

CHAPTER TWENTY-TWO

COLE DROPPED TO the couch and cradled his head in his hands. Baxter, sensing his distress, licked the back of one hand. The gentle concern broke Cole's downward spiral into the dark recesses carved out by his childhood, and pulled him back to the present. Cole patted him distractedly, then stood and paced halfway around the living room, stopping in front of one of the large picture windows to look out along the length of the Sangre de Cristo Mountains. Hands on his hips, he sighed in frustration.

Kelli couldn't have been that upset over just seeing Jenna walking across the property. It must have been something Jenna said to her. It was the only explanation. He stormed to his phone and scrolled down his list of incoming phone calls from the other day. Coming to a local number he didn't recognize from two mornings ago, he hit dial.

"Hey, Cole," Jenna answered on the second

ring. She must have his number ID'd. He could hear she was driving.

"What did you say to her?" He spat the question at her like the accusation it was.

"Say to who?"

She said it so innocently he wondered if he'd been mistaken. Removing as much venom from his voice as he could, he tried again. "Did you see Kelli here before you left?"

"Sure. I ran into her as I was leaving."

"Did you talk to her?"

"Just for a minute."

He clenched his jaw. He'd pull it out of her word by word if he had to. "And what did you say to her?" he said slowly.

"Um, I don't know. Let's see, I told her I'd been riding with Dustin and we'd just gotten back."

"You said you were with Dustin?"

"Geez, third degree much? I don't know. I might've said *I* just got back, or *we* just got back. Why? What's up?"

She knew very well what was up, he was sure of it. "By the way, I really liked that mustang," she said into his silence. "I was hoping I could set up some barrels in your arena and see how he does. Maybe tomorrow?"

"No. Not tomorrow," he said roughly. No one had witnessed Jenna and Kelli's conversation, and he couldn't outright accuse her of something of

which he had no proof. "That's all I called about."
He was anxious to end this conversation.

"Okay. Well, don't forget I'm going to be at the
Longhorn Friday night if you change your mind
about showing up."

"I'm not going to change my mind, Jenna. Not
now. Not later. You need to go find a boy your
own age. And if you see Kelli again, you clear up
this misunderstanding with her."

They hung up. He was going to have a lot of
apologizing to do if he was wrong about her, but
he wasn't. He knew her type. She was young and
foolish. She'd been hurt by some guy, and he'd
been in the wrong place at the wrong time, and
now she'd set her sights on him. Based on what
her mother said about her competitive spirit,
imagining herself in competition with Kelli had
probably only encouraged her. He swore and
tossed the phone back on the table.

Troy was off somewhere with Jan, and Sally
had left for the day. Cole rattled around the house,
feeling like one of those little silver balls bouncing off the walls in a plastic maze. He finally
stopped himself to keep Baxter from walking
too much as he followed him to and fro. Toss-
ing his hat to the coffee table, he stretched out
on the couch and patted his chest. Baxter didn't
need to be asked twice. He hopped up, stepped
on Cole a few times trying to find the right spot

222 HER COLORADO COWBOY

and flopped down between the back of the couch and Cole's hip.

Cole tried to shut out thoughts of what Jenna might have said and what Kelli might be thinking or feeling right now. Frustration roiled in him like a tide. He'd never been so keen to impress a woman in his life. That first day she'd helped with the breech calf, he'd felt the renewal of an old and profound connection with the beautiful and caring woman his childhood friend had grown into. A woman who loved the things he loved and dedicated her life to tending to animals.

He'd hoped too hard this was something that could build into the kind of relationship he'd sought all these years. True and lasting love; the kind that could be counted on never to waver. The kind that would never drag his trust and emotions through the ups and downs he'd experienced his first seven years of life.

When Amy had pushed him away and pulled him back it had triggered old cycles of depression and need. But for Kelli to do this felt like the sun falling out of the sky. Like drowning on dry land. His world had changed in some fundamental way, and he might never trust it to be the same again.

THE FRONT DOOR SLAMMED, waking Cole. Morning light filled the living room.

"Either you had too much fun last night, or not enough," Troy said.

"That second one," Cole said, sitting up stiffly from the couch where he'd unintentionally spent the night after getting up briefly to feed Baxter.

"What's up?"

He hauled himself vertical, shaking his head, still unable to believe his situation. "Kelli and I had a fight."

"What? You haven't had enough time with her to screw this up. What did you do?"

"I didn't *do* anything. Dustin met up with Jenna yesterday about the mustangs, and I guess Kelli saw her here. I'm pretty sure Jenna said something to her, but I couldn't get it out of either one of them."

"But why'd she take off? It's not like she caught you in some compromising position." He paused. "Did she?"

"No. I never even saw Jenna." Cole stood and shuffled to the kitchen to start a pot of strong coffee. "I don't know. She didn't believe me, I guess. Now she wants to *dial it back a bit*."

Troy's ceaseless movement and chatter stilled for the space of a breath. Cole glanced over to see his brother chewing his lip in thought. Noticing Cole staring at him, he dropped his jacket onto the couch and followed him into the kitchen, moving on from whatever he'd been thinking.

"I'm really sorry. I've never seen you as hung up on anyone as you've been with Kelli." He leaned against the counter and reached out to slap

224 HER COLORADO COWBOY

Cole on the shoulder. "Don't worry. She's bound to come around in a day or two. Trust me, I have some experience in this area."

He must have been wearing his heart on his sleeve if his normally oblivious brother had picked up on the depth of his feelings for Kelli. Cole wanted out of this conversation before Sally arrived and chimed in.

"If you want to do some real work today, we're going to vaccinate a couple hundred more cows. We could use the help."

"I would but I'm beat. I was up a little later than you." He winked.

Cole just nodded and Troy headed upstairs.

He toasted a couple of pieces of bread and poured coffee into his thermos. At the barn, he saddled Jet instead of taking the four-wheeler. He needed the tranquility of his horse today as well as the connection to a trusted friend. By the time he reached the squeeze chutes, Dustin was there waiting for him.

They worked through the day, moving the new Angus cattle out to pasture, then starting on vaccinating the main herd against common diseases and administering their dewormer. It would take most of the week to finish the whole herd, all the while trying to keep up with the day-to-day routines. The only upside was that the busy day helped him shut out thoughts of Kelli.

Late in the afternoon, he rode past the small

pasture where they'd turned out the Angus. He stopped Jet at the fence line and took in the scene; the first big piece in his plans for the future of the ranch. The only sounds were the light breeze, creak of saddle leather, cows tearing grass and a soft snort from Jet. In the quiet and solitude, his thoughts wandered back to Kelli.

Amy, in Texas, had been the closest he'd come to what he imagined he was looking for. Confident, capable and beautiful. And in the end, a hot and cold landmine that had nearly demolished him. Amy doing that to him had been bad enough, but he couldn't take it from Kelli—she had the potential to destroy him. The only solution he could see was to get out before she pulled him like a whirlpool, down into a cycle from which he might never break free.

He was leaning on his saddle horn, staring into the middle distance when it registered that two of the new Angus were lying down but not chewing cud. He dismounted and led Jet through the gate. Most of the cattle ambled away from him, but the two on the ground didn't get up. He came closer, trying to spook them. "Hup," he shouted, waving his hat. Nothing. He pulled out his cell phone and called Dustin.

"I need you over at pasture six." He hung up and within minutes he heard the rumbling of a four-wheeler.

"Problem?" Dustin said, walking toward him.

226 HER COLORADO COWBOY

Cole nodded at the two cows and saw concern dawn on his foreman's face. "How long they been down?"

"Don't know," Cole said. "Last time I checked was only a little while after we moved them. Maybe around ten this morning. You?"

"After lunch, about one. I passed the bull's corral less than an hour ago and he looked fine. Do you think it's the change from feed to grass bothering them?"

"I don't know what to think, but I'm going to call a vet."

Cole removed his phone and pulled up his contacts. He scrolled down to Bill Salem's number, hesitated, then scrolled on to Kelli's number. This was too important for personal feelings to get in the way; he needed the best vet he knew. The dozen cows had cost $19,000 and the bull another $9,500. Those Angus represented the first business decision he'd made without his father's approval and an investment this ranch couldn't afford to lose. If this turned out to be something contagious that could threaten the regular herd, the damage could be catastrophic. The phone rang for the fourth time. He wondered if she was call-screening him, but she answered just before the voicemail was due to pick up.

"This is Kelli," she said.

Her voice lanced through his armor. He'd expected to be stronger than this.

ELIZA D. COLLINS

"Kelli, it's Cole. It's about my cows."

"What's going on?" She sounded hesitant, as if she thought he might make a game out of this to get her to come out. And if she did think that, then maybe she really didn't know him at all.

"Those new Angus. I've got a couple that are down. I don't know if it's something viral from the auction hitting late or something else."

There was a slight pause and then, "I can be there in a few minutes."

Cole hung up. "Gather up all the hands. We'll move them back into the corrals. Sick cows in this near one and unaffected ones at the other end of the pasture. Get a couple of spotlights set up for tonight too. Tell everyone they'll be taking shifts through the night to keep an eye on them."

CHAPTER TWENTY-THREE

KELLI PULLED UP to the corrals amidst a flurry of activity. Two ranch hands were mounted, moving a single cow in with another pair of Angus, while the rest of the workers secured gates, loaded hay into feeders and set up portable lights for the fast-approaching evening. Cole's broad shoulders and trademark black hat were easy to spot in the commotion. He left his foreman and a wrangler to finish with the lights and headed over to meet her as she got out of her truck.

His manner was distant and he dispensed with any greeting. "We just now got them all off the pasture," he said. "We put the two sick ones in this closest corral but then a third one went down." He looked at the corrals more than at her. She tried to tell herself it was worry for the cows rather than discomfort from being around her.

Feeling as uncomfortable as he looked, she grabbed her kit and headed for the corral holding the sick cows while he filled her in on what they'd observed so far. She took temperatures, listened to heart, lungs and stomachs, and drew blood. Then she did the same with the seemingly healthy Angus in the other corral. Cole brought her the vet certificates from the auction and gave her the details of their feed and the timing of their move from the corral onto pasture grass. She asked him for hay, grain and soil samples.

Finished with all that, she looked at her watch. "If I hurry, I can get the blood and feed samples over to the lab before they close. It could be a little colic from the new feed, but their gut sounds are good. Make sure you check your corrals and that pasture thoroughly for any toxins. Lead paint on buildings and old batteries are the most common. You know cows, they'll lick anything."

"I had the ranch hands check already, but I'll look again myself," he said.

He helped her pack her truck while she talked, conscious of the time. "It's possible it's nothing serious. Let me know if you see any new developments, and I'll call you as soon as I get the results."

Driving away, Kelli hoped this would turn out to be something minor, but she had no strong feel for what might be going on. Worry for Cole and his ranch wormed in her gut. On the other hand, she felt proud that she'd been able to set aside her jumbled feelings and act like a professional around him. But then, she'd always do her best for any animals. It was why she was a vet. He'd been professional, too, and though he'd been lukewarm around her, it was a good sign he'd called her out here today. It reassured her that she hadn't permanently damaged things between them; a worry that had kept her up last night.

She relived the events of yesterday afternoon for the hundredth time and still felt she'd done her level best at handling the Jenna situation. Her request to slow down hadn't been a euphemism for breaking up. It had been the best she could do under the circumstances to give him a fair chance while still protecting her heart.

Once she'd gotten home yesterday and had the space to think about his story versus Jenna's, she'd calmed down considerably. After that, she'd spent an hour on the phone with Sienna. The conversation had calmed her still more, and ended with Sienna's promise to let her know if her rumor network turned up news about Cole and Jenna, or if she spotted Cole hooking up with any women on the dating site.

Kelli still had a fair bit of soul-searching ahead about what she wanted in a man and what she wanted from Cole, but today at the ranch had been a good start to getting things back to normal. They could go slow and easy from here, and if Sienna turned up nothing new, then maybe he really was a different sort of man than the others she'd dated. Slow and easy, though. That was the key to not getting hurt again.

BY MID-MORNING FRIDAY, nearly all the lab results were in. Kelli took a break between her clinic patients and headed for the house to pour herself a big cup of coffee and give Cole an update call. Her heart gave a little squeeze when she heard his deep voice on the other end of the line.

"How are your cattle today?"

"Two more Angus down. The ones that went down yesterday got on their feet for a little bit, so we aren't looking at dehydration or nerve damage yet."

Whatever the root cause of the illness, downer cow syndrome could end up being even worse. Cows were unable to lie recumbent more than twenty-four hours without risk of permanent nerve injury. Every time a cow went down at Tillacos, the clock started ticking.

"Fever or cough?"

"No. Still no sign of either."

"Well, the good news is the tests and lack of fever have ruled out brucellosis." The highly contagious disease posed serious risks to both cattle and humans and caused a wide variety of symptoms. "The metabolic panel looks normal, which is good, but it also gives us no clue to what's going on. Their white blood cell counts aren't especially elevated, so viral and bacterial infection are unlikely. And unless we start seeing a cough, fever or any other sign of bacterial infection, I have a hard time believing this is something an antibiotic would help. If I thought it would, I'd suggest it in a heartbeat, but I know you want to avoid them if you're planning to sell to natural beef markets. I just don't see any indication for it right now."

"Okay. I agree with holding off."

"The hay, grain and soil tests that came back so far are normal too. No toxins, nothing high in heavy metals, no unusual deficiencies. Honestly, Cole, I'm not sure what's going on. I have a couple of calls out to some specialists and I've blocked off time today to do more research. In the meantime, I'll plan to come out this afternoon for a follow-up exam, but I'll have my cell phone with me all day in case of emergency."

He thanked her and signed off, sounding even more distant than he had yesterday. He was worried about his herd, she knew, but she detected something more; a lifeless quality to his voice that left her uneasy. She feared that asking to slow down might have brought their relationship— maybe even their friendship—tumbling down like a house of cards, after all.

She held the warm cup of coffee between her hands and breathed in the aroma while remembering the weekend with him. He'd been so gentle. He was everything that set her heart racing but also the things that set her alarm bells clanging.

It was so much more than merely physical with Cole, though. He'd been a gentleman that night at the bar, and then had given her an amazing first date and an even better second date. He'd made a solid case about Jenna but hadn't gotten mad or persisted when she told him she needed space. And at his ranch yesterday, he'd left any emotional baggage out of the way and helped her do her job.

Could he really be one of the most macho men she'd met in her life and still have the morals and loyalty she'd always sought? It felt like yet another bait and switch, something too good to be true. It seemed hard to imagine a man with his looks and skills could be so different from the other arrogant players she'd known—but not once she recalled Cole as a child. A boy, curled around his pain and his loneliness. Perhaps those childhood experiences had sculpted him into someone as invested in genuine love and fidelity as she was herself.

Ever since she'd told him she wanted to slow down, her stomach had been queasy to the point she'd finally bought a bottle of Maalox this morning. Maybe it was her body's way of telling her what her mind refused to see—that she'd made a huge mistake and if she didn't fix it soon, it might be too late.

CHAPTER TWENTY-FOUR

COLE TOOK A short break from work and returned to the house to find Troy eating lunch at the kitchen island and Sally washing dishes. She retrieved a plate of BLT sandwiches and homemade coleslaw from the fridge and set it on the counter for him.

"Thanks, I'll probably eat later," he said.

"You should eat now," Sally said, in a tone that meant business. "You look like you could use the fortification." Her piercing green eyes held his, seeming to read his levels of stress like a book.

Far from the boys' expectations when his father announced he'd hired a cook and housekeeper for their household ten years ago, Sally had come on as a "tough as nails" retired mountaineering guide. She and her husband had both been world-class mountaineers, leading expeditions around the globe, but she'd lost her lower right leg to frostbite when she stayed with a weaker climber in a storm. Now in their fifties, her husband lectured and wrote mountaineering books and Sally worked for the ranch during the week, and hiked fourteeners and taught rock climbing at the weekends. She was also a phenomenal cook.

"Yes, ma'am," he said. He unwrapped the plate and Sally headed upstairs to vacuum.

"You've been away a lot," he said to Troy, draping his coat over a chair and heading to the sink to get a glass of water. "Things going well with Jan?" Other than Troy waking him on the couch yesterday morning, Cole had hardly seen him on his run of days off.

"Mostly, yeah. Until today, anyway. I think she got tired of me hanging around."

It was just as well Troy was here. It was Cole's first chance to tell him about the sick cattle.

"We've got a problem with the herd."

Troy looked up from his lunch. "What's up?"

"I don't know. Some of the cows are starting to get sick and we don't know yet what it is."

"Sick how?"

Returning to the island counter, Cole set his glass down and faced Troy like he might a tornado he couldn't outrun. He briefly explained what he'd seen the last two days and what steps Kelli had taken. "We've checked for any toxins on the property and Kelli said the labs and the feed analysis didn't show anything unusual. She'll be back out later today for a follow-up."

Troy set his fork down and turned on his barstool. There was a blistering silence for the space of one breath.

HER COLORADO COWBOY

"You called Kelli for this? Having Kelli out for your dog is one thing, Cole. Having your girl-friend treat our herd instead of Bill Salem is another."

"Kelli is an excellent vet."

"Based on what? Delivering one calf and taking care of Baxter's leg bruise? She graduated last June, Cole."

"Based on the fact that I've talked to her extensively and you haven't," he shot back. "Besides, being a recent graduate is an advantage in my book. I had Bill Salem out once right after I moved back. He looked half asleep through the exam, wasn't up on any of the new research, and when I needed answers, I couldn't even reach him the next day. Remember that? And in case you've forgotten, he doesn't do evening calls or weekends anymore. I called Kelli at the end of her day and she came straight over."

"What I remember is thirty years of Bill treating our cattle. I remember Dad trusting him. And today is Friday. You could have scheduled him out here this morning instead of having Kelli come back. I get you wanting to fix things with Kelli, but not like this. Not with these kinds of stakes."

Cole couldn't deny that her rejection of him stung. He felt as if he'd held a winning lottery ticket that had blown away in the wind on a crowded street. But his feelings for her weren't why he'd called her out for his sick cattle.

"This has nothing to do with my relationship with Kelli. And I understand the stakes better than you do. You went off to be a firefighter instead of helping Dad all those years I was away at college."

Cole knew he was pushing the boundaries here, but it was his job to find out what was wrong and take care of it, not Troy's. Yes, Troy was part owner in the ranch. Yes, this was his inheritance, too, but their dad had entrusted him with the management.

Troy pushed away from the island and stormed two steps toward him, closing their distance. He might wear uniform blues and steel-toed boots at work, but his attitude now was all cowboy. And cowboys didn't back down.

"Running this ranch isn't a right, Cole. It's a privilege. Dad left it to you, but you still have to earn it. In the first three months since you took over, you've changed up the mix of the herd, the pasture management and some of the basic practices we've had in place for decades." Troy gestured, stabbing his finger on each point, but avoided touching Cole. He had to know if he'd stabbed his finger into Cole's chest, the fight would have come to blows. "We have fifteen hundred head of cattle and you *had* to go out and buy new stock, three months in, barely even settled into taking over here."

This was an argument Cole needed to win, not

out of pride, but for the sake of the ranch as well as his future here.

"I told you the situation five minutes ago and you're ready to declare me unfit to run the ranch? Yes, I've changed things that haven't been changed in decades. Stagnation kills ranches. Dad was a good rancher, a great rancher, but he wasn't moving ahead with the times. What worked in practice fifty years ago, believe it or not, doesn't hold today."

Now Cole was the one stabbing his finger with each point. "The cows aren't the same. Breeding has evolved new traits, new strengths and weaknesses. The land isn't the same. Using the same fertilizers or the same fields year after year will cause long term decreases in yield. The water rights aren't the same. We may have a high water table and senior call out for irrigation rights, but Southern Colorado's been in drought more often than not for the past twenty years, and that affects how we need to manage the land."

Shoulders squared, Cole continued, "I've studied this in school and in my internships for years now. And like Kelli, my knowledge is current, not stale and outdated. Bill Salem has been a good vet over the years, but all that man thinks about these days is a countdown to retirement. I ended up with Kelli on that breech calf because he was out of town. But for this, I chose to stay with her.

She's looking for a cause, and I'm going to trust her."

Troy stewed a long moment, then said, "You'd better hope your trust isn't misplaced."

Cole hoped for it more than Troy could have imagined.

COLE SKIPPED LUNCH after all, grabbed his coat and headed back out. Things immediately took a turn for the worse.

His walkie-talkie squawked. "Mister Tyler?"

"Go ahead, Dustin."

"Jake saw a few Herefords down."

Herefords? The regular stock? Cole swore. "I'll be right there."

Ten minutes later, he and Dustin were closing half a dozen cows into the last available corral when a truck drove down the county dirt road that bisected the pastures. It wasn't Kelli's white Toyota, but Bill Salem's dark blue Chevy. Dustin shot Cole a look, but his clenched jaw stopped his foreman from asking any questions.

Cole walked to Bill's truck, fighting to keep his temper in check. Troy had thrown Bill into the middle of this, and Cole wouldn't take it out on the vet.

"Bill," Cole said by way of greeting.

"Cole." The old vet extended a shaky hand. Cole wondered if he might be in the early stages of Parkinson's disease. It might explain a few things. "What do you have going on?"

"How much did Troy tell you?"

"Not too much. It sounds like you brought some new cows back from auction and they've probably passed some illness on to the others."

"It's not looking viral at this point. Did he tell you Kelli Hinton was out yesterday?"

"No. He didn't mention it." Bill's eyes grew wary, sensing the tension.

"She took blood from the first of the Angus to go down. BMP and chem panel came back normal this morning. Feed tests too. No brucellosis and we've found no source of toxicity."

Bill nodded. "Do you still want me to look?"

The man was here already, and Cole could expect World War III with Troy if he sent him away. "Sure. A second opinion is always welcome."

All three men walked out to the Herefords they'd just quarantined. Cole filled him in that a wrangler had radioed a few minutes ago that one of the new Angus cows was no longer getting up. Downer cow syndrome was the biggest concern now. They had less than twenty-four hours to figure things out before he started losing cows to permanent nerve damage.

Bill went through the standard exam.

"Lungs are clear, hearts sound strong and the temperatures are normal. I'd expect to see fever or respiratory issues and I'm not, but I'm still going to say the most likely thing is some infectious disease that the new cows brought in."

He repacked his instruments and stood again with some difficulty. "My guess is you're going to start seeing respiratory symptoms and temperatures over the next few days. I'd recommend a general spectrum antibiotic right now. We can dial it in with a specific antibiotic once the symptoms get more pronounced."

Cole looked down at his boots. Antibiotics could set his plans for natural meat back a whole year and Kelli had felt they weren't indicated at this point. On the other hand, the drug might save lives and had little downside other than affecting his long-term plans. The decision was the hardest he'd ever made.

"I think I'm going to hold off, Bill."

Bill looked affronted.

"I don't recommend it. By this time tomorrow, you could be dealing with fever and cough. We could get out ahead of it now, so you aren't fighting a bigger spread and higher losses."

"I understand," Cole said, not budging.

"Your choice," Bill said, sounding like it really shouldn't be. Since Troy had been the one to call their old vet out, Cole would bet everything he owned that Bill would be on the phone with Troy before he left the property. He'd trusted Kelli with his heart and she'd let him down by not trusting him back, leaving him as hollow as a burned-out

242 HER COLORADO COWBOY

tree trunk. Now he was trusting her with his herd, his livelihood and his family's legacy.

Dustin stood at his shoulder, watching Bill drive away. His foreman never said a word. He was Cole's man, just like he'd been his father's man, and he would follow whatever decision he made. A decision that kept getting heavier for Cole to carry.

CHAPTER TWENTY-FIVE

KELLI TALKED TO Cole midafternoon and learned that two dozen from the main herd were now in trouble, and also that Bill Salem had been out and recommended antibiotics. He told her that Troy had been the one to call Bill, but learning that Cole had stuck with her opinion over Bill's advice and experience added even more pressure to her decisions. As well as an emotional lance piercing her, reminding her that when she'd been given the chance to believe in him, she'd wavered. If she let herself slide down that path of worry and regret, though, she'd never focus on the problem at hand with the cattle. She'd assured Cole that she'd be out before dark for one last checkup, but that her time was better spent researching right now.

She reviewed all her notes yet again, spoke with one of her old professors, then pulled down her reference textbook and paged through the relevant sections to see if it jogged any new ideas loose. Following research rabbit holes down less and less common issues, she read until the wheel

244 HER COLORADO COWBOY

in her brain was spinning so hard she should have seen smoke coming from her ears. Still, she could feel a puzzle piece floating just out of reach.

Suddenly, she had a thought. It was a long shot, but worth checking. She dialed the number for the Animal Health Laboratory in Broomfield and asked for a lab tech whose Doberman she'd treated at the university hospital two years ago.

When Beth came to the phone, she asked, "Did any of the results for the Tillacos Creek cattle come from your lab?"

"Yes. We got blood samples by FedEx this morning from the Alamosa lab for a couple of tests they don't handle down there. I ran them myself first thing today. Didn't you get the results?"

"I did. But I'm wondering if you still have the sample. I'd like a couple of additional tests."

"Depends on what you want."

"Some additional micronutrients. I got the basics with the metabolic panel—iron, calcium, magnesium and phosphorus—but I want to look at some others. Could you run copper, cobalt, manganese, iodine and selenium with the vials you have?"

"Sure."

Kelli glanced at the time. It was after three on Friday and some of those tests took two or three days under normal, nonemergency conditions. Worse, the lab was closed on the weekends.

"Would you be able to run them stat? We've got a large herd going critical."

There was a long pause. "Sure," Beth said, coming to a decision. "They won't finish today, but I can start them now and come back in tomorrow. I'd probably have results for you around nine or so tomorrow morning."

"I really appreciate it, Beth. Thank you so much."

"Well, I seem to remember you spending one of your rare weekends off staying at the hospital with Trident to make sure he didn't go into respiratory failure when he got toxicosis from that garbage binge of his."

"And I'd gladly do it again. Still, thank you. This means a lot."

Kelli hung up, grabbed her jacket and drove to Cole's for the follow-up exam she'd promised. She drew more blood for the Alamosa lab and gave what suggestions she could for watching the cattle tonight. If it had been one cow, she could have transported it to her hospital and tried IV therapy and various treatments, but with three dozen sick animals now, there was little they could do at this point other than try and figure out the cause.

Back home again, she had dinner, checked all the door and window latches, as usual, then took her laptop to the couch and tried to shed a bit of her stress over the cattle and worry about Cole by opening dog rescue sites. Predictably, she wanted

246 HER COLORADO COWBOY

to take home nearly every dog she saw, but once she'd filtered them by size and breed, she tagged two as favorites with heart icons.

Dog rescue sites were more fun to look at than online dating sites any day. But once that thought was in her head, it was all she could do not to go hunting for the dating site where Troy had put Cole's profile. She didn't know where to start, though, and seeing it wouldn't help her mood any. Kelli couldn't imagine any woman seeing his picture and not wanting to meet him. And here she'd had him, and she'd pushed him away.

CHAPTER TWENTY-SIX

A LUCKY RANCHER might go years without a major issue. On the other hand, disasters were a risk every year. There were blizzards, fires, diseases, and there were threats to running the ranch itself in the form of new zonings, litigation, fights over water. Cole hoped it was bad luck rather than bad decisions that had led to something this big hitting him so soon after taking over. Either way, this was the job he'd chosen and the life that had chosen him. All he could do was his best.

Dark had fallen about an hour before, and Billy had shown up for the weekend. All the wranglers were taking shifts through the night again, watching the herd and separating sick cows. As he walked up the front steps to the house, Cole was so far past hungry he realized he didn't care about eating anymore.

He was reaching for the front door when his phone rang. A sinking feeling hit him in his gut when he stared at the contact name.

"Hi, Lane."

248 HER COLORADO COWBOY

"Cole." His older brother's tone was chilly, telling Cole everything he needed to know. "Troy told me about the infection in the herd."

"We don't know that it's an infection. White blood cell counts are normal and there's no cough or fever."

"What else could it be? You bring home new stock from the auction and a week later the whole herd is coming down sick. Do you even know the source you bought them from?"

"Of course I know the source. What do you think, that I bought them blind? That I bought cattle from some two-bit auction with locals passing off their sick animals? I've researched this breed for two years and searched since I got here for a reputable ranch producing a good size. I got them because we need more weight at market to bring in more income. But you wouldn't know that because you're not here. I am."

"Just because you're there, doesn't mean you get to experiment with everything you read about in some book."

Cole paced down the long front porch and leaned against the wood railing, looking out into the dark. The silhouette of the mountain hung heavy in the sky to his right and the vast fields stretched to his left. "I've already had this discussion with Troy, as I'm sure you know. I'm not experimenting. The first thing I did when I moved back was update with the accountant. We're on the verge of owing more than we can scrape together to pay."

"So you decided to go out and spend, what, twenty or thirty thousand on new stock?"

"Yes. And different fertilizers for the fields, and a different feed mix for the cows. All of it to improve the ranch and turn things around."

"And how's *that* going for you?"

Cole gripped the log rail of the deck like he might crack it with one hand.

"The new stock came from one of the best Angus ranches around, and I got them at a good price. I could look at a hundred ranches and not find better. They were vet-checked and I've called the rancher. His cows aren't experiencing anything like this."

"You think it's something they contracted through the auction yard?" Lane was starting to sound slightly calmer. Slightly.

Cole sighed and flopped into one of the heavy wooden chairs on the deck. "I don't know. I'm looking into it, of course, and so is the auction manager and the Wyoming and Colorado Livestock Commissioners. I'm serious when I say this isn't anything I've seen before."

"And you think Kelli Hinton is going to figure it out for you?"

"I do. If I didn't, I'd be using Bill. He was out here today anyway. Troy's doing. He wanted to

250 HER COLORADO COWBOY

start shooting up with a broad-spectrum antibiotic even though there's no indication for it."

"Well, it's not like I can do anything from here. But I'll promise you this, Cole, if you hurt our ranch through arrogance or stupidity, I'll beat you into the ground when I get home."

"If I hurt the ranch through arrogance or stupidity, I'll let you."

Lane huffed a short laugh at the implication that he couldn't do it unless Cole let him. "Keep me informed, all right?"

"I promise." Cole turned his phone off, sighed again and laid his head back against the log wall. He'd known when his father died that it was going to be tough taking over the ranch. He'd badly underestimated just how tough it would be. Gaining and then losing Kelli's affection had left him as beat-up and desiccated as roadkill. He couldn't endure the thought of losing the love and respect of his family as well.

CHAPTER TWENTY-SEVEN

KELLI'S PHONE RANG at 9:05 a.m. Saturday morning.

"Manganese and iodine were normal," Beth said, "and your selenium was only slightly low."

"Oh," Kelli said. If the results all turned out to be normal, then she really was at a loss about what was going on with the herd.

"The big surprise," Beth continued, "was your cobalt came back critically low and copper dropped right off the scale." She gave Kelli the numbers and the values for normal, then said she'd fax over a copy.

Kelli thanked her profusely and grabbed her tablet. She double-checked the feed analysis from the ranch and the hay wasn't low in either element, but either copper or cobalt deficiency alone could explain the downer cow syndrome and all the symptoms they were seeing. She might be grasping at straws now, but she had a wild idea where the deficiency might have come from.

She called Cole.

252 HER COLORADO COWBOY

"You don't have an infection. You've got a bad mineral deficiency," she said as soon as he picked up.

"What would cause that?"

"I'm not certain yet. The good news is both mineral levels are easily reversible. The problem is, we still need to figure out the root cause. I've got a pretty far-fetched idea. Did your cattle get anything recently besides their 7-way vaccination?"

"A dewormer, but nothing else."

"And those new Angus hadn't received this year's vaccinations from the rancher who sold them?"

"No. I talked to him myself before I left and double-checked it in their paperwork."

"Neither the dewormer or the vaccine itself should cause anything like this, but I have an idea I want to pursue. Do you have a vaccine bottle handy?"

"Sure. I'm in the barn now. We had to stop inoculating them when we were dealing with everything else. Most of what's left to give is stored here."

"Read the label to me, including the manufacturer, lot number and expiration." She heard his footsteps on the dirt floor, then a cabinet door banging.

He read the information off to her and she wrote everything down.

"Have all the affected cows been given the vaccine?"

There was a long pause. She could picture him staring at the high ceiling of the barn, lost in thought.

"I don't know. Hang on one sec." She heard the click of a hand-held radio. "Dustin," he said, "have any cattle in pastures two or four gone down?"

"No, sir," she made out in the static. "Not as of an hour ago at feeding."

"I heard," she said. "And for the cows that have gone down, did it start in the same order you did the vaccinations?"

He was silent again. "You know, I think it might have. We did the small group of Angus Monday, then started the Herefords the next day. The Angus started getting sick Thursday, and the first Herefords got sick yesterday. Not all the cattle that were vaccinated are sick, but I think the cattle that are sick were all vaccinated. Man, how did I not see that?"

"Don't worry, neither did I until just now. I've never ever heard of a vaccine causing an issue. My guess is it isn't the drug itself, but if a batch got contaminated or destabilized for some reason, it might explain everything. Can you find some of the old bottles and give me lot numbers off them?"

"I can do better than that. I have it all in the log-

254   HER COLORADO COWBOY

book, down to lot numbers and expiration dates for each cow." She could hear him jogging. There was a thump as the door to the house opened. A moment later, he was reading a different lot number to her. "It looks like the new Angus were all one lot, and some from our first couple of Hereford vaccinations were as well. Maybe a hundred and fifty cows all together got the same as the Angus. Almost the number we have ill."

"One of the reps from that vaccine company came up and did a presentation at the vet school. I've got his card somewhere. I'm going to see if I can reach anyone at Vetmore Innovative now. Meanwhile, get your people out to every feed store in the area and buy all the dissolvable cobalt pellets and copper you can find. Dose it in the water tanks according to the instructions on the bag. Try to hand water the cows that can't stand. We can force water by tube for any that won't drink. I'll be out as soon as I can with a B-12 supplement, which will give them a boost and help them absorb the cobalt. I think I have some copper compound on hand to inject the sickest ones."

She heard Cole yell to Troy, probably somewhere in the house, that he needed his help.

"Get mineral licks in each corral where you have animals quarantined," she added. "Get extras out in the field too. They may not have enough of the right element, but it can't hurt."

They hung up. She'd be burning a candle of

hope for any client, but for Cole she'd light a bonfire. Helping him save his cattle—seeing some light return to his eyes and life to his voice—it was the only thing she could focus on now. She flipped through her folder of business cards, page after page slotted into their individual plastic sleeves, and found the one she was looking for. She packed all the B-12 and copper sulfate she had, then dialed the number and let it ring while she headed for her truck. A recorded message said the company would reopen Monday at eight o'clock, and that she could dial her extension at any time. She remembered the extension number from the card and tried it.

There was hold music, then a click. A man with a strong West Texas accent answered. "This is Robert."

"Mr. Greaves, my name is Kelli Hinton. You gave a talk on the need for livestock vaccinations at the College of Veterinary Medicine in Fort Collins a couple of years ago. I'm calling because one of my ranchers just used your 7-way vaccine and there's been a problem."

She started her truck and explained the situation and her suspicion on the way to Cole's ranch.

CHAPTER TWENTY-EIGHT

COLE CALLED DUSTIN on the walkie-talkie and told him to get the wranglers to collect all the mineral blocks they had stored. "Mineral only, not salt licks. Don't forget the storage shed. I'll need you to stay close to the barn. I'll be out in a minute.

"Troy," he yelled for the second time.

Troy appeared from upstairs dressed in cowboy boots, jeans, padded coveralls and a Western shirt. As he trotted down the stairs, he threw on his heavy canvas jacket against the snow predicted for today. He even had on the cowboy hat he rarely wore anymore.

Under different circumstances, Cole would've enjoyed seeing his brother dressed for ranch work. The last time they'd ridden together had been a single day last summer when Cole had come home for vacation and they'd moved cows up Blanca Peak with their dad. Today felt nothing like that day. Troy evidently planned to shadow him, and the lack of trust stung anew.

"The cows are going down from a mineral deficiency," he said, cutting Troy off before he could speak.

A variety of emotions played across his brother's face: surprise, doubt and finally uncertainty.

"Troy, whatever you think of my recent actions, I can't change that. But I want you to know that I would never base decisions about this ranch on my feelings for a woman. Not even Kelli. You know what this ranch means to me. More than that, I hope you know what family means to me. Dad's belief in me. You and Lane, you're all the family I have left. I'm not going to do anything to endanger any of it. Not now and not ever."

The last of Troy's arrogant stance deflated.

"I know I've been making changes," Cole said before Troy could speak, "and it's not easy asking you to trust me. I can't promise that I'm not going to make a wrong decision someday, but if I do, I'm the one who has to live the rest of my life with it."

Troy sighed. "I know. And I know it would eat you alive. But this… Are you sure this is a deficiency and not an infection?"

"Yes. Nothing about it has played out like an infection. Kelli's following up to see if it's tied to the 7-way we gave this week. She may not have been in practice for decades, but she thinks like some of the best vets I worked with in Texas. The labs proved the deficiency and she's on her way

258   HER COLORADO COWBOY

here to start administering injections to the sickest cows."

"All right. I'll put my faith in you, at least for today. I can't swear to tomorrow. But for now, you do what you think is best for the ranch, brother."

Cole couldn't remember the last time Troy had called him brother. His eyes burned with salt from sudden tears. Since their father's death, it had been a daily emotional struggle for Cole, hoping that his father had known how much he had appreciated and loved him. That he'd told him often enough, clearly enough, how much his adoptive family meant to him, and the changes it had made in his life. He clapped Troy on the shoulder.

"Then let's get to it, brother. We have a busy day ahead."

CHAPTER TWENTY-NINE

KELLI ARRIVED AT Tillacos under a slate gray sky. The air held the chilly ozone scent of impending snow. Ranch hands were loading mineral licks onto four-wheelers and trucks to drive out to the corrals and fields. Cole and Troy were both on their phones, calling every feed store in a hundred-mile radius for cobalt pellets and copper and checking closing times as it was Saturday.

Cole sported dark circles under his eyes and his face looked thinner than it had yesterday. She hated seeing him like this and could only imagine the stress he was under. Besides the fact that he obviously cared for his animals, she knew too well what a shoestring most ranches ran on. That tractor in the driveway probably had payments on a $150,000 loan and wouldn't be the only machinery they owned. Ranch assets were all in the buildings, the land and the livestock. It wouldn't surprise her if Cole had little more in the bank after buying the new Angus than she did herself.

260   HER COLORADO COWBOY

If even a fraction of his sick animals died today, it could hurt the ranch badly.

"We found some supplements in Alamosa, but more in Trinidad and Pueblo," Cole told her. "Are you okay being here with Dustin and the rest of the ranch hands if Jake, Troy and I leave to get them?"

"Yes, go. We'll be fine."

"Jake, you take Alamosa. Hit all three feed stores there. Troy, you want Pueblo or Trinidad?"

"Pueblo's farther and you drive like an old lady. Besides, it's better if you're back here sooner than me."

Kelli's phone rang and she glanced at the screen. "Wait a minute before you take off." She had a short conversation, listening more than talking, then hung up.

"That was the vaccine manufacturer. They got their research department involved and have confirmed that what we're seeing is a contamination problem with one of the stabilizers in one specific lot. They'll get back to us with recommendations in the next hour. They're chasing down the exact cause of the reaction, but just this morning they heard from another ranch with a similar issue. They're in the process of sending out a recall notice to every ranch that might have an affected batch. They agreed with the B-12 shots and the cobalt and copper treatments."

Troy gave Cole an enigmatic look, then punched

him in the shoulder. "Good job." He turned to her. "Both of you." He pulled his keys from his jacket pocket and headed for his truck.

"I'll call you as soon as I get the amounts calculated so you know how much to buy," she said.

"The Angus are in the same pens as before," Cole told her. "The last two cows are on the ground now. The bull is still standing, but he's off his feed. Dustin is up to date on everything here. He'll help you while I'm gone."

"Drive safe. We'll be fine here." She reached out and put a hand on his arm. "I have a good feeling about this, Cole."

He nodded but didn't respond to her touch.

She'd wanted to see hope coming to Cole's face, or even a connection of shared concern between them—an acknowledgment that she was on his side, that she cared about the cattle *and* about him—but his dark eyes were full of tension. He knew as well as she did how little time they had. Even if this wasn't an infection and even if it was reversible, the cows could suffer multiple system damages from those heavy bodies lying on the ground too long. She had to get them up and moving. Fast.

CHAPTER THIRTY

BY THE TIME Cole returned from Trinidad, snow was falling. He'd heard by phone that Dustin and the ranch hands had all the mineral blocks out. Kelli had finished with the Angus and was giving B-12 and copper sulfate to the Herefords. He drove to the corrals holding the Angus, but when he parked, he could hardly believe what he saw. All the Angus were on their feet again. He gave a loud whoop and drove for the next corral.

Kelli walked out to greet him when he arrived. Cole hopped out of the truck and threw his arms around her, lifting her off her feet. He spun her in a circle, but the feeling of her in his arms and the lavender scent of her hair brought him to himself abruptly. If he didn't wall off his feelings for her like an iron fortress, she could seep through the smallest joints and tear all his battlements down. He set her down and stepped back. She'd smiled at him when he spun her, but he'd betrayed a physical barrier he'd set for himself.

Sobered now, he said, "I can't thank you enough,

Kelli. You know what a disaster this could have been for the ranch."

"Are you kidding? Days like this are the whole reason I became a vet."

She'd looked concerned when he stepped back but smiled up at him now, anyway. She was smart, she was beautiful and she was caring. And she had more potential to hurt him than anybody had in a long, long time.

Dustin was setting up a test kit Kelli had brought to measure the level of cobalt in the water tanks. Cole called out to Billy to start unloading the bags in his truck. Kelli took one of each to read the concentration on the label and sat on the ground to do the dosing math on her tablet.

"I talked a couple of times to the R&D team at Vetmore Innovative about recommended treatment levels of the minerals while you were gone," she said as she worked. "Looks like we'll need one bag of cobalt and a quarter bag of copper per fifty gallons of tank water. It dissolves and suspends well, so mix it going in and then it should be fine."

Dustin had stopped to listen as well and was shouting orders before Cole could tell him to get started.

She continued, "I'd like to keep a couple of bags of copper aside to do drenches on the Angus that were affected the longest. They won't absorb much through the skin, but it'll help speed their recovery."

He rested one foot on the lowest rung of the corral and leaned his arms on the top rung, soaking in the view of the cows eating and drinking and moving around normally. "Will there be any lasting side effects?"

"The company doesn't think so and I'd agree. The effects from low cobalt and copper are both reversible if caught soon enough. I know it didn't feel like it, but we actually got on this pretty quick."

"Yeah, well, again, thanks to you."

"Once it was obvious that the unvaccinated cows were staying healthy, the cause would've been obvious. By tomorrow, you would've figured it out."

"But by then I would've had anywhere from a dozen to five dozen cows dead from the deficiency or with nerve damage from being down so long."

"I'm so glad you didn't lose any."

Looking up at him from the ground, the light snow catching on her hood and knees, she took his breath away with her shining smile. His gratitude, and admiration, and love for her were conflating into a single emotion beyond his ability to name, making him look away to regain control.

"And no antibiotics either," he said, making himself turn back to her. "We're still on track to qualify for the natural beef program by fall. Okay, what's next?"

"I have a lot of Herefords left to inject. When your ranch hands finish dosing and testing the water, they could do that drench treatment for the Angus."

While she worked, Cole intermittently combed through his logbook to make sure they had every vaccinated cow from the main herd separated, even if they were still on their feet. It felt wrong to sit in his truck, dry and warm, even for short periods, while Kelli worked through the afternoon in the off and on snow. Like him, she'd worn her quilted coveralls and heavy gear, but it couldn't counteract being outside that many hours with the temperature plummeting. The best he could do was make sure Kelli got in the truck frequently with the heater blasting, and Troy helped by bringing hot coffee out for everyone.

By the time all one hundred and forty-two cattle had been treated, it was seven o'clock and dark outside. The snow had accumulated at least four or five inches.

"You look frozen," Cole said to Kelli, standing with her at the corral railing.

"I'm okay," she said. "It's part of the job."

"You should come to the house for dinner and a stiff drink to warm up," Troy said, looking almost as chilled as Kelli. He'd worked shoulder to shoulder with the wranglers getting all the water

266 HER COLORADO COWBOY

tanks filled and dosed properly, then helping to get the affected cows hydrated.

Kelli glanced at Cole, but in the shadows cast by the headlights, flashlights and headlamps, he couldn't read her expression. Flinching internally, he wondered if Kelli would think the invitation to dinner was something he'd planned with Troy.

"Home isn't that far. I think I can last a bit longer," she said with a smile. When she turned back to Troy, Cole clearly saw her face in the light, tight with cold and hunger.

He'd vowed to himself to be professional about working with her but inviting her in was simple common courtesy. She was welcome to come to dinner if she wanted, as friends and nothing more—whatever Troy might have in mind.

"You have at least a ten-minute cleanup here," Troy said, "a twenty-minute drive home, and then you still have to make yourself something to eat. On the other hand, Sally will have stockpiled meals for us for the weekend. All it'll take is a couple of minutes of reheating. Come on. You know you want to say yes. Besides, we need to celebrate." He never once glanced Cole's direction for approval.

"That does sound good," she said, sounding grateful and rubbing her gloved hands together.

They caravanned their trucks back to the house. Once inside, they shed their heavy outer layers and hung them by the door. Baxter danced his greeting and Troy poured a stiff drink of brandy for each of them.

"I owe you an apology," Troy said, handing Cole his drink.

"No, you don't. You were concerned about the herd and the ranch, same as me."

"Well, I won't doubt you so quick again. Or Kelli either," he said quietly. "You," he said more loudly to Kelli, "drink your brandy. I'll start heating up a meal and you two can talk while Cole gets a fire going."

Kelli followed Cole to the fireplace as he knelt and stacked logs on kindling.

Relief that things were all right between him and Troy and between Troy and Kelli melted the second of the three stressors that had sat like a bar of lead in his belly over the past twenty-four hours. The first had evaporated earlier this evening at seeing the cattle recover. If he and Kelli hadn't derailed, this would be the perfect evening. Instead, the tension over the change in their relationship made him self-conscious when he spoke to her and awkward when she came too near. Having her so close to him felt like a starving prisoner watching a feast; everything he wanted and needed just out of reach.

Once the fire was going, they both took a seat on the couch. Baxter hopped up between them, tail wagging, turned three times, then plopped down facing Kelli. Cole put his stockinged feet up

268 HER COLORADO COWBOY

on the granite coffee table, crossed them, leaned back into the couch and sipped at the brandy. It warmed him from the inside out, like sparks from the fire blazing down his throat to his gut. He closed his eyes for a moment, breathing in the truth that his livestock were out of danger.

Baxter whined, bringing Cole back to full wakefulness from what was quickly sliding toward a nap. Baxter wasn't looking at him, though. He slapped one paw on Kelli's leg, encouraging her to pet him.

"He likes you."

"Well, I like him too." She acquiesced to Baxter's demands and petted him. "I've actually been looking for a dog myself. It's been a long time since I've had one, and I've missed it." Her caresses turned to a professional palpation of his shoulder, checking his reflexes and range of motion. "I'd say he's one-hundred percent again. He should be safe going out with you as long as you start with short days. I wouldn't let him work cattle for another week or so."

"Okay, you two, break it up," Troy said, looking at Baxter rather than Cole. "Dinner's ready."

They took their seats at the large oak dining table. Their grandfather had built it more than fifty years ago, solid and big enough to comfortably seat eight, but Troy had set their dishes close together at one end.

After dinner, Troy pushed Cole to get his gui-

ELIZA D. COLLINS 269

tar, though everyone looked ready for sleep. Cole finally relented and sang a couple of songs while Troy poured an after-dinner brandy. His brother's tactics were obvious, but instead of working, it only made his time with Kelli more bittersweet.

Troy raised his glass. "To Kelli, the smartest vet in the county."

Cole raised his glass as well. He drank, admiring her. Loving her. The perfect woman he would never have.

CHAPTER THIRTY-ONE

KELLI ARRIVED HOME at 10:30 p.m., exhausted. She checked the window and door locks, then dropped onto her bed, fully clothed, sitting up against the headboard. So many workdays were difficult: losing animals that she'd tried to save, people choosing to forgo care for an animal due to the cost, dealing with people's grief or her own frustrations and doubts. Days like today were one in a million.

Helping Cole had made her happy. It had been so comfortable, spending the evening with him and Troy. Troy was a joker. She suspected his clowning might hide some inner struggles, but he was a good person and she liked him. She'd had no idea Cole could sing, and the three of them listening to Cole play guitar and laughing and telling after-dinner stories had felt like family to her. It reminded her of her childhood, growing up with a mother and father who made the most of their family time together.

And as happy as tonight had been, it had been poignant too. Cole put on a good face, but the rare times he met her eyes all she saw was hurt and wariness. She'd had her reasons for pushing him away, and they were good ones, but the more time she spent with him, the more she knew all that goodness and kindness was no act. If she hadn't acted rashly the other day, tonight might have ended very differently.

She wondered how a man that handsome, that buff, privileged enough to be raised on one of the largest cattle outfits in Colorado and macho enough to rodeo could genuinely be so unlike all the good-looking, buff, macho jerks who had hurt her in the past. But she knew the answer. Even if growing up good at sports and handsome and popular held the same potential to turn him into an arrogant and insensitive man, there was that core she knew so well. That sensitive child who'd craved friendship and love.

KELLI WOKE IN the same good mood that had lulled her to sleep last night. She couldn't recall her dreams, but a warm feeling and fleeting sensory memories of physical closeness enveloped her. The ghost of an image of Cole's face near hers; the impression of a kiss. The misty wisps of a conversation that even now, awake, still rang some emotional bell deep in the pit of her stomach.

By 8:00 a.m., she was headed to Tillacos, driving through eight inches of rapidly melting snow.

She'd let Cole know last night that she'd be out today to recheck the cows and then would need to do a final recheck the following day when the lab was open, with a blood draw from at least one Angus and one Hereford to be certain they were recovering. She called on the way there and they arranged to meet at the Angus corral.

On examination, all the cattle looked to be improving. She tried to make light conversation as she worked and even flirted very slightly to see if he'd respond. If anything, he grew increasingly uncomfortable, which left her feeling as uneasy as when she'd examined the Angus the day after the Jenna incident. She finished up quickly and left.

Maybe he wasn't picking up on her abysmally incompetent flirting. Or maybe he was being understandably cautious after her reaction to him the other day, when he hadn't done anything wrong. If he'd decided they were finished romantically, she'd regret it forever; but if she'd done irreparable damage to their friendship, it would break her heart.

Going home to waste away her Sunday with morose thoughts of what a failure she was at relationships held little appeal. Before she'd even hit the highway, she was dialing Sienna's number. Between everything going on at the ranch in the last half of the week and Sienna working nights and sleeping days, she had hardly spoken to her friend lately.

ELIZA D. COLLINS

"Hey, you," Sienna answered, "haven't heard from you in a while. What have you been up to? No good, I hope."

How to answer that one…

"Good and bad, I guess."

"Whoa. I know that tone of voice. Things still haywire with Cole?"

"I'm about ten minutes from your place. I was kind of hoping I could swing by and get you caught up."

"I'll start a pot of coffee."

SIENNA NEVER JUST "made coffee." She was basically a home barista with an espresso machine that cost as much as Kelli's new couch, milk steamer, powders, syrups, drizzles and toppings.

Kelli walked in the front door to a strong aroma of dark roast and cacao. Sienna met her by the kitchen door and placed a giant ceramic mug filled with a steaming mocha latte in her hand. She gestured to the assortment of additional choices lined up neatly on the counter. Kelli added a splash of toffee nut syrup and another of caramel. She took a sip to make certain it was sweet enough.

"Yowza, that's good." The words came out on a sigh of pure bliss.

Sienna picked up her own cup and led the way to the living room couch. They sat at either side of the short sofa, facing each other, legs tucked up cross-legged, same as they'd done for years.

"Heads up that I promised my mom I'd be over by ten to untangle her taxes," Sienna said.

"Weren't those due last week?"

"Did you not catch the part where I said *my mom*?"

"Got it."

Sienna had been the parent in that relationship as long as Kelli had known her.

"Okay, spill," Sienna said.

"I think Cole and I broke up."

"I thought you just asked him to slow down. And what do you mean you *think* you broke up?"

Kelli detailed the whole messy ordeal since seeing Jenna at the ranch on Wednesday and wrapped up with a recap of the dinner last night and Cole's emotional distance this morning. The heavenly sips of mocha as she talked were the only comfort while relating the timeline. Well, that and having found the cure for the cows.

"Dang, girlfriend. That's an awful lot going on in just a few days."

"Tell me about it. So, did I just blow the best thing ever over absolutely nothing?"

"You didn't blow it. You're just damaged."

"Gee, thanks."

"Not damaged like damaged goods, and you know it. Damaged as in traumatized by multiple jackasses who didn't deserve to exist in your shadow."

"Yeah. And then I took it out on Cole."

"You protected yourself. You made decisions based on past experiences and the information you had on hand. Anybody with your history would've done the same thing. All you asked was to slow down. He's the one who overreacted and isn't getting over it."

Kelli shrugged. She'd overreacted, too, and wasn't going to judge who was "more wrong."

"What do you think about the Jenna thing? Think there's anything to it?"

"I don't know, sweetie. You know him a lot better than I do. I asked Lisa at work and she hadn't heard anything about it. The important thing is what do you think?"

"I want to believe him, but I've gone down that road before."

"How about him seeing anybody else?"

"I don't think he is. Last week, when he took me on that picnic, he told me he wasn't with anyone else. And he's been so busy with the ranch I don't know when he would have had the time."

"Want to check?"

A flock of butterflies launched in Kelli's stomach. She'd had the same thought recently about looking at the dating site. What if she found proof that Cole had moved on without a back-

HER COLORADO COWBOY

ward glance? Or worse still, proof he'd been active on there these last three weeks.

"I'm scared to," she finally said.

"Denial isn't a river in Egypt."

"I know, I know."

"I checked the site after we talked, like I promised, but I haven't looked lately. I thought things were okay again when you said you were treating his cows. I'm going to go out on a limb and say that I don't think you're going to see anything bad. And you know I'm never wrong. But theoretically, if you looked and found out that he's a serial womanizer, wouldn't it be better to know rather than mooning over him?"

"I guess you're right." Kelli downed the last sweet sip of her mocha and said, "Okay, let's do this."

Sienna went into her spare bedroom and came out with her laptop.

"Hey, I forgot to ask, did Cody Sanders ever ask you out?" Kelli said as Sienna fired up her computer.

"We went out once and then he was off to Oklahoma City for a rodeo, followed by one in Tucson and one in Nevada somewhere."

"Yeah, I guess the pro-rodeo lifestyle is pretty much like that about eleven months a year."

"Yep. He's all kinds of good-looking and it was a fun date, but that life's not for me."

It felt like the internet took forever to load.

Sienna clicked on the dating site, then a book-marked page.

"And you have Cole's profile bookmarked why?" Kelli teased, though inside molten jelly churned thick swells through her stomach.

"Because I look out for you."

She opened the profile. The moisture sucked out of Kelli's throat and she clasped her hands in her lap to keep from fidgeting. The first thing she saw was a drop-dead gorgeous picture of him, worse than she'd imagined. He must have been herding cattle and had pivoted in the saddle to look at whoever took the photo. It had been cropped to avatar size; his hat pulled low over his dark eyes and the collar of his heavy canvas jacket turned up against the cold. There were cows just faintly visible in the background.

Sienna scrolled down past his bio to the winks; a little pink heart with a number in it. Fifty-six freaking women had winked at him in the past three months. The number glared at her from inside the heart. It meant nothing, she told herself. It didn't indicate the number of women he was in touch with or had responded to.

Sienna clicked on the heart and it opened up a details page where people could make initial con-tact. If he answered, then they'd have the option to contact each other privately or could continue the conversation in comments until such time as one or both decided to go private.

278   HER COLORADO COWBOY

Kelli scanned down for recent comments and her stomach dropped right down to her socks. He'd told her he'd been out with three women from the site, so it didn't rattle her to see that in the past month or so he'd interacted with some Italian woman who was in Colorado for the skiing and some woman named Barb. Barb had been about three weeks ago—about the time she went out to his ranch to deliver the calf. Those she could deal with. What jumped off the web page at her was the line below Barb's. Cole answering back to a new woman. Thanks for getting in contact. I love that one of your passions is skydiving. So cool. Hope you stay in touch.

The comment was dated three days ago. Thursday. *The day after Kelli had seen Jenna at the ranch.*

"Dang, I hate being wrong," Sienna said under her breath. "That must have been right after I checked it." She closed the laptop without shutting the page down. "Troy put him on this site, right? You do know that could have been Troy responding for him. Cole might not even know about it."

"Cole said Troy set the site up for him. He didn't say his brother impersonated him there." Kelli got up, feeling her way past the coffee table because her vision had blurred with sudden tears. It could have been Troy, but Sienna hadn't been there last night to see Troy trying to push her and

Cole together all evening. "You need to take off soon to meet your mom. I better go."

She threw her jacket on and Sienna hooked a finger in the collar, stopping her from heading for the door.

"Okay, but listen to me first. I don't say this about a lot of guys, but I still think, despite some flimsy evidence to the contrary, Cole is one of the good ones. You two have been on crossed wires from the start. Even if that was him responding to a wink, it isn't the end of the world. Maybe he did it because he was hurt. And I don't mean in a 'revenge wink' way, I mean in a 'lonely and hurt' kind of way."

"I think it's better I just accept this for what it is."

"You don't know yet what *this* is. Look, I'm not going to be at my mom's for long. Just long enough to get some kind of late extension thing figured out. I'll probably be home by noon. I don't want you moping around alone. How about doing something this evening? Tostadas and margaritas?"

"I have some paperwork to catch up on, but maybe," she said, though she knew she wouldn't come over for dinner. She wasn't going to break down or go to pieces over one wink, but she needed to be on her own for a while. "Don't worry, I'll be fine."

CHAPTER THIRTY-TWO

AFTER KELLI LEFT the ranch, Cole thought wistfully about taking the rest of his Sunday off for once. It would have been nice to get out of town and have some time to himself, try to stop thinking about Kelli for a minute, but he was so behind from losing those few days to the cattle illness that it just wasn't possible.

With Troy on the last of his days off for this "go-round," it was no surprise when he headed inside with Baxter and found his brother having a late breakfast. What did surprise him was a plate of bacon, eggs and toast warming in the toaster oven for him. Troy really *must* have felt guilty about the way he'd acted recently.

Cole retrieved the plate and sat with his brother at the kitchen island. Normally, he would have had something light to eat first thing, then a large lunch, but this morning he hadn't been hungry, knowing Kelli was showing up.

"So," Troy said without preamble, "when are you seeing Kelli again?"

"She'll be back again tomorrow to do a last follow-up on the cows."

"Yeah, that's not what I meant. When are you going to *see* her again?"

Cole sighed, not wanting to get into this. "I tried that, remember? She didn't want to keep seeing me."

"You said she wanted to slow down. That's different. Besides, I saw the two of you last night. She has feelings for you, you have feelings for her, and the two of you still dance around each other like a pair of feral cats."

"Seriously, Troy, what's it to you? You didn't even want me to use her as our vet."

"I know. And I was wrong about that. I said so. A few times. But I always liked her as a person. More, now that I actually got to spend time with her yesterday. Cole, you could look for the next ten years and not find anyone as right for you as her."

"Drop it, Troy."

Kelli wanting to backpedal after two dates. Troy and Lane not trusting him with the ranch. This wasn't the week for Troy to push him on this. He dreaded having to be around her again tomorrow afternoon, pretending that everything was fine.

Troy fell quiet and sipped his coffee, then said, "Remember that time—you must have been around eight, 'cause you'd only been living here a year or so—and you decided to help Dad by mowing one of the pastures with the tractor? He and Mom were in town, and I was supposed to be watching you. You started the tractor and had no idea how to drive it. You got it into Neutral and it rolled and tore down part of the fence. Cows got out all around the house. Do you remember how much trouble I got into over that?"

"What on earth does that have to do with anything?"

"If I'd been the one to start the tractor and break the fence, even with the good intentions of wanting to help Dad, I would have been grounded so hard I'd probably never have seen the sun again. Instead, I got grounded for not watching you close enough, and you got a *stern talking to*. And by the way, I really resented you for that."

"I was three years younger than you."

"You still are. But that wasn't why they were harder on me. Mom and Dad understood the one thing that would tear you down quicker than anything was if you thought, even briefly, that you'd lost their love."

Cole looked down at his plate and pushed scrambled egg around with his fork. "I don't need you to tell me how good they were to me. And I still don't know why you're bringing it up."

"I'm bringing it up because I think it's tied to you not giving Kelli a fair shake."

Cole tossed his fork down and pushed the plate away from him. "You're hardly the person I'm going to take love advice from. At least I know I can settle down when I find the right person."

"Don't try and twist this into something about me. I know my shortcomings better than you do. I also know that Jan and I aren't right for each other, even though we keep trying. I just don't want to see you regret this for the rest of your life." Troy wagged his fork at him. "Someone like Kelli isn't going to be alone for long, and I can't imagine any two people better for each other than you two. She'd just had some jerk of a boyfriend cheat on her and then Jenna did whatever she did. You're punishing her too hard. I think you need to decide if it's because of her emotional baggage, or if it's because of your own."

"I'm not punishing anybody, Troy. I'm grown up enough to know that *let's slow down* is code for *I'm not that into you*."

Troy pushed his plate away as well and leaned his forearms on the table.

"You go into everything heart and soul. You always have. Not everybody can commit as fast or as wholeheartedly as you do."

Troy picked up both their plates, scraped them and put them in the dishwasher. He turned to leave. "Just think about it, okay? She's going to be out here tomorrow. If you let this opportunity slide, you may not get another."

BILLY AND THE rest of the Sunday crew were out feeding horses and cattle but Dustin, as always, was waiting for Cole at the barn. His foreman took care of the wranglers' schedules, but Dustin worked every day that Cole did—which was most every day, whether Cole told him to take the day off or not.

Yesterday's snow was melting quickly, and the grass underneath had been thick enough to keep the fields from getting too muddy. "We'll catch up on fertilizing the alfalfa fields today," Cole said.

Still stinging from Troy's "unasked for" advice, his words came out more briskly than he'd intended. Then again, this was the way the ranch needed to be run. His emotions might be in upheaval, but he could take control of this part of his life. He couldn't be the boss of the men and still be one of them, however much he wanted or preferred to. He pictured his dad out here, how he'd commanded the respect of everyone working for him. It was a good day for him to start doing the same.

He tried his best to block Kelli from his mind, focusing on work, but couldn't stop himself from remembering their first kiss in the cabin. More than the physical, though, he remembered the sweetness of her smile when the waiter began singing at the Italian restaurant. Her pleasure in the ride up the mountain. Her easy conversation. Her pure joy at something as simple as chocolate cupcakes.

Maybe Troy wasn't completely wrong in the things he said, but his brother couldn't understand what was at stake for him. Letting her in again, getting sucked into that destructive cycle of wanting more love than he'd get. He didn't dare risk it.

CHAPTER THIRTY-THREE

KELLI FUMBLED WITH the key in her front door, then slammed and locked it behind her like she could lock out the whole world. Flopping onto the couch, still wearing her coat, she finally drew a deep calming breath.

Sienna was right, seeing Cole post one comment on that dating site wasn't the end of the world; but it might just be the end of her trying. The intensity of her reaction to seeing that wink online scared her. She wasn't even acting like herself these days. Allen's betrayal seemed to have kicked off a cascade of reactions in her, from not wanting to be alone to feeling certain she would never pick the right man. Cole had appeared in her life like the miraculous answer to everything. He loved animals, he treated her well, he genuinely seemed to want to be with her. But above all, he'd seemed kind.

What she needed was a good heart-to-heart with herself about her goals at this juncture in life. But not now. Right now she wanted a pint of

Ben & Jerry's, internet pictures of baby animals, and maybe an animated all-ages comedy. And a dog. She really, really needed some nonverbal, unconditional love. She got her laptop from the office and scrolled through the rescue websites.

She still wanted every dog she saw, of course, but neither of her favorited ones hit her like a gong. She returned to the main page and clicked on new arrivals. The page loaded and showed eight results. Scrolling down, she passed the Chihuahua, three bull terriers and the husky mix.

At number six, her hand froze on the mouse. A large cream-and-brown dog looked back at her, either a longhaired shepherd with unusual coloring or some kind of mix. The deep brown eyes were soulful but happy. Kelli clicked on the name, Millie. They listed her as a shepherd cross, eighty-five pounds, approximately two years old. She'd been found running loose on the streets of Denver and had gone to a kill shelter where no one claimed her. The rescue had pulled her from the shelter. In foster, she'd been found to be people-friendly, house-trained, and good with dogs and children. Kelli wanted her immediately. She was perfect.

The gut feeling held such absolute certainty that she paused to examine the reaction. What made her believe Millie was the perfect dog when she hadn't known what she was looking for? Is that how these things worked? That the

288 HER COLORADO COWBOY

heart knew even when the mind didn't? Maybe regardless of Jenna or the dating site, this was what she needed to do with Cole. Quit thinking and let her heart decide.

She closed her laptop and emailed the rescue address listed, hoping someone would answer on a Sunday. If they did, she would listen to her heart and try her best to get Millie today, before she risked losing her to someone else.

KELLI RECEIVED AN email back within minutes from an ecstatic rescue worker, thrilled that a veterinarian had applied for the dog she fostered. She called the private number the woman provided and discussed the dog with her. The more they talked, the more convinced Kelli became that Millie was the perfect fit for her. Unfortunately, two other people already had applications in, and the woman wouldn't commit over the phone.

The rescue was outside Monument, north of Colorado Springs. It meant a three-hour drive each way from Burgess, but today was the perfect day to go. Besides, it would give her something to do other than think about Cole.

She grabbed what she needed and left. The truck radio played, but every country song seemed to reflect her relationship ups and downs and her anxiety at the thought of losing Cole forever. She finally turned the music off, plugged her phone in to her car speakers and listened to a veterinary journal podcast.

Traffic through Colorado Springs was less congested than regular weekday traffic, but still busier than she'd navigated in months. She'd gotten used to it when she'd lived in Fort Collins, but it was amazing how quickly she'd fallen back into small-town life since graduating.

Kelli arrived at the woman's home surprisingly close to the time she'd guesstimated. The rescue was on the outskirts of town and the setup not too unlike her own; a house on a small piece of acreage with a few kennels out back. The woman's name on the website was Francine but she'd said on the phone to call her Franny.

Franny answered the door, surrounded by an assortment of breeds, both large and small. Kelli felt a stab of pleasure when she spotted the big ginger-and-cream longhaired shepherd among them. "Come on in," Franny said. "Sit down."

"Are these all up for adoption?" Kelli asked, pushing through the furry mass.

"No, four of these are my regular crew. Foster fails. The hazards of fostering lots of dogs. You can't help falling in love. I usually get the kids into foster homes as soon as possible, but Miss Millie has only been here a couple of days. She would've been a foster fail for sure except I knew she wouldn't be around long enough. I've already had another call on her this morning. Good thing, as I certainly don't need another dog of my own."

Millie hadn't barked when the door opened and she'd wagged her tail as she followed Kelli to the couch. She sat prettily now, alert and interested.

"Let me put the others in the bedroom so you and Millie can get to know each other." The woman called the dogs and they all trotted behind her, but when Kelli called Millie back, she came running happily to her. Kelli tried a sit command and was pleased to see Millie respond quickly.

Franny returned from the bedroom.

"Any health issues?"

"None that we know of, but we don't know a lot about her. She was a stray when she got picked up by animal control. They held her for ten days, but no one came to claim her. They said she's spayed, but that's all they knew. Our rescue has a good relationship with a lot of the shelters around here. They'll usually call us if they get a good adoption candidate whose time is running out on death row. It's a win-win. We free up shelter space for them, and the good-natured ones are easy to place in foster and easier for us to get adopted so we can take more out of the shelter."

"Aww. Poor girl. Ten days in jail—it must have seemed like forever. It's surprising, since she looks well cared for."

"And she may have been. She might have gotten lost from people passing through the area or might have been owned by someone who loved her and died. She could have been stolen and dumped, or wandered off if a gate got left open. I wish they could talk. It's hard not knowing their history. In any case, she's not microchipped, didn't have tags and no one claimed her."

"Well, I'd love to take her home."

Kelli dug her vet license out of her fanny pack, then pulled up photos of her home on her phone. Franny had explained that they were supposed to do a home check by having a dog adopter in the area come inspect the house and property, but she was willing to waive that requirement if Kelli brought a copy of her vet license and photos.

"Did the other two people come see her yet?"

"They both came this morning, while you were on your way up here." Franny looked apologetic. "I told them we'd check their homes, plus there's the other person that just called."

Here with her now, having seen her and touched her, Kelli couldn't imagine her going to someone else. She rubbed Millie's ear, then scratched inside when the dog tipped her head into the experience and grunted with pleasure. Kelli didn't want to risk losing her. She turned to Franny, determined not to give up and leave this to chance.

"When I was young, I had a longhaired German shepherd. She passed away from gastric torsion when I was seventeen. She was only seven. We didn't get help for her fast enough because no one in the family knew the signs of bloat. I think it was a pivotal factor in me choosing to become a vet. Miss Millie doesn't look exactly like Bella, but something about her eyes and her personality reminds me strongly of her. I'd very much like to adopt her. I'd love to take her home today, and it's no problem to hang out the rest of the day in town if you need to look at the other places, but I also understand if you can't make a decision today. Coming back up for her isn't a problem. I'll make the time."

The woman watched as Millie slapped her big paw in Kelli's lap, asking for more scratches. The silence stretched. Franny pursed her lips.

"I think the two of you will make a good pair," she said at last. "It's hard to imagine a better home for her than with a country veterinarian who loves shepherds."

Delighted and relieved, Kelli grinned and gave Millie a happy scruff on the head. She wrote a check for the adoption fee, knowing the money would help bring other dogs out of the shelter and pay for their sometimes-extensive health care needs along with the spay and neuter fees the rescue shouldered. She clipped a leash she'd brought along onto Millie's collar, and her new dog happily followed her out to her truck.

Millie had obviously ridden in a car before and sat, excited but obedient, on the front seat. On the drive out of town, Millie settled in for the trip, finally lying down and resting her head on Kelli's leg. Kelli stroked Millie, honored by the trust and affection. The bond was mutual, and Kelli couldn't help but remember what she'd been thinking earlier, that sometimes you just needed to let go of all the questions and listen to your heart.

And sometimes you needed to fight for what you wanted most.

CHAPTER THIRTY-FOUR

FIVE HOURS OF clinic Monday morning felt like fifty.

Between patients, Kelli's gaze kept ticking up to the clock on her office wall instead of staying trained on entering her exam notes. Other than Kelli's patients, Millie proved her only distraction from the whirlpool in her brain, spinning her thoughts into a confusion of feelings about seeing Cole this afternoon. Padding from her office, Millie would pass through the shared doorway to Rikki's desk—enclosed on three sides by the reception counter—visit Rikki, check out the new sights and smells, then return to Kelli for reassurance and cuddles.

Giving up after her third try to finish a note without thinking about Cole, Kelli bit her upper lip, ignored the cramping in her stomach and opened the dating website. Pulling up Cole's profile, she clicked on the picture and enlarged it, studying those dark guileless eyes. The half smile on his face when he'd turned in the saddle, maybe hearing his name and seeing the camera. Her heart swelled just like it had when she'd seen Millie's photo.

If she could have just stopped all the chatter in her brain weeks ago and listened to her heart, it would have told her what she needed to know. And maybe it had. When she was a child, it had told her to connect to him; that they were tethered in some way deeper than either of them understood. And in a couple of hours, she'd be seeing Cole again. It would be her final recheck on his cattle, and quite possibly her last chance to ask her questions, listen to his answers and, with any luck at all, save their relationship.

She didn't want to lose him; she knew that now. If he'd responded to someone who winked at him, maybe he *had* done it out of hurt, like Sienna said. *Maybe he really hadn't been the one doing it at all.* Bottom line, though, it didn't matter. The overthinking going on in her brain could take a long walk off a short pier; her gut believed what he'd said about Jenna. Her heart believed he cared for her. Wanted her. Loved her.

When she pushed down her own fears enough to see him for who he was rather than what she projected onto him, she didn't care about one stupid comment on a dating site. She was listening to her heart and her gut now. She'd been willing to fight to get Millie. She was more than willing to fight for Cole.

296 HER COLORADO COWBOY

One o'clock finally rolled around, and her last patient left. Rikki had offered to watch Millie while she went to check Cole's cows, so Kelli braced herself, girded her loins, held on to her reins...and headed out the door to win back her man.

CHAPTER THIRTY-FIVE

KELLI SHOWED UP at the ranch right on time. She emerged from her truck looking freshly scrubbed, well rested and so beautiful that Cole felt pins and needles in his belly, like she'd cast a fishing line and the hook had snared him in the stomach. He'd slept poorly last night, which was unusual for him these days, and his remembered dreams had all seemed to be different forms of angst brought on by the things Troy had said to him yesterday.

The combination of sensations decided for him. This needed to be her last visit to the ranch. After this, he'd go back to using Bill Salem. Once Bill retired, he could make do with Carlos and Sam. He was going to miss Kelli's outlook and quick mind, but this was too uncomfortable. Probably for them both.

"How'd they do yesterday?" she asked brightly, as she opened the topper boxes on her truck. She took out needles, syringes and blood vials.

"Great. They've been eating and drinking well and seem anxious to be let out to pasture."

298 HER COLORADO COWBOY

"Good to hear. Well, we'll hope these blood samples come back showing all their micronutrients back to normal." She tucked the needles and syringes into her coat pocket and came to stand near him at the corral gate.

He took half a step away from her, not realizing what he'd done until Kelli took a half step the opposite direction, shifting casually, as if to see one of the cows better.

There were so many levels to body language between two people attracted to each other; it boggled the mind to think about it consciously. And all were different depending on the situation. Whatever he and Kelli were to each other now, a wariness had entered the game. Each touch became a question and each reaction an answer.

"I've got more good news for you," she said, still cheerful, though he detected a slight forced quality to her smile. "The vaccine company has promised to pay all veterinary costs involved with this incident, plus your entire vaccine cost, and to FedEx you a new batch of vaccine double-checked for contaminants. I'll give you the rep's phone number and let you work it out with him if you want to accept their offer."

"Okay, thanks." She obviously knew as well as he did that the company wasn't making this offer out of the goodness of their hearts; they were trying to avoid a lawsuit.

"Well, let's get to it," she said brightly. She removed a syringe from her kit, opened the sterile packaging and screwed the needle on the end, leaving it capped. She fished a blood tube out of her pocket. "Any cows in particular you want tested?"

"Number 462 was the first one we saw down." He opened his logbook. "And 475 was the last to get up."

"Okay. Those sound like good parameters."

She quickly and deftly drew blood on the two cows, stopping to label each vial, but she looked to be deep in thought, her expression determined. When she climbed out of the corral, she asked where the affected Herefords were.

"They're in the next pasture. You can follow me over there." He turned to head for his truck.

"I only need a handful of supplies. Would you mind if I rode over with you?"

That uncomfortable fishhook tugged at his belly again. Why didn't he want to be near her? He was a grown man, capable of being friends with her. *Wanting* to be friends with her. But he also wanted distance between them, at least for now. With her here, working side by side with him, all he could think about was what might've been.

"Sure." It came out gruffer than he'd meant it to, and he tried a tight smile to mitigate it.

She nodded, looking less cheerful than before. Placing the filled blood vials in a cooler

300 HER COLORADO COWBOY

in her truck, she gathered a few more supplies and climbed in with him. The truck rattled and bumped across the field.

"Listen, Cole," Kelli said, looking down at the floorboards.

Crap. She was going to bring it up.

"I've been doing a lot of soul-searching these past few days. I know that I blew it by letting fear get in my way. I'm so sorry if asking to slow down hurt you. That was never my intention."

"No. It's fine," he said, gripping the wheel. "I get it."

"What I've realized, though, is that this isn't about time. It's about trust. Not me trusting you. Me trusting me. I've had it all wrong. I always thought it was all about whether I could trust the other person. I believed it so much that when the right man finally came along, I got in my own way. Honestly, though, I think I've been in love with you for twenty years."

He turned to her, surprised by the word *love*. Electricity hummed from his hands, where they gripped the steering wheel as he drove over the bumpy ground, up his forearms; a frisson of adrenaline straight to his brain. The layers of complexity that he'd always associated with that word hit him like a punch to the gut. He remembered his birth parents and how they would sometimes get clean for a while and then do and say

ELIZA D. COLLINS 301

all the perfect, happy things—until they didn't
again. This felt a lot like that.

"Well, that's the problem, isn't it?" he said.
"Trust. It's the same for me. You know that trust
doesn't come easy for me. I'm not saying you did
anything wrong and am definitely not saying that
we can't be friends, because one thing I know for
sure is that I always want to be your friend but…"

"Cole, I need to stop you there because I have
to know when I leave here today that I did my
very best to say this right. If your answer is still
the same when I'm done, I'll accept that. I promise. I've been giving this a lot of thought, so just
let me talk for a moment, because I have a feeling
I know what you're about to say and, if you do,
we may not get this chance again." She twisted
on the seat to face him.

"I think children understand things intuitively,
and I think as we get older, we start interfer-
ing with that intuition. We know too much for
our own good and we overthink and project old
feelings on new situations, like I did with you.
Children don't have the world experience and the
language finesse and the filters to corrupt information like we do. They're instinctive creatures."
She drew a deep breath and let it out, but he remained silent.

"When you came to school that very first day,
I knew that something inside me fitted together
with something inside you. We needed each other.

302 HER COLORADO COWBOY

You were brave in all the ways I wasn't. You were so very brave. And I… I don't know, I guess I just had extra room in my heart for you, and maybe that's what you needed. Whatever it was, we completed each other in some important way back then. It was something crucial for us both that happened at that time in our lives, and then we both moved on."

They came to the county road bisecting the ranch and he turned right. A few hundred feet down the road, they arrived at a large corral holding nearly fifty of the Herefords that had been ill. Dustin, on the four-wheeler, was just leaving the field. He returned and parked near the corral. Cole turned the truck off. Kelli fidgeted with her hands in her lap, then set her left hand on the seat between them, as if bracing herself. He thought for a moment she was going to reach out and touch his leg, but she didn't.

"We beat the odds already, Cole. Both of us moving back to Burgess, coming together when we were both single. And then you reached out to me across this gulf of years apart and I pulled back. And I'm so sorry. My heart knows you. It knows that you're the right person for me. And I don't mean that in any scary way. I'm not putting any pressure on this. I don't have any long-term expectations for us. But I want this chance. I hope you'll let us have a shot at seeing if this works and if we're as good together as I think we might be." She gave a half laugh and turned to look out the windshield again.

"So, yeah, that all kinda came out pretty heavy. All I'm really saying is that I would very much like to go out on a date with you again. No expectations and no baggage. I believe you about Jenna and I don't care if you've been on that dating site again. I'm just asking you to give me another chance first, then decide what you want. And, I hope I'm not blowing this in a whole new way, because if I can't have another shot at dating you, then I really do want your friendship."

Cole sighed and dropped his hands from the steering wheel. He wanted to say yes to her more than anything, but the ragged holes inside him wouldn't allow it. They gaped and bled, whispering that this might be nothing more than the upswing of that up and down seesaw.

"Kelli, I want you to know I hear what you're saying, and I know you mean it." He watched her face go from hopeful to stricken to ashen as she realized what he was about to say. "I hate to say 'it's not you, it's me,' but that's the truth." He continued while he still could. "I'm not saying no to friendship, and I certainly don't want to hurt you. I realize that all you asked for was to slow down, but we've both had bad breakups recently, and they've taken a toll. I think my breakup with Amy affected me more than I realized. And Allen's cheating is still fresh for you. Why don't we just leave it at this for now and see what happens in the future, okay?"

She was looking away from him, out the side window, biting her lip. "Yes. Sure. Okay," she said in a tight voice. She turned back and studied her hands in her lap. He could see the tear that filled her left eye. "But what I think will happen in the future is that neither of us will know how to start this again and that the odds of the timing being right aren't very good. I guess I'm just going to have faith that if this is meant to be, it'll be."

She sounded unconvinced by her own words. The tear spilled over her eye and flooded his heart with her sadness, but he stayed silent.

"Okay," she said, the strength returning to her voice. "I better get on with my work, right?"

Before he could say more, she jumped out of the truck.

She was right and he knew it. People seldom got back together after an uncomfortable break. It was like trying to force two magnets to touch. Cole sighed, dismayed at how badly he'd handled all this, and unsure anything he'd said or felt since the day of their second date was actually right. Done was done, though. He wasn't sure why she'd brought up that dating site again, but if she assumed he was moving on, then that was for the best.

He got out of his truck, but Kelli was already through the gate and trying to close it behind

ELIZA D. COLLINS 305

her. She was having trouble latching it, as if she couldn't see well. Dustin came over and stood next to Cole, saying nothing about the wait or the long conversation they'd had in the truck.

"Do you want any help?" Cole called to her. She waved him off.

As Kelli approached the herd, a truck came into sight down the road. He took a quick look behind to check that Dustin had pulled the four-wheeler well off to the side, the same as he had done with his truck.

The oncoming truck grew louder. The RPMs were revving up.

"It's those kids again," Dustin said. "I'm surprised they're opening it up with us right here, though."

Dustin was right. They didn't need some kids farting around or losing control while Kelli was in with those cows. Cole stepped into the road and waved his hand palm down in a slow-down gesture. The teens, full of themselves, apparently, moved to the far side of the road and pushed the truck faster. They were nearly level with him now.

"Stupid kids," Cole said, stepping back. He wasn't in the mood for this. Even though he and his brothers had done the same, they hadn't been careless enough to do it near people, vehicles or livestock.

He got a good look at the truck, the license and the kids as they roared past. He committed it all

306   HER COLORADO COWBOY

to memory. Just before the truck passed the four-wheeler, the driver shifted down, then accelerated again, preparing to skid around the corner ahead. The old truck backfired like a cannon going off. Even Dustin flinched.

Everything happened at once. Cole heard the cows bellow in alarm, the sound of gravel spraying as the kids took the corner, and the hoofbeats of running cattle as he spun to check on Kelli. He didn't see her. She'd slung a halter over a cow's nose to hold her head while she drew blood. The cow must've spooked with the rest and pulled her off her feet.

Cole's heart leaped into his throat. He yelled her name and Dustin ran stride for stride with him. They vaulted the rails, not bothering with the gate. Cole spotted the sleeve of her orange sweater on the ground and ran, arms waving to keep the cows from trampling her. Dustin ran to her other side doing the same.

The cows ran a few steps, but as soon as it became evident there was no life-threatening danger from the noise or the men, most of them turned to stare with their wide dark eyes and placid bovine faces. Within seconds, they were drinking from the water trough, chewing and ruminating, or grazing at the hay in the feeder at the side of the corral.

Cole dropped to his knees and pressed one hand to Kelli's cheek. She was unresponsive. Next to him, Dustin had his cell phone out, talking to a 911 operator. While Dustin gave the details, Cole tried to remember his basic first aid.

Kelli was smart enough that she would have been cautious under normal circumstances if a truck drove by fast, but her mind had probably been elsewhere and her vision blurry. If so, he knew why.

"Oh, no, Kelli. I'm so sorry."

She had a cut at her right temple and a bruise already darkening to maroon red. She'd probably caught one of the short horns when the cow she was drawing blood from threw its head in alarm. He should've been out there with her, holding the halter. Whether she wanted him with her or not, he should've been there.

In the distance, he heard the town's emergency siren blare. The town of Burgess had one ambulance and one fire truck, both manned by community volunteers who responded from home or work when the siren sounded. He probably knew as much about emergency medicine as they did, but it saved time as they wouldn't have to wait for an ambulance to come all the way from Alamosa. Still, the wait felt interminable. He couldn't stop stroking Kelli's face and apologizing. He wanted nothing more than to see her open her eyes and tell him she was all right.

She was breathing normally and her heartbeat felt strong, but the fact she wouldn't wake up scared the hell out of him. He'd seen plenty of unconscious cowboys at rodeos. The ones who were out for a few moments were usually fine. The ones who were carried away unconscious... They often weren't fine at all. There'd been a bull rider who'd taken a terrible blow to the forehead that put him in a coma for seventeen days. Only his youth had saved him, but the last Cole heard, he still couldn't walk without a rolling walker and his personality had done a U-turn from affable and congenial to angry and impatient.

"Come on, sweetie. Come back to me."

Out on the highway, Cole could hear the wail of the ambulance siren.

THE HOSPITAL MADE Cole stay in the waiting room because he wasn't family. Troy and his crew had shown up in the fire engine when Cole called to tell him about the accident. The other firefighters ate lunch in the cafeteria and then the captain said with a wink that the hospital's sprinklers and alarms needed inspecting. Dustin had lined out work for the wranglers, then dropped off the blood samples from the cattle at the lab in Alamosa before joining everyone in the waiting room.

A doctor came out to say that Kelli had regained consciousness, but they were sending her to radiology for an MRI. Cole belatedly thought of her parents and looked up their number. There'd been no answer and he'd left a message. After that, he'd called Rikki at the clinic to let her know what was going on. Troy sat next to him and tried to console him, but Cole had no words left to share except with Kelli.

Inside his head, though, Cole was nothing but words. Words of anger and dismay for himself and for how he'd acted. He'd tried his whole life to overcome his past and be grateful for the family who'd taken him in. Three-quarters of his life had been lived with strong, loving people. It was long past time to stop allowing those first seven years to overshadow all the good.

He'd botched things up so badly with Kelli he didn't know how to begin to fix it. All she'd asked was to slow down when she'd been unsure, and he'd overreacted. He saw it now; now that it might be too late. An hour ago, Kelli had said everything he could have ever wanted to hear, but he hadn't been able to respond to her because he hid his heart in a shell like a hermit crab.

What more could he want out of life than a relationship with her? The generous soul that had drawn him to her as a child and the beautiful, intelligent woman she'd become that drew him to her as a man. If he was responsible for lasting harm to her, he didn't know how he'd live with himself.

The double doors leading into the emergency department pushed outward and everyone looked

310 · HER COLORADO COWBOY

up, as they had all done each time for the three and a half hours they'd been waiting. At last, this time it was the doctor again. It had been evident when they checked her in that Cole was the closest person to her, and he jumped up as the doctor approached him.

"The contrast dye shows a small area of injury on the MRI, but she's awake and responding appropriately, so we're optimistic it's a minor concussion. You can come back and talk to her now if you want to." Cole surged forward.

The glass doors to the outside whooshed open just then and Kelli's parents came rushing in. Her mother's eyes were red from crying. Her father held her hand in both of his. They looked around, seeming overwhelmed, then headed for the check-in desk. Cole had focused for nearly four hours on seeing Kelli, touching her, apologizing. If he went with the doctor right now, that could happen. But he couldn't do it.

"Those are Kelli's parents," he said, pointing.

"Oh," the doctor said, swiveling his attention. In a heartbeat, Cole was forgotten as the doctor strode toward them. He began filling in the Hintons as they pushed through the doors into the emergency department where Cole wanted so badly to follow.

Troy and Dustin had been near enough to hear the update.

"That's good news, Cole," Troy said. "The biggest takeaway is that she's conscious and responding appropriately, and the MRI didn't show anything serious."

Cole nodded numbly. Nothing was going to make him feel better except seeing and talking to Kelli himself. The first priority was her well-being. Next, his apology. How could he not have understood her fears when he was so filled with his own? He should have spent more time trying to make her understand about Jenna, and maybe she would never have left the ranch upset. He should have allayed her concerns about that stupid dating site. Explain that it had all been Troy.

But he *had* told her that last bit...

"Troy, when I started seeing Kelli, did you take down that dating site like I asked you to?"

Troy's face was all the answer Cole needed.

"What makes you ask that now?" his brother said.

"Kelli mentioned it today out of the blue. Said it was okay if I was still on it."

His brother's expression slid from blame-deflecting to mortified. "Oh, man." He tipped his head back and squeezed his eyes shut in dismay. "I hadn't gotten around to it, and then when I found you on the couch Thursday morning and you said you'd broken up... You looked so gutted, so I got on there, and someone had sent you a wink." He winced. "I wrote back. I'm so sorry. I thought it would help you feel better. You know,

312   HER COLORADO COWBOY

before she came over Saturday and she was so great and all, and I knew you guys belonged together. And then I forgot about it."

Cole didn't have the energy to be angry. Besides, he had more to account for than Troy by a large margin. He just nodded. "It's okay. Thanks for being here for me today."

With Kelli awake now, Troy and the other firefighters returned to their station, and Cole sent Dustin back to the ranch. Time dragged on. He'd been in the emergency room once or twice himself and knew how these things worked. You could probably come in for a toothache and it would still be five hours of red tape and paperwork before you finally got released.

About twenty minutes later, Kelli's father came out to the waiting room. Cole stood.

"Cole," Mr. Hinton said, extending his hand. They shook. "They were talking about keeping her overnight but she's more than ready to leave. They're going to sign her out now as long as she stays overnight with someone who'll keep an eye on her. Momma wanted to bring her home, but…" He hesitated in a meaningful way.

Mr. Hinton had been a Colorado state trooper for nearly thirty years. He knew people and read them like books. He always had. It used to put the fear of God into all of them as kids.

"I'd like it very much if she'd come to the ranch with me," Cole said. "I feel responsible for this.

ELIZA D. COLLINS   313

Also, her truck is there, so no one would have to bring her out later. We have two spare rooms, and I promise to keep a close eye on her."

"Hmm. Well, I'll have to see what Momma says about it. But I'll let Kelli know you offered."

Just then, the doors opened again, and Kelli was pushed out in a wheelchair with Mrs. Hinton at her side, holding the paperwork and a plastic bag of hospital paraphernalia. Kelli looked well, except for the white bandage taped over the cut on her forehead.

Mr. Hinton walked over and spoke with them both. Mrs. Hinton looked to Cole and then down to Kelli. They spoke in a huddle before they all approached Cole, the orderly still pushing Kelli's wheelchair.

"She says she'd like to go to the ranch," Mr. Hinton said.

Kelli smiled up at him.

Cole breathed a sigh of relief. "I'll take good care of her."

"You have to wake her every two hours," Mrs. Hinton said. "All her instruction papers are in the bag, along with her medication."

"I'll follow all the doctor's orders. You have my word."

"I don't doubt you'll take care of her, son," Mr. Hinton said.

"I'll bring my truck to the front," he said. He squeezed Kelli's hand.

314 HER COLORADO COWBOY

Her father wheeled her outside and she said her goodbyes to her parents when he parked at the curb. Cole promised them again to look after her and call if there were any changes. Kelli pulled away when he took her arm to help her up, seeming embarrassed by her infirmity.

"I'm fine, really," she said.

He respected her independence and let go, fighting the urge to be wildly overprotective.

"I feel silly I let that happen," she said, once they were both in the truck and on the way to the ranch.

"You didn't let anything happen. It was those dang kids showing off that are to blame."

"I agreed to go to the ranch because I didn't want my parents to worry, but you can just take me to my truck if you want. I'll be fine at home."

"Not a chance. I gave my word."

She glanced at him, as if trying to understand his change of heart about being around her. "Then I need to ask if we can go by my house first. I have some things I have to pick up."

"Of course."

Driving to her house, Cole finally got to repeat the apologies he'd given to her while she lay unconscious in the dirt.

"I'm so sorry this happened to you, Kelli. I'm sorry I wasn't there helping you." His chest nearly burst with all the other things he wanted to tell her, but now didn't feel like the right time.

ELIZA D. COLLINS 315

He pulled into Kelli's driveway and Rikki came from the house out to the truck to greet them.

"I wanted so much to come to the hospital and see how you were," Rikki said, "but I know you needed me here. Everything is fine with the clinic. I fielded a couple of calls that came in, nothing urgent. Shadow and Inky were both picked up this afternoon. That leaves the kennels cleared out for the night, so I closed the office. I moved tomorrow's clinic patients out to Wednesday, but I warned them that you might not be back this week."

"Thanks, Rikki. They said the concussion is mild. No blurred vision, no memory issues. I have a splitting headache, but I'm sure I'll be back at work tomorrow."

"But we'll have to wait and see," Cole put in for her.

"I'm just glad it wasn't worse," Rikki said. "By the way, there's somebody here who missed you a whole lot while you were gone. Apparently, I was a poor substitute." They'd reached the front door and Rikki pushed it open. Cole was surprised to see a large longhaired shepherd on the other side, prancing from one foot to the other in excitement.

"This is Millie," Kelli told him.

Cole squatted down on his heels and scratched her neck, but the dog was preoccupied snuffling Kelli's legs up and down, tail wagging. "When did this happen?"

316   HER COLORADO COWBOY

"Just yesterday. If you'd be more comfortable with me staying here instead of the ranch, you can see I won't be alone. I know Sienna would take the night off and come stay with me if I needed her, but really, I know I'll be fine. You used to play football. I'll bet you got knocked out once or twice."

"Yes, I did. And I know that a concussion is nothing to mess with. I was kept home with my family looking out for me and my mom watching me like a hawk for days."

"I could stay here with…" Rikki began.

Cole shot her a "don't you dare" look. He was going to be the one to take care of Kelli, no matter what.

"I could stay here while you're at Cole's ranch," Rikki smoothly amended. "Catch the phones and dog sit for you."

Kelli gave them both a funny look, picking up on the fact that hadn't been what Rikki originally planned to say.

"Really, Bethany would be fine with it. She can take care of things at home for as long as you need me here."

"Thanks, anyway," Kelli said, "but that shouldn't be necessary, and you two have enough of your own animals to take care of. If it's not okay to have Millie at the ranch, I can call Sienna or go to my parents if I need to. Millie and I just started bonding. I don't think I can bear to leave

ELIZA D. COLLINS   317

her with someone else on her second night here. I don't want to confuse her."

"Of course, Millie can come with us," Cole said. "Baxter would love to have a friend for a sleepover."

She studied his face again, then nodded and went to pack.

Rikki said her goodbyes while Kelli bundled a few things into a small daypack. Cole carried her bag out to the truck and Millie hopped onto the back seat, tail wagging and a big grin on her face.

CHAPTER THIRTY-SIX

KELLI WASN'T AT all sure about her decision to go to Cole's instead of her parents', especially considering all the awkwardness earlier today. But then the awkwardness was the point, really. She'd been resigned to Cole not wanting a relationship with her but had lost none of her determination to fix things between them if she could. If he wanted her near him now, even out of guilt, she'd take it. If nothing else, maybe they could talk things out enough to feel relaxed and comfortable around each other again. Friendship, like they both said they wanted.

Arriving at the ranch, Millie ran all through the house, sniffing everything, then she and Baxter ran and played like puppies. Cole reassured Kelli that he'd closed the dog door in the mudroom, so she couldn't run off.

He showed Kelli the two guest bedrooms. Lane's room had been turned into a dedicated guestroom, large and elegantly decorated, while Cole's old room had been left intact for him to return to after college, back when his father had still been alive.

"I really hadn't planned on moving into the master bedroom," he said, "but Troy convinced me it would get harder with time and eventually it'd be a mausoleum if I didn't."

Kelli chose Cole's room. It seemed homier than the guestroom. Also, it had been his.

He put her daypack on the bed. "You must be hungry," he said.

For once she wasn't.

"Don't go to any trouble for me. A couple of pieces of toast would be fine."

She had never in her life eaten nothing but two pieces of toast for a meal, but to be honest her stomach did feel queasy—whether from the head injury or the awkward situation with Cole, she wasn't sure.

"Nonsense. Besides, it's genuinely no trouble. Sally cooks for us, remember? Troy and I are hopeless bachelors. She makes enough for both of us whether Troy's on duty or not. Would you like to rest and I can bring you something, or come see for yourself what we have on hand?"

He was being so solicitous over her that her head spun from more than the concussion. She studied his expression and his eyes yet again, trying to figure out if it was misplaced guilt over her accident or genuine concern for her. Who knew? Like the vaccine company, maybe he was just try-

320   HER COLORADO COWBOY

ing to avoid a lawsuit. No. That was stupid; she knew Cole better than that. Besides, they both knew perfectly well that Colorado laws prevented lawsuits over livestock accidents.

"Okay. You talked me into it." Queasy stomach or not, the prospect of a proper hot meal was starting to sound good.

Dinner turned out to be chicken fried steak with country gravy, mashed potatoes and what looked to be fresh steamed green beans. There were also rolls and butter and homemade peach pie for dessert. She glanced at the clock, 7:10 p.m., an hour later than her normal mealtime; no wonder hunger was winning out. Cole was telling her about Sally and that she'd been with the family since his late teens while he heated the food up in the microwave. The aroma turned her stomach from queasy to rumbling and her brows pinched together.

"What?" Cole asked. He hurried over to her, looking concerned.

She laughed at his protectiveness. "I just realized why I'm suddenly so hungry. I was knocked out through lunch. I haven't eaten since breakfast."

He visibly relaxed. "I love a woman with a good appetite."

Conversation was sparse during the meal while Kelli dug into everything. Millie and Baxter lay at their feet, beneath the table.

ELIZA D. COLLINS

"I better not," she said, one hand raised, as he pulled the pie toward them and offered to cut her a large slice. "I'd love some in just a bit, though." He took a slice for himself.

From this afternoon to this evening, the atmosphere between them had changed as abruptly as the weather over the Colorado mountains. Cloudy and brooding to sunny and calm so fast that it hardly felt like the same day. Things between them now were like that first morning in the barn, and the tensions of their recent cross-purposed emotions had dissipated over the course of the meal and conversation. She wasn't sure where this was headed, but she planned to enjoy the camaraderie while it lasted.

"Do you ever miss when things were simpler?" She hadn't meant to head down this path again when the evening was so nice. It just popped out, thinking of their childhood; the days when talking was just talking. Well, simpler days for her maybe, not for Cole. "I don't know, though," she amended, recalling her own stress and fears at that time. "Maybe life is never simple."

"I think I'm finally starting to learn that life is seldom the smooth sailing we hope it'll be," Cole said. "It's fluid and changeable and I keep hoping I'll learn that the easiest way to handle it is to flow with it."

She steered belatedly away from the conversation, not wanting it to become heavy again.

322   HER COLORADO COWBOY

This was too pleasant. It was hard, though, not to picture herself living here, with this their normal dinnertime after a hard day of work. Troy at the fire station, and the house to themselves. She shook herself out of the thoughts, stood and gathered the dishes.

"Hey, I'll do that," Cole said. "Doctor's orders." He pointed to the couch.

"I thought I was the doctor here."

"Not tonight you aren't."

"Yes, Nurse... *Ratched*," she said, under her breath.

"I heard that." He lowered the dishes into the sink with a clatter.

Kelli picked up a ranching magazine from the coffee table and pretended to flip through it while she furtively watched Cole at the sink. He rolled his sleeves up to his forearms and she admired the bunch and flex of his arm and shoulder muscles as he rinsed the dishes and set them in the dishwasher.

Drying his hands on a towel, he turned unexpectedly and caught her looking. She couldn't stop the grin. "So nice to see a man in a kitchen. If you want to kick off your socks so you're actually barefoot, it would complete the picture for me."

He wadded up the damp towel and tossed it at her.

She threw up a hand, fending off his good aim, and laughed out loud.

ELIZA D. COLLINS

"So, anything you want to do this evening. We have a TV in the den. Or are you tired?"

"Yeah. A little tired, I guess. Weird how a blow to the brain can make you feel like you just ran a marathon. I'm torn, though. I don't want to miss out on my pie."

"I can warm it up now and you can take it up to the room with you."

"Ooh, that sounds *so* perfect."

She hadn't been kidding about her fatigue. Each step on the staircase sapped her strength a bit more.

Back in her room—Cole's room—she changed into the cotton shorts and baggy T-shirt she used as pajamas and ate two bites of pie before deciding she was even too tired for dessert. She brushed her teeth and climbed gratefully into bed. Her eyes were achy, so she set aside the magazine she'd brought from downstairs and turned out the light.

SOME UNKNOWABLE TIME LATER, a silver bar of light woke her, shining in like a new moon. She saw a large figure looming against the brightness. She couldn't remember where she was and, for a panicked moment, her mind flashed to her childhood bedroom and the break-in. She pushed upright, startled, her only thought to find the closet so she could hide.

"Hey, sorry. It's just me," came Cole's soft,

deep voice. "I'm on my way to bed, but I promised your folks I'd check on you every couple of hours."

Millie, lying next to her, lifted her head. Kelli's memories of the past twelve hours came rushing back. "Oh," she said a bit shakily, "it's okay. I'm a light sleeper." It seemed weird, Cole standing there in silhouette and her in the darkened room. "You can come in if you want."

The door pushed open farther, illuminating him better and unkinking that small knot of fear she got with any strange occurrence at nighttime.

"I sort of wanted to talk to you anyway," he said, "but maybe it's not the best time."

Her heart seized a little, wondering if he was about to pull away again. She didn't know if she could bear losing ground on their tentative progress back to friendship. But if he didn't tell her what was on his mind, she was going to lie awake all night wondering what he'd wanted to say. If it was going to be bad news, they might as well get it over with.

"Sure. We can talk anytime, Cole. I hope you know that."

"I have some things I've been wanting to say and didn't know how. So, I'm just going to blurt this out."

Kelli nodded. She braced herself for the worst. Whatever it was, this was obviously difficult for him, and she wanted him to be able to say it without interruption. She propped the pillows up and sat back, one hand on Millie's furry shoulder for reassurance.

"You know more about my past than just about anyone," he began. "We both know that I'm one of the lucky ones." He paused again, seeking the right words or the right direction. "Plenty of children live their entire childhood in situations as bad as mine was or worse. I got out at seven, and I came to a family that was more loving and supportive than I ever could have dreamed possible. By high school, I was settled enough and popular enough that I could lie to myself that it was all behind me, but even then, I knew better. Even then, any correction from my parents, any alienation from my brothers or friends, hit me like a gut punch."

They hadn't talked about this in years. The thought that those emotions lived on so raw inside him made sympathy well up in Kelli until she could hardly breathe.

"In high school and college, I pulled back a lot when anyone got too close because the thought of having something good and losing it scared me too much. And then I met Amy. I'd decided by then that I really wanted to try, that I needed to risk more to gain more. I've always wanted to be in love. I've always wanted commitment and family. I thought if I gave everything I could, I'd get the same back. But Amy wasn't like that. The more I gave, the more she took. Once in a while, probably when she felt me slipping away, suddenly she was one hundred and ten percent into our relationship. For a day, or three, she was everything I thought I wanted. And then it would start over. It was too much like my early years, and it threw me back into a bad mindset."

Kelli reached out and put her hand over his but said nothing to stop his flow of words. He tipped his head away from her, not meeting her eyes, staring somewhere beyond the wall into his past.

"You'd think that breaking up with Amy would've been the easiest thing in the world, but it wasn't. I was hooked into an old cycle of trying to win love—as addicted to that need as my birth parents ever were to their drugs."

His parents' addictions had stolen the affection he'd needed in his early years. Ben and Cora had tried their best to make up for it, but now, as an adult seeking a different kind of love, she could see how his old injuries had flared up again. It was like he'd been shot through the heart at birth and had waited all these years for the right person to come along and stitch up that gaping wound so he could finally heal.

His gaze returned to her. "And then I moved back here, and you came into my life again, and my soul remembered your sweet soul. It's like we were joined by some mystical binding in those grade-school years, and seeing you again reawakened that in me. I knew that first day you came out to the ranch that I wanted you more than anyone I'd ever known or would ever meet. You're special to me, Kelli, and when it seemed you wanted me as much as I wanted you..." He paused again and looked down at their hands resting together. "Anyway, it's why I pulled back so hard, even though all you said was that you wanted to go slow, which makes all the sense in the world if we're going to try to build something that lasts."

The tentative elation that had been growing in Kelli opened its wings and soared in full-feathered joy. "You want to try again?" Her voice was almost a whisper, rising in uncertainty on that last note.

"No," Cole said, plummeting her into a new bout of apprehension, but he squeezed her hand reassuringly.

"I don't want to try. I want to *do*. I get it now. Love, even true love, isn't going to look like a jet on takeoff. It's going to look like a wagon train crossing the Sierras. Ups and downs, hills and valleys. I've always known that on some level, but I think I'm finally ready to deal with it. I can hold on for the ride this time, with you, because you're the love of my life." She squeezed his hand back, but he had more to say.

"I did hear what you were telling me this afternoon, Kelli. I was in a valley then, like you were the other day. I'm better now. I can see the horizon again, and you there waiting for me. I know

328 HER COLORADO COWBOY

I'm a mess, and I don't know if it's fair to you to ask this, but if you'll have me, I'm yours. I love you, and I hope that your good heart will make me a better man."

"You're already a good man, Cole," she said with tears running freely down her cheeks. "You're the best man I know."

Everything her heart had told her all along was true. He was and always had been her soulmate.

"Of course I want you, Cole. I love you too. So much. I can't swear that I won't accidentally hurt you again, or that I'll never have a bad day, but I can promise you—" she squeezed his hand again, hard "—that I will always, always be there for you. You can count on me."

She leaned into his shoulder and nuzzled his muscular neck. Tears continued to fall as he wrapped his strong arms around her. Tears of joy. No more words were needed and the two of them remained entwined, him sitting against the headboard with her snuggled against his chest. She'd never felt so happy, so complete.

Sometime later, Kelli opened her eyes, unable to remember when they'd closed. Cole swung his legs off the bed, supporting her shoulders as he eased out from under her.

"Sorry to wake you. I was actually trying to do the opposite, leave so I wouldn't disturb you. I'll look in on you again around midnight."

"I have a better idea," she mumbled, still only half awake. "Why don't you stay here with me? You can keep an eye on me all night long, and I won't get spooked if I wake up to someone in the doorway."

He was standing now, looking down at her. He tipped his head to the side, considering her proposition. "Are you sure you wouldn't rest better on your own?"

"I'm not on my own." She reached behind her hip and patted her dog's warm chest. "I have Miss Millie to kick me in her sleep and move around. I'd like you to stay too." Fully awake now, she held his gaze, willing him to say yes.

"All right. It'll make me feel better to be where I can keep watch on you. But only if you promise to send me packing if I keep you awake or if you decide you'd be more comfortable having the bed to yourself."

"Promise," she said.

Not for all the chocolate cupcakes in the world, she thought.

Leaving the door ajar and the hallway light on, he sat on the bed again and pulled his boots off. She watched his every move, knowing he could do this every night for the rest of her life and she'd never get tired of seeing him settle next to her.

Millie grunted, stood, shook and moved to a spot by their feet. Cole lay on his back on top of

330 HER COLORADO COWBOY

the blankets. Kelli rested her head on his chest as his arms enveloped her again.

"Where's Baxter?"

"He's probably asleep on my bed. He'll come in if he wants, but I'm sure he's enjoying having a whole king-size bed to himself more than sharing this queen with the three of us." He pressed a series of buttons on his watch, setting an alarm to check on her.

Cole's strong arms cradled her against his side and her free arm rested across his ribs. She lay curled against him with her head on his chest, listening to the drum of his steady heartbeat. That big heart, so sturdy despite the deep wounds it suffered in his childhood. A heart where she belonged and was loved. Fatigue and a throbbing headache tried to pull her toward sleep, but she kept adjusting her head minutely, listening to the dual cadence of his heart beating, sliding her hand to a new position, feeling the rise and fall of his chest with his breath.

"Are you comfortable?" he asked, when she shifted slightly again.

"I'm more than comfortable. I'm so happy that I don't want to get up ever again. I never want you farther from me than this." Tucked beneath his chin, she could feel him tip his head to look at her.

"Then I won't be." He said it like a promise. "As long as you want me, I'll be here for you. If we're across town from each other or across the world, I want you to feel me next to you, holding you, because I will be." The congestion that came with the sudden return of tears in her eyes made her head throb, and she didn't care one bit. "When something really wonderful comes into my life, I may take a while to get it through my head that it's real, but once I do, I hang on with everything I've got. I love you, Kelli Hinton, and I'm yours until you say I'm not."

"Then you're mine forever," she said.

They held each other tighter, there in the semi-darkness.

Kelli fought to stay awake to revel in the sensation of being here with him like this, but her fatigue won out at last. She felt herself slipping toward sleep, but it was all right. Her last thought as she drifted off was the surety that she and Cole would love each other till the end of their days.

* * * * *

Don't miss the next book in Eliza D. Collins's
Tillacos Ranch Romance miniseries,
coming June 2025
from Harlequin Heartwarming.

Harlequin Reader Service

Enjoyed your book?

Try the perfect subscription for Romance readers and get more great books like this delivered right to your door.

See why over 10+ million readers have tried Harlequin Reader Service.

Start with a Free Welcome Collection with free books and a gift—valued over $20.

Choose any series in print or ebook.
See website for details and order today:

TryReaderService.com/subscriptions